LOVE ACROSS THE TABLETOP

LOVE 💜 💜

ACROSS

THE
TABLETOP

KAIT DISNEY-LEUGERS

4 Horsemen
Publications, Inc.

4 Horsemen
Publications, Inc.

Published By: 4 Horsemen Publications, Inc.

4 Horsemen Publications, Inc.
PO Box 417
Sylva, NC 28779
4horsemenpublications.com
info@4horsemenpublications.com

Cover & Typesetting by Autumn Skye
Edited by Jen Paquette

Library of Congress Control Number: 2024938009

Paperback ISBN-13: 979-8-8232-0514-6
Hardcover ISBN-13: 979-8-8232-0515-3
Audiobook ISBN-13: 979-8-8232-0517-7
Ebook ISBN-13: 979-8-8232-0516-0

DEDICATION

To the Inhumans, the best damn D&D adventuring party!

Linda, Jordan, Jacob, Lori, Peter, and Henry, thank you all for the years of adventure, dumb decisions, and love. And yes, this time I remembered to check for traps!

TABLE OF CONTENTS

CHAPTER 1 1
CHAPTER 2 11
CHAPTER 3 19
CHAPTER 4 30
CHAPTER 5 42
CHAPTER 6 54
CHAPTER 7 65
CHAPTER 8 75
CHAPTER 9 87
CHAPTER 10 110
CHAPTER 11 124
CHAPTER 12 135
CHAPTER 13 149
CHAPTER 14 163
CHAPTER 15 178
CHAPTER 16 196
CHAPTER 17 209
CHAPTER 18 225
CHAPTER 19 240
CHAPTER 20 252
CHAPTER 21 260
CHAPTER 22 273

Epilogue 285
BOOK CLUB QUESTIONS 289
AUTHOR BIO 291

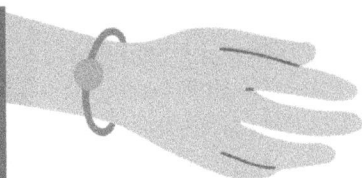

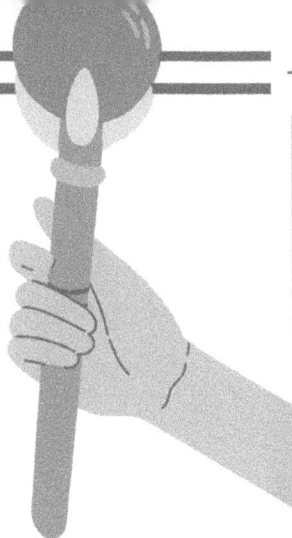

ACKNOWLEDGEMENTS

Back in the summer of 2022, my friend Elle Stewart and I challenged each other to write a Dungeons and Dragons romance. She finished hers; I did not. Not for a while, at least. So really this book is all because of Elle. But it goes back much further than that. One evening in 2016, I went to my local game store at the time, Isle of Gamers in Santa Clara, CA, and played D&D for the first time. I ended up at a table DM'd by Elle, and not long after, the Inhumans were born, an adventuring party full of non-human chucklefucks.

I also need to thank my dad. When I was a kid, he and his friends used to play D&D in our basement. I used to hang around playing with the dice since I was too young to play with them. The adults stepped on a lot of d4s thanks to me. D&D has brought me and my dad closer together.

I also have to thank Jordan Bunnell for the ridiculous door mod. That was evil and I loved it!

Finally, to Makara Fiernas, my tiefling rogue, and first character. You led me on a journey that broke my heart, made me laugh, and made me a better story-teller. We made it to level 20, and you basically became a shadow god.

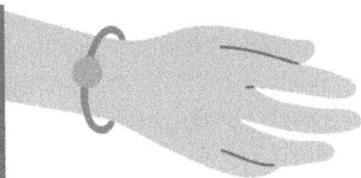

CHAPTER 1

MIKA

"And I crit! Take that sucka!" I punch the air to a chorus of joyful yells.

"Okay, with a powerful stab of her short sword, Merida delivers the killing blow and Salzared the Serpent of the North falls down dead. The Swamp Lords return to Everlonter as heroes," Marco announces behind his GM screen.

"Free drinks forever for the Swamp Lords," Stella shouts, keeping with the heart of her ogre bard character. She pulls out the elastic she used about halfway through the final battle to pull up her long blue-black hair, letting the strands cascade around her shoulders.

Even standing from the table, Stella Cordero doesn't reach much higher than the rest of us sitting. She may be compact, but she's a total pit bull, sweet when she wants to be but will sink her teeth into you and not let go if you fuck with her. Not that she would actually bite someone—she's been doing Brazilian Jui-Jitsu for years, and she can be scary.

"And that's the end." Marco closes his binder. "Holy shit. Can't believe it's over after two years." He runs a hand through his shaggy, dark brown hair shot through with a few greys. He claims our character shenanigans are making him go prematurely grey.

It's probably true.

"And with a critical hit to bring it all home. Nicely done, Mike." Marco started calling me Mike within the first hour of meeting me, despite my name, Mika, having the same amount of letters.

Marco Perez is the best damn GM in the whole DMV. And easily one of the best friends in the world. He owns exactly five pairs of the same jeans, and the only shirts he owns are ones that advertise his own podcast, *Be Kind, Rewind*. His following is pretty substantial, considering he talks about 80s movies and TV shows. I think the current run is on *Quantum Leap*. The original, with the dreamy Scott Bakula.

We are all riding a high from the end of the game. This campaign of Battles & Bargains has gone on for the better part of two years, and it's bittersweet to see it end. I've grown so attached to my elven paladin character.

But now is not the time to be sad. Now we celebrate all of our characters making it out alive and ending a wonderful storyline.

"So, who's up for real drinks to celebrate?" Nico McLeod, our resident bard, asks as he starts to place what looks like the hundreds of dice he pulled out back into his bag. Three quarters of his d20s are in his little dice jail box, but he snatches them up quickly. His unruly ginger curls fall over his eyes as he does. Nico is the kind of guy who is handsome in a bad-boy rocker kind of way.

But he's definitely a pecs-out, head-empty kind of guy. Nico is our very own King of the Himbos.

"Wish I could, but I still have to finish editing this week's episode, and Lena just texted me to pick up burgers on my way home. I am already loving her pregnancy cravings." Marco laughs as he packs up his stuff.

Marco's wife Lena is three months pregnant and already changing cravings on a weekly basis. Last week it was chocolate cake. She baked this colossal layer cake, but after one slice, she threw up, and we ended up with most of the cake at last week's session.

I shove my own dice bag and character sheet binder into my bag. "I have some work to finish too. I'm transcribing this speech, and I swear the guy whispered the entire thing. My headphones don't go high enough." One of the pitfalls of being a transcriber: I don't always get quality audio or coherent people.

"Yeah, I have an early morning in the lab. Maybe tomorrow night? I'm going to need it after being stuck with the undergrads all morning," Stella whines. She loves to complain about academia even though she'll never leave it.

Everyone starts cleaning up the mess at the table. It's a custom design, with dice tray inlays and a sunken part for the maps and attachments that go on top so it can function as my actual dining table. My dad made it for me a few years ago when I got my own place. It's my most prized possession. I got him to play with us once, and he didn't quite understand the game, but I love him for trying.

"Why don't we discuss it over the group chat so you can all get the fuck out of my house?" I say, giving Nico a playful push toward the door. I love having my friends around, but we could easily spend another hour just trying to sort out schedules. It's hard enough to keep a standing game going when we all have professional lives. Adding more is just as much of a hassle. Not to mention, Marco will flake at the drop of a hat if Lena needs anything. We don't hold that against him though. It's their first kid and we're all excited.

"Ugh, fine. But don't forget my band is playing at The Old Nut House on Friday. Drinks are on me if you come," Nico says as they all head out the door. We just nod our heads. His band is pretty good—don't get me wrong. It's just that we've all seen them play a million times, and they don't exactly change up their set list all that often.

When I'm finally alone in my house, I finish up the cleaning, washing the few dishes left behind. I then settle on my couch to finish up the transcription project. I should work at my desk, but I'm feeling lazy after hours of playing Battles & Bargains.

It's going to be a late night, but I'm still riding the high of the end of the campaign, so I don't really care. The perks of making my own hours mean I can sleep in tomorrow.

[Marco: Don't forget we are taking next week off]

[Stella: good didn't want to see you anyway]

[Marco: Rude]

[Nico: why are you all awake]

[Me: It's noon, Nico!]

[Nico: noon on a Saturday]

[Stella: you're such a bum]

[Marco: Anyway, my cousin just moved to town and needs to get out of his apartment more]

[Marco: Would you all be okay with him playing?]

[Me: Sure, unless he's a total ass. Or one of those guys who argues every rule.]

[Stella: or is a total misogynist]

[Me: Or that]

[Marco: He's definitely not a misogynist. He's a solid guy]

[Marco: He's actually never played before]

[Stella: We've got ourselves a virgin!!!!]

[Nico: He can play so long as you all stop texting, my head is killing me]

[Me: Get your ass out of bed and drink some water, you dehydrated, but capable bitch.]

[Nico:]

I've been agonizing over my character sheet for the last hour. I was originally going for a warlock, but I didn't really want to play such a squishy class. Plus, I played a warlock years ago, and I wanted to try something new.

Flipping through the classes in the *Player's Tome*, I thumb through the worn tabs I placed there years ago.

My hand stops on a class page. Hm, I've never played a rogue before. That could be fun. A little squishy, but not so much that I couldn't still use melee in combat. I've already decided to play a divine-kin, so that settles it.

Just like that, Uriel the divine-kin rogue is born.

I pull out my dice to roll up some stats and hope for some good rolls. They end up being decent enough, and I quickly fill in the rest of my sheet, though she's definitely not packing much muscle. See, that wasn't so bad. I really don't know why it took me so long to settle on all of this.

Now I can spend the next week agonizing over a backstory, and I'll be good to go for the next campaign. It's exciting. One of my favorite parts of the game is coming up with a new character, someone new to explore, a way to channel a piece of me. I can be anyone—do anything when I'm playing B&B.

I decide I should make a huge meal for the kickoff of the campaign. Since our last one lasted two years, who knows how long this one will be? It's a milestone in life if you look at it a certain way. And my Bubbe always says it's good to start something new with a big meal.

I absolutely love to cook and really nothing makes me happier than cooking for my friends. Unlike some home cooks out there, I also really love to eat my own food. When I'm good at something I always champion myself, and I am good at cooking.

This means I should probably ask Marco if his cousin is allergic to anything. I shoot off a quick text. Marco is the kind of guy who will respond right away unless he's recording, and then it's anyone's guess when or if he'll respond. He tends to forget after he finishes up with the podcast.

Luckily, I catch him at a non-recording time because he responds within two minutes. It looks like I don't have to worry about allergies, which makes my life a little easier.

Now I have a week and a half to work on my back-story and plan a meal on top of my normal workload. That's all manageable. I should probably clean the place too. While my friends have seen my place in arrays of cleanliness, Marco's cousin has not, and I want to make a good impression on the new guy in case he sticks with us for a while.

We always play at my place. I live alone and have plenty of space. With Lena pregnant, we don't want to keep her up by playing at Marco's. Stella's girlfriend is a nurse, so it's a toss-up if she's at work or passed out from working too much. And Nico's apartment is so tiny it barely fits him, and that's without all the records piled around him.

Since we're not playing the next Wednesday, I grab drinks with Stella after she gets out of class. It's nice to keep some semblance of structure to my schedule, even though we're not playing. I take the green line to U Street and head to the Gibson.

I get there first and have already received my vodka cocktail by the time Stella stomps into the bar. Her wedge heels are sky high, but that barely gets her over five foot three inches. It's always hilarious to see Stella with her girlfriend Elise since Elise is six feet tall. She could easily lift Stella and carry her around. Tall and Smol, we call them, and they are the cutest.

Stella flings her bag into one of the open seats and flops down on the chair next to me. "You will not believe who I saw today!" I slide the cocktail I already ordered for her across the table. I'm dreading what she's going to say because I already know who she saw, and I try not to think about her.

"Fucking Quinn!" she practically yells after taking a drink of her cocktail. "Where does that bitch get off showing her face around town after what she did?" Stella is going to work herself up into a full fury if I let her. And I really don't want that today.

Mostly, I just don't want to think about Quinn. She was the one who got me into playing Battles & Bargains with this group. That was almost six years ago. Being introduced to the game and the other players was the best thing that ever happened to me. I thought Quinn was included in that. I loved her, and I thought she loved me too.

That was until I found her in our bed with her yoga instructor. So, I guess she didn't love me that much after all. I found out she had also been sleeping with one of her professors in the political science department and some random girls she met at the bars when I was working late.

But even though Quinn had known them longer, after a year of playing with the group, they took my side and kicked Quinn out. Marco made it very clear to Quinn that he and the rest of the group would not support her behavior.

I know it was hard on all of them, but they never made me feel guilty for it; instead, they made me feel wanted and loved at one of the hardest moments of my life. But I don't regret them kicking Quinn out. Or replacing my mattress afterward. I mean, who cheats on someone in the bed they share with their partner? Assholes, that's who.

I shake my head because I really don't want to think about Quinn. It's been almost five years, but there's still that small pang of hurt that I think will always be there when I think of her.

"She's a congressional aide. She kind of needs to be in DC," I say with a sigh. A part of me really hates that Quinn is successful. I'm petty enough to admit that.

Stella rolls her eyes. "Doesn't mean she needs to be around GW's campus! She came to pick up one of the kids from the lab, so she's like dating babies now." She downs the rest of her drink, a clear sign she's in a really bad mood. That would be the undergrads' doing more than seeing Quinn. She always calls them the kids, but really, they are third and fourth years. And the poor souls have Stella for a TA—as if chemistry wasn't hard enough without a tiny, grouchy Filipino PhD student watching their every move.

I shrug because I really don't want to hear about Quinn. "So, she's robbing the cradle. That's her business. But if she says anything to you, you have my absolute support in bludgeoning her with your ridiculously high shoes."

"I'll expect you to have an alibi for me when I hide the body," Stella says before standing up to head to the bar for another drink.

That makes me laugh. "Girl, I will be holding the shovel."

When she returns to the table with another cocktail, sipping slowly this time, we start discussing the upcoming campaign. Turns out Stella has made three characters and can't pick between them. I offer to help, but she waves me off and just tells me about each one anyway. She'll have it figured out by the time the game rolls around.

Stella is the type of player who makes characters for the sake of making characters, even if she never gets to actually play them. She has a whole binder of filled out character sheets and printed backstories. She's our legacy player. Her mom and dad met at a game store back in the early 90s and taught Stella and her brothers how to play when they were young. Hell, the story goes that her mom went into labor while sitting at the gaming table. Knowing Mrs. Cordero, it's probably true.

"I'm so ready for next week," I say, setting down my empty glass.

"Me too, and I think it'll be fun adding a new player. If he's anything like Marco, he's going to fit in just fine." Stella throws her arms against the back of her chair and lounges.

"I really hope he's like Marco because if he's a total douchecanoe, I might actually feel bad about making him leave." I don't want to be the asshole who throws someone out of my home, but douchecanoes will not be abided.

"Here's hoping!" Stella raises her glass in a toast.

CHAPTER 2

ASH

"I don't know about this game idea, Marco," I say to my cousin before taking a drink of the coffee Lena just offered me.

My cousin and his wife have been nothing but kind to me since I moved to DC a month ago. Leaving New York was hard. My whole world is there: my mom, my siblings, my work, my girlfriend.

No, not my girlfriend anymore. My ex-girlfriend. I had to get away. I know that. Doesn't mean it doesn't still hurt like hell.

But I have Marco and Lena and my Tia and Tio here in the city, so at least I still have some family around. And literally no one else. I don't make friends easily. It's not from lack of trying; it's just the minute I'm around other people, I clam up. I start to get all sweaty, and the urge to run away overwhelms me. Every situation, every conversation, even if it's simple pleasantries, I can't handle. I overthink it, I panic, and then I avoid it altogether.

Maybe moving was a bad idea. I got so focused on a fresh start that I didn't think about the whole actually having to restart my life from the ground up thing. Which absolutely sucks.

Marco must see the panic in my eyes because he lays a comforting hand on my knee. It's grounding, and I'm thankful. Marco is older than me by a few years, and despite the distance, we've stayed close. He's more like a brother than a cousin to me. "Hey, don't worry. I don't want to push you beyond your comfort zone. It's a really low-key game and Mike, Stel, and Nico are my absolute best friends. They won't judge you or anything. I just think it'll be good for you to know a few people in the District."

"It's not so much meeting your friends. It's the whole role playing I'm nervous about. I've never done anything like that before." Honestly, it sounds a bit like my own personal nightmare. It's hard enough to interact with people being myself, but playing Battles and Bilbos or whatever it's called, socializing as a made-up character... Yeah, I don't know about that.

I'm pulled from my own head by Lena thrusting a plate piled high with chocolate cherry cookies. That's just my plate as I notice she hands a similarly laden plate toward her husband before settling down with her own.

"Hon, why don't you try it one time? Who knows? You might have fun." She takes a bite of one of her cookies and moans loudly, placing a hand over the small bump just starting to form.

It sounds almost indecent, but she's been having some weird cravings, so I don't let it bother me. From what Marco has told me, Lena has had some terrible nausea. She's tall and incredibly thin, so the bump that would be tiny to nonexistent on anyone else is noticeable. Mixed race with brown curls and big brown eyes, she's the kind of person who takes one look at you and decides you're one of hers. She's from Baltimore and somehow from a larger family than the Perez clan—and there are a lot of cousins in the Perez family. Lena is going to be a great mother.

"Why don't you play, then?" I ask her.

She shoves another cookie in her mouth before responding. "I tried, but it turns out I have no imagination whatsoever. I'm more of a video game girl." As if the ancient and faded *Legend of Zelda* shirt wasn't a dead giveaway, though the size suggests it's Marco's or it used to be.

"One game, hon. You'll like the gang. And if it's not for you, then you can always hang with me on game night. We'll eat crazy things and then you can hold my hair while I puke it all up." She laughs and polishes off her plate of cookies.

Marco hands over his barely touched plate to his wife, and Lena smiles brightly at him. I'm glad my cousin has someone who loves him the way Lena does. He's been so great helping me get acclimated to the city, I can at least try out the game for him.

"Here, you'll like this class. Druids get to shape change into animals, so you won't have to talk to anyone in animal form." Marco points to a page which has a man covered in shades of forest green, a roaring bear at his side.

I've already picked a demon-kin character since they are seen as outsiders and avoided by polite society. Seemed fitting. "Okay, demon-kin druid. Sure, that's fine. Now what do I do?" Marco and I are sitting at my kitchen table. He has several books spread out across the table, and before me is a sheet of paper with several empty sections. It's supposed to be my character sheet, but so far, I've only come up with class and race. This thing doesn't even have a name.

"So now we'll add your stats. I usually have my players roll their own—makes it more fun that way. But I think for you we'll just keep it easy and do a standard array." I have no idea what any of that means, but I nod and let Marco show me the ins and outs of stats. Then we move on to armor and weapons. It's all a bit much, but I let him show me everything I need, and my character sheet gets progressively more filled.

Marco stands finally and stretches out his back. "Alright, Ash. You just need to come up with a fun backstory, and you should be good to go. Don't worry about making it elaborate. Keep it simple." He grabs his stuff and heads toward the door, pulling on his scuffed-up navy blue Crocs where he's left them by the entrance. He's the only grown man I know who wears Crocs outside of a professional kitchen. "I'll see you Wednesday. Oh, and I'll text you Mike's address. Come hungry. Dinner will be provided."

I'm alone now in my one-bedroom apartment. It's my first time living alone. I've always had roommates, and then Adele and I lived together until two months ago. Then it was a few weeks back home where chaos reigned and silence was unheard of.

But here, the silence is deafening.

Washington DC is not nearly as loud as New York. Even NoMa where I live, trendy as it's becoming, is no match for the Bronx. I miss home already.

My apartment is all set up. I couldn't stand to see boxes laying around and unpacked everything in one night. It's a tiny place. Even with my decent graphic design salary and book cover design side hustle, DC is still crazy expensive, and this was one of the few places in my budget that wasn't outside of the city. Being the only person to pay rent put a real damper on my housing prospects.

I take a seat on my couch, which takes up a large portion of the living room and settle in to watch whatever World War II documentary I can find. Once I do that, I pull out my phone and order some Indian takeout for delivery. It's what I need right now. I wish I could paint to fill up the silence and strangeness of my new surroundings, letting myself get lost in splashes of color and line definitions.

But I can't.

My art supplies are in the one box I haven't emptied yet. I haven't painted anything since I left the apartment I shared with Adele. Something within me is broken, and I don't know how to fix it.

Maybe playing this game with my cousin will be good for me. I've never lacked imagination, and I always enjoyed fantasy stories. And maybe there's a chance my spark will come back, and I can actually make art outside of work again.

Or maybe not. I'm getting ahead of myself already, and I haven't even started playing. One thing at a time. I need to first half-ass a backstory for my demon-kin druid, play the game, and hopefully not completely embarrass myself.

My phone pings, and I see it's a text from Marco. It's an address for a place in Petworth. That must be Mike's place. Hopefully the guy won't be put out by having a Perez cousin invade his house.

I send Marco back a thumbs up emoji and then settle back on my couch to wait for my food. I have a few days still to not think about this upcoming social interaction. That's a problem for future Sebastian to deal with.

I've made a horrible mistake.

I can't do this.

I have been paralyzed on the sidewalk for five minutes now, holding my bike next to me. Several people have stepped around me, shooting dirty looks over their shoulders. But I don't care. Walking up the steps to the narrow brick home is daunting. It's ten minutes to 6:00 p.m. I made sure to arrive early.

Early enough to totally psych myself out.

I clutch the strap of my worn leather bag across my chest. The bag is stuffed with the *Player's Tome* Marco lent me, the character sheet I agonized over for a few nights, some pencils, and my first ever set of dice in emerald green. Marco said I would only need the one set tonight, implying that I'll need more later, but I'm not sure why.

Finally, I convince my feet to move, and I walk up to the front door, carrying my bike up the steps of the porch. As I raise my fist to knock, I notice a mezuzah attached to the doorframe. I've had enough Jewish neighbors to recognize what it is. It's a bit faded, and there's a dark line surrounding it like it's been there forever. Mike or one of his roommates is Jewish. That's cool, I think in passing as I finally knock.

The door opens within seconds to reveal a woman about my age with long bubblegum pink curls pulled up in a ponytail. She's wearing a pale-yellow dress, fitted at the top and flaring out to land mid-thigh. The color contrasts well against her light skin. Her gray-green eyes are wide and accentuated by a bit of liner and mascara. She's cute as hell, and I can already feel the sweat forming on my body as my nerves fray. I think about running away, but I can't move my feet.

"Hey, you must be Ash, right? You're early. The rest of the group always shows up fashionably late. I'm Mika, by the way. Come on in. You can bring your bike in. I have extra wall hooks," the bright woman says. She's a flurry of words and hand gestures. Then she steps aside to let me through.

I can do this. A pretty girl just invited me inside her house to play a game. No problem. But then I feel like an idiot because I've been thinking of Mika as a guy since Marco only referred to her as Mike. Well, that's on me for assuming. But I'm also not prepared to be around a cute girl I've never met.

"If it's easier, you can wait for Marco out here. I totally understand. You don't know me, and I'm just like 'Come inside my lair, random stranger.' I have to run back to the kitchen to finish up dinner. So why don't you hang out on the porch until the others get here? You want something to drink?" She barely takes the time to breathe, her words streaming out.

It's only then that I realize I'm completely rooted to the spot. I haven't moved an inch toward her open door. At this point, I haven't said anything to her either, just stared. God, I'm a total creep.

"Uh... sure." I somehow manage to force the words from my lips.

She points to a wooden chair on the porch and smiles brightly at me. "Cool. You take a seat, and I'll be right back." She ducks back into the house, bubblegum curls bouncing behind her with each step.

There's no way I'm going to make it through this game.

Chapter 3

MIKA

So, he's handsome. *No big deal*, I think as I pull the mac and cheese casserole from the oven. I grab a can of soda and a can of flavored seltzer from the fridge and walk back to the porch.

The porch where the hot guy is sitting perched nervously on the edge of one of the chairs. "Coke or bubbly water?" I ask around the edge of the door, holding up both.

Ash gives me a wide-eyed, deer in the headlights look, and I feel like I have to approach him with extreme caution, lest I spook him.

"Uh... the water is fine." He mumbles a thanks as I hand it over and quickly retreat to the door, giving him space. He seems so nervous; I just want to hug him and tell him we're all family here. But not in the gross way.

I look at him for a second too long before I head back in. His deep brown hair is styled in an undercut, if newly cut sharp lines are any indication. Long thick lashes frame beautiful hazel eyes. He has a runner's build, long solid legs barely contained in tight fitting jeans, ripped at the knees, and a defined torso wrapped in a black t-shirt. There's a hint of a blush on his tan cheeks, and I realize I'm probably making him uncomfortable with my staring.

Way to treat him like a piece of meat, Mike!

"Sorry, I'll just..." I'm saved from being a total awkward creep by Marco's arrival.

"Hail and well met, my dudes! Who's ready to roll some dice?" he calls loudly, bounding up my front steps.

I see Ash's shoulders release some tension. He stands up, clutching the unopened can in one hand and the strap of his bag with the other. His knuckles are turning white from how hard he's holding onto the bag.

Oh, you sweet baby deer, I am so going to be your friend. Nobody comes into my house and doesn't feel like they belong. This is a safe space, dammit!

Marco steps up next to his cousin, leans his arm on Ash's shoulder, and addresses me. "Lena tried to send me off with some blueberry pie, but I reminded her that, one, Nico is allergic, and two, you would definitely be making babka and would be sending me home with some for her."

I laugh because it's true. I did make babka, and there is indeed a whole second one just for Lena. There's no better way to tell people you love them like cooking for them.

And I love Marco and Lena. They welcomed me into their lives with open arms. Held me when I cried over Quinn. Laughed with me over dumb work things and family shenanigans. Hell, Lena took her first pregnancy test in my bathroom, and we cried for like ten minutes together before she even called Marco.

Marco and Lena are family.

And now, for the first time in five years, something is changing in our little group. I'm conflicted between being excited to introduce someone new to the wonders of B&B and also extremely protective of our group dynamic. But Ash is Marco's actual blood family, so I should be welcoming to him. He's not going to hurt the group balance.

Not like Quinn did.

I let the guys slide through the door before shutting it behind me. I point to the spot near the door where Ash can hang his bike above mine. Marco already knows where he's going and heads straight back into the kitchen to get first dibs. Ash trails behind him after he hangs his bike, his head darting around as he takes in the hallway, the living room off to the left, and the stairs on the right. We always play in the dining room, directly next to the kitchen. It's a large cozy space with a working fireplace, and of course, my amazing table.

Marco is already standing over the casserole dish when I enter seconds later. He's eyeballing it like he's planning to stick his whole face in the still bubbling cheese. Ash stands next to the counter, clearly unsure of what he should do or where he should stand. He's still holding onto the water and his bag strap.

"You're welcome to go sit that down in the dining room if you want. That's where we play," I say, pointing to the open doorway into the next room. I smile at him, hoping it helps. It doesn't seem to do much.

"I'm good," he mumbles and doesn't meet my gaze.

Okay, I'll give the guy a break. He's probably just nervous about meeting all of us, so I turn my attention toward Marco. "Hey, want to grab some salad dressing from the fridge for me?" It gets him away from the mac and cheese and also helps me. Win-win.

I grab the bowl of salad I prepared just before Ash arrived and set it next to the cooling casserole dish of cheesy goodness. Marco comes up beside me and sets down three bottles of dressing because, of course, none of us like the same dressing. There's Green Goddess for me and Stella, Catalina for Marco, and ranch for our resident twelve-year-old boy Nico. Hopefully, Ash finds one he likes.

I pull out the covered cake stand where I stored the babka, two loaves of chocolatey cinnamon goodness in bread form. One is wrapped in foil for Lena. Marco is already pulling down plates from the cabinet and setting them at the start of what has become a small buffet line.

"Hey Ash, can you grab silverware? It's in the drawer next to your hip." I point to the large drawer next to him. He's been watching us move around the kitchen, but my words seem to startle him.

He points to the drawer I've just indicated. "This one?" I respond with a "yeah," and he sets the can of seltzer on the counter and finally lets go of his bag strap. "How many sets?" he asks, though he keeps his focus on the silverware drawer.

"Five. Wait, no, six. I forgot Elise is stopping before work. That's Stella's girlfriend, FYI." Because he doesn't even know who Stella is, so obviously he doesn't know her girlfriend. I listen to the clink of silverware as I turn and pull out napkins.

Just as everything is set out, my front door bursts open, and Nico loudly announces his presence with a warbling "Honey, I'm hooooome!" He's in the kitchen a second later with Stella and Elise coming up behind him.

Nico sweeps into the room, spots the food, and is suddenly lifting me up off the ground. I place my hands on his shoulders for balance, laughing.

"Mika, babe, you made my favorite. Why don't you just marry me now?" He spins me around, and it's lucky the kitchen is big because the man cannot spin in one spot. The skirt of my dress flairs out behind me, and I just keep laughing.

When he finally stops spinning us and puts me back down on the floor, I give his chest a playful backhanded slap. "Because we agreed on forty-five for our marriage year. Besides I might meet someone who doesn't eat all my leftovers before I get to them, and who doesn't live in a place that looks like it's the inside of a record player." It's true. You can't see any floor space in Nico's place due to all the vinyl albums around.

"I would like to amend our deal, then. If you meet a nice girl, we can be a beautiful throuple!" He laughs with that glint in his eye. He would just love that, wouldn't he? Not that Nico and I have ever or will ever harbor any romantic feelings for each other. After my breakup with Quinn, he jokingly suggested we get married if we are still single at forty-five, and I tearfully accepted. It's become our thing ever since. With the way my love life has been the last few years, it'll probably happen, and I'll have to move Nico and his entire record collection into my house.

From the corner of my eye, I see Ash's cheeks turn pink and his gaze falls to the floor where a minute ago he was staring at me and Nico.

I focus back on Nico. "And what if I meet a nice guy instead? Going to join us in a throuple?" I joke, knowing full well Nico is all about women.

He pretends to think for a moment. "Only if he's hotter than me. Tall order, I know. But if I'm in a power throuple, it better be with a total hunk and my best girl." He chucks me under the chin. For all his golden retriever energy, Nico is a completely wonderful person who has never had any reservations dropping his life to help me, or anybody, really.

"So, who's going to introduce the new guy?" Stella yells out, directing our attention toward Ash. The poor guy turns completely white, and once again, his hands scramble for his bag like it's a lifeline.

Luckily, Marco saves him from having to speak. "Gang, this is my cousin, Ash Aguila. He just moved here from New York, and he's going to be our druid tonight. Stella, be nice." He directs his gaze to Stella and points a finger at her for emphasis.

I see Ash look gratefully at his cousin. It's not hard to see that he is having some social anxiety. Not that I can blame him; together, our group can be a lot. We're loud, we're loving, and we've all been together so long that the lines of appropriateness are virtually non-existent. We'll just have to ease Ash into the craziness, but once he's in, I'm sure he'll be fine.

"Okay, right, so the small one there is Stella Maria Evangelista dia Codero, and the giant behind her is Elise Dorsey, her girlfriend. She doesn't play. She's just here for dinner before work. The loud little rockstar is Nico McLeod. And then of course, the rainbow is Mika Levenberg, but you already know that." Marco points us all out in turn. Ash gives a head nod as each person is introduced but still doesn't say anything.

"Alright, chucklefucks, come eat," I announce to the assembled group. We take our time loading up plates and head to the dining room. Marco takes his place at the head of the table since we'll start playing right after we eat.

"Here, sit next to me," I say to Ash as I take a chair on Marco's left. Better me than Stella. I love her, I really do, but she will lay into Ash so hard with questions or force him to talk. She means well, but her approach is heavy-handed, and she'd scare him off for sure.

We spend the meal chatting about our individual days. It feels like a proper family dinner. I love it. Ash is completely silent and singularly focused on his food.

"Don't worry about talking if you're uncomfortable. This is just a low-key hangout, so no pressure, okay? Besides, Nico and Stella talk enough for everyone." I lean over and whisper to Ash. I want to give his leg a reassuring squeeze. And okay, yes, I want to touch those muscled thighs of his. I have eyes, you know. But I don't because I instinctively know that would be way over his comfort line. I may be a touchy-feely person, but I respect boundaries.

Ash looks over, gives me the barest hint of a grateful smile, and we lock eyes for just a moment. He has such beautiful hazel eyes. I could absolutely lose myself in them. The pink returns to his cheeks. This man blushes a lot, and it's so adorable. I want to make him blush more.

"Oh my god, I can basically hear you talking about me!" Stella glares across the table at us. I straighten up in my seat, pulling away from Ash. His eyes drop back to his plate.

Thanks a lot, Stella. We were totally having a moment.

"I'm always talking about you," I say with a smirk, but my eyes are giving her that glare, like *bitch, you threw off my groove.*

The Cheshire Cat grin creeping across her face tells me she gets it. "Riiiiight, of course you are." Her eyes flick to Ash, but luckily, his face is pointed toward his plate.

Elise stands from her chair. She's definitely picked up on the situation and is going to reign in her girlfriend. "All right, you lot, I've got work. Take care, and try not to start any tavern brawls in the first ten minutes," she says in her thick west London accent. She grabs her plate, kisses Stella, and rounds the table to me. She places a kiss on my cheek. "Great meal, as always, Mikey."

"I've already filled a Tupperware bowl for you to take to work. It's in the fridge," I call as she heads to the kitchen with her plate. She throws me a beaming smile and a thank you over her shoulder.

"Bring the wine in, please, babe!" Stella calls out. She stands up and heads to the small cabinet holding an assortment of tankards I've acquired over the years especially for game night. Some have come from renaissance faires and more than a few as gifts from the assembled group.

Elisa brings in two bottles of uncorked wine while Stella hands a tankard out to everyone. Then Elise kisses Stella once again and waves goodbye. A few minutes after Elise leaves, I stand to clear plates. It's time to start playing. Let the game begin.

I go to grab Ash's plate, but his hand beats me to it, and our fingers brush. It's like a little electric shock to my fingertips. I jerk my hand back, and he does the same.

"I can clean up. You went through all the trouble of cooking." His voice is so rich and deeper than I would have thought. But he's practically whispering, so it comes out soft. It's a nice voice. I look at him, my gaze catching on his gorgeous eyes again. He's actually looking back and holding eye contact this time. He's very cute, and I realize he has a small smattering of freckles across his nose. His face is perfect.

Then my brain catches up and finally understands what he's saying. "Oh... yeah, that would be nice. Thank you. Just dump them in the sink. I'll take care of them later," I say, sitting back down and handing him my plate. He goes around the table and collects plates before disappearing into the kitchen.

Marco gives me a look and leans close to whisper to me. "He just got out of a bad relationship, Mike."

I lean toward him to whisper back and give him a weird look. "Okay, that doesn't sound like my business."

Marco raises an eyebrow. "I'm just saying, maybe keep your heart eyes toned down for a bit. Until he's settled, okay?" He's not being harsh; his tone is just concerned.

"Tell him to stop making heart eyes back at her then, Marco," Stella whispers across the table because of course, none of our whispering is particularly subtle or quiet.

I sit back in my seat. "There are no heart eyes anywhere," I hiss at them.

Nico, bless him, pipes up at a normal volume. "Why are we whispering?"

"Okay, time to turn this bad boy into play time," I shout as Ash walks back into the room. We all stand up, set drinks off to the side, and pull off the sectional top of the table, revealing the sunken part in the middle and the carved in dice trays. Dad even included drink holders at each station.

We all start to pull out our things: character sheets, dice sets, or in Nico's case, way too many dice sets, pencils, and small figurines to represent our characters on the board. Marco unrolls a large mat with grid lines printed on top, starts pulling intricate little set pieces from a bulging bag, and sets them up on the map in the center sunken part of the table.

"This is a pretty cool table," Ash says to me quietly as he takes his seat again.

"Thanks!" I beam. "My dad made it for me. He doesn't exactly get Battles & Bargains, but he knows it makes me happy, so he made me this." I will hype my dad all day, every day because this table really is amazing.

"Enough chit-chat. It's time to get this thing started. Ash, I know you and I went over the basics, but if you have questions, just ask Mika. She seriously has all the rules, spells included, memorized." He laughs like it's a joke. It's not. I really do have most of the spells memorized. I am a compendium of B&B knowledge in human form.

Once Marco is satisfied with his setup behind his GM screen, all we can see is his head and shoulders, he does a once over of his notes and looks up at us, ready to begin.

"Welcome to Galimere, adventurers. We begin our story in the Sleeping Gnome Tavern on the seedier side of Galimere City. Each of you has received an anonymous summons to come to this tavern. There was no other information other than the place and date. You are all waiting for your mystery contact to appear." Marco begins to set the scene, and so the campaign begins.

I peek over at Ash who is watching his cousin with rapt attention. Ash's shoulders are less tense, not totally relaxed, but without the focus on him, he seems more at ease.

I let my attention linger too long because his eyes shift over to mine, and I quickly look back at Marco.

Head in the game, Mika. You are here to roll some dice and get into shit, not ogle the cute new guy.

My attention stays on Marco for the rest of his introduction, though I still catch Ash's subtle fidgeting in my periphery. There will be plenty of time to look and talk to him as the game progresses. I mean, we'll have to roleplay these characters, after all. Nothing wrong with a bit of flirty banter for the sake of the game, right?

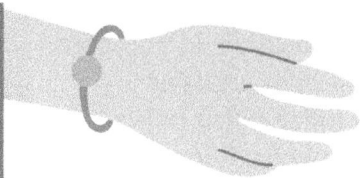

CHAPTER 4

ASH

I am simultaneously awed and terrified of what's playing out around me. Everyone at the table has fallen completely into the story Marco weaves, stepping into character voices and actions like a second skin. I can easily believe they are all professional actors.

At first, it does seem a little hokey—grown adults doing voices and sometimes acting out scenes without standing from their chair. But then I find I kind of like it. It's like immersive storytelling, not much different from going to the theater. Except this time, I'm part of the show, and I have no idea what I'm doing.

"Here, roll this one." Mika's voice draws me out of my head, staving off the bit of panic rising there every time it's my turn. She sets one of my dice in my hand, the twenty sided one, her fingers brushing my palm, and I instantly feel my face burn.

She leans close to me. "We're rolling initiative to determine what order we go in for combat. So, roll your d20." I look at the die in my hand and then let it drop onto the table. Mika smiles at me, and it's one of the most beautiful smiles I've ever seen. It takes over her whole face. I'm blinded. "Your first roll! And look, it's pretty good too."

I look at the number facing up. It's a twelve. "What does that mean?" I ask, feeling incredibly stupid. I went over the basics with Marco, and I still feel like I know absolutely nothing.

But Mika doesn't let me wallow in my stupidity; she's patient and isn't condescending. "It means we're going to take that number and then add your initiative modifier." She points to a box on my sheet with a +2. "Every time you roll for initiative, you add two to whatever number you get. See? Easy."

I nod my head. I guess it does make sense.

"I need numbers, people." Marco looks around the table and then trains his eyes on Mika. "Uriel, whatcha got?" He refers to Mika by the name of her angelic rogue character.

"Sixteen," she responds, and Marco does something on the tablet behind his screen.

"Alright. Kilris?" I jolt when I realize he's asking me now. Kilris, my demon-kin druid, was literally the first name I saw on a name generator.

"Fourteen," I mumble, and my cousin gives me a thumbs up before focusing on the tablet again.

"Lay it on me, Varic," he asks Nico who is playing an elf bard.

"Well, it's not great. I got an eight. Not a good omen for the new game." He looks forlornly at the twenty-sided die in his hands, then he reaches down into his bag and pulls out a small box that looks like it has bars. It reads

Dice Jail on the front, and he drops the die into the box. I have no idea what that's about.

"Damn, the dice jail is coming out early tonight. Alright, last but not least, Tamotur." Marco refers to Stella's half-orc barbarian.

"Fuck!" Stella growls next to him. She stares down at her roll angrily. "I crit on initiative. The rest of my rolls tonight are going to suck." I don't understand anything she just said.

But here's Mika again, picking up on my questions before I can even ask them. "She rolled a twenty. We call it a crit or natural twenty. It's a good thing. But Stella is notorious for getting only one good roll in, and then it's all shit after that." She laughs when Stella flips her off with a scowl.

"Alright, kids, settle down. So first up is Tamotur. What are you doing?" Marco waits for Stella to respond.

Stella smirks, and in a snap judgment, I know this means trouble. "I'm going to *rage*!" She yells the last word, then throws her head back and her arms up like she's actually going to go into a frenzy. I'm more than a foot taller than Stella, but I know without a doubt that she could easily kick my ass—probably while wearing the huge shoes she came in wearing. It's not surprising that I jump in my seat.

I feel a warm hand on my forearm, grounding me. I turn to look at Mika, but she's not facing me. She's looking at Stella, though her hand remains where it is.

"Seriously? There's like two dudes, and you're going to rage in round one?" Her other hand is gesticulating wildly, and I'm glad I'm sitting on the other side of the flailing appendage.

"Hey, no meta gaming. Uriel can talk it out with Tamotur in character," Marco says, getting the two women back on track. Stella finishes her turn, and Marco shifts his attention to Mika.

I feel a pang of loss when she finally removes her hand from me. I don't think she realized it was still there until she needed to use her hands again. Part of me wishes she would put her hand back. It was nice to have someone touch me with no other intention than to offer comfort. I don't remember the last time someone outside of my family has offered such a simple gesture. Adele never did anything like that, at least not in the last year or so. Maybe not ever.

It's pathetic to think I'm so touch-starved after only being broken up a few months. Then again, I had been craving a comforting touch long before that. Adele just never cared because if it made me feel worthless, then it was good for her.

I force myself to breathe and push thoughts of Adele and our life in New York away. If I don't, I'm going to start spiraling in front of a bunch of strangers. I need to be in the here and now. And anyway, it's my turn next. Mika helps me by pointing out my weapons and how to roll to hit.

Which I don't because I roll a three.

"Want to put that in dice jail?" Nico asks me, holding up the little box and giving it a shake. The one die in there rattles against the sides.

I shake my head. "I only have the one set," I mumble. At least I'm looking at him. One thing at a time. Nico sets the dice jail box back down and shrugs.

Next to me, Mika starts to rummage through a large bag she must have left on the floor. I hear the clinking of dice, and by the way the bag bulges, she must have quite the collection. After a second or two, she pulls out a small clear cube with a set of sparkly blue dice inside.

"Here, take these. Hopefully, they will give you more luck." She hands them to me, and I stare at the box. The dice are a translucent blue with flecks of glitter, definitely not something I would pick for myself. Still, I'm grateful for Mika. She's trying to make me feel included, and I appreciate it. I should have believed Marco when he said his friends wouldn't judge me.

We continue playing for several more hours. By the end, while I'm not exactly comfortable with the group, it doesn't seem so bad now. The game was fun, and I actually enjoyed myself some. My cousin is a brilliant story-teller, which I guess means he's a great GM.

Everyone is buzzing with a post-game high, talking excitedly about their characters. I gather up the dice Mika gave me and drop them back in the cube. "Thanks for letting me use these," I say to her, and I'm actually able to look her in the eye for more than a blink. She spent all night helping me through, not even getting frustrated when I asked her the same thing over and over. I couldn't stop myself from looking at her occasionally.

I haven't really looked at another woman in years. Adele made sure to make me feel like I was a cheater just for acknowledging another woman, even family members. But I'm looking at Mika now as I try to hand over the dice.

She smiles at me, and it's so big and luminous that my face heats up. I'm sure I've turned completely red. "Keep them. Consider it a little welcome to B&B gift. Besides, they seemed to roll well for you." She gives me a wink. While I know she's referring to the higher rolls

I made using her dice the rest of the night, part of me is reading too much into that wink.

I need to get out of here.

But first, we all help to remove tankards and replace the top of the table, then pack up our stuff. Everyone offers to help Mika with dishes, but she waves us off. I feel a little guilty about leaving her alone to clean up, but I think if I spend any more time in Mika's presence tonight, I'm going to combust.

I walk down the front steps with Marco after saying goodbye to Mika, Stella, and Nico. It's later than I realized, and I'm half tempted to take the Metro home. But my bike will be faster, so I strap on my helmet as I walk with Marco to the station.

"That wasn't so bad, right?" he asks, and I can tell by his tone he's hoping that I'll want to come back. And strangely, I do.

"Not bad. A little awkward, but not bad," I say, feeling like I can breathe fully for the first time in hours. We don't say anything for a moment, only the sounds of Marco's Crocs creaking with each step and the clink of my bike spokes as they rotate.

"Sooo," Marco draws the word out, "you and Mika looked quite cozy tonight." I stop and turn to him, panic rushing through me. Marco stops too and gives me a grin.

"What?" A brilliant response.

Marco starts laughing and resumes walking. I stay still a beat longer, then increase my stride to catch up. "I'm just saying—looks like you two were enjoying each other's company. That's all. Neither of you could stop making eyes at each other," he says, still laughing.

"I wasn't making eyes. She was just helping me out with the game. I was grateful." I sound truly pathetic to my own ears.

Marco makes a noise that sounds like *mmhmm*. "I'm the GM, Ash. I see all."

I snort. "You see nothing. A pretty woman helped me figure out how to play a game because we were sitting next to each other. There's not much more to it."

But of course, my cousin picks up on only one word of what I say. "So you think she's pretty? You know, she's single if you want to ask her out."

"I want out of this conversation," I respond but tuck the knowledge that she's single away to ruminate over later.

This time Marco is the one to stop, and I do too. He puts a hand on my shoulder. It's one I'm used to, a familiar pat. Nothing like the heat from Mika's hand earlier. Marco looks me square in the eyes, "Listen, Ash, I know Adele did a number on you, but it's okay to—"

But I cut him off. I don't want to hear it, and I think I've pushed myself well outside of my comfort zone for one night. I shrug off his arm and keep walking. "Don't, Marco. Just don't, please."

He nods and we walk the rest of the way to the Metro station in silence. I'm not angry at Marco. I know he just wants me to be happy. Not just happy, either. He wants me to feel like I'm worthy of being happy. Something I haven't felt in a long time. Years, really.

But everything is still so raw. I'm still raw. And as much as I think Mika is cute as hell and fun to be around, I'm not ready for anything.

My cousin gives me a hug when we reach the station, and I hug him back tightly. "See you Friday for dinner, right?" he asks me.

I nod. "Yeah, I'll see you then." Hopping on my bike, I take off toward home, thinking of gray-green eyes and bubblegum pink hair.

I'm putting the finishing touches on a design for a book cover a few days after the game. It's a thriller, which seems to be my wheelhouse lately. My graphic design day job pays the bills, but designing covers for indie authors brings me more joy. The pay is decent enough for the amount of work I do too.

My phone vibrates next to me, and I see that it's Marco texting.

[Marco: Drinks tonight with the gang?]

Drinks? Like out at a bar on a Saturday night? When was the last time I did that?

It's been years at this point. Adele never liked to go out to bars, not with me anyway.

[Me: Sure]

[Marco: Awesome. 7pm at the Gibson, U St metro stop]

[Marco: Seriously, don't bike around here]

[Me: Ok. See you then]

I'm doing it. I'm actually going out on a weekend to a bar. With other people. There's no one around to guilt me out of going now. I can do whatever I want.

Then why am I already regretting saying yes?

Because it's easy to stay home. I let Adele convince me that it was wrong of me to live my life outside of her for so long. And now I'm broken. Now I want to bail on my cousin and his friends when all they have been is welcoming to me.

I consider texting Marco back and canceling, but then I think of Mika. Her beautiful smile and colorful hair. After meeting her one time, she has already become something like a bright beacon in my life. I've thought about her every day since I left her house Wednesday. I haven't thought about another woman since college.

Okay, so maybe it wouldn't hurt to spend a little more time outside my apartment. Maybe it'll be good for me to hang out with people and make friends. And if one of those people happens to be a pretty woman who is patient, kind, and funny, that's totally okay too.

That doesn't stop me from feeling guilty the rest of the day.

I've walked past where the Gibson should be at least twice, but there's no sign. Normally, I would think I just got the address wrong, but I've triple checked it. I'm about to give up and head home when I turn, and there's Mika coming out of a non-descript door.

Her pink hair is down tonight, curled around her bare shoulders. The form fitted top she's wearing is forest green and off the shoulder, starting at mid bicep. I can't help but let my eyes travel over her, from the modest heeled boots, up miles of long lean legs, to her short black skirt. There's so much skin on display, and honestly, I just want to stare at her all night. But then it finally dawns on me that I'm being a total creep and look away.

"Hey, I thought you might have trouble finding the place." She walks up to me with that big smile of hers.

"Come on, we already have a table." Before I can do anything, she grabs my hand and tows me through the door.

I barely register a host stand before I'm tugged off to the left into the bar proper. *It's a speakeasy*, I think, but my brain is focused on the most important thing: Mika's hand around mine. It's like I can feel nothing but that one point of contact. Her hand is soft and warm in mine, and I hope she never lets go.

My feet are on autopilot, going one then the other, following wherever Mika leads. I see the rest of the group sits at a corner table, crowded up against each other on L-shaped benches. Elise and Lena are also there, and it makes me feel a little better to have Lena's comforting presence around.

"Move over, lazy ass," Mika says to Nico, even as she starts sliding onto the bench beside him, dropping my hand. I miss her touch already. They move down until there's enough space for me to fit. Mika could have very well pushed me into the space next to Nico, but she didn't. She gave me the end, an out if I need it.

Or maybe it just happened that way and she put no thought into it at all. People just naturally want to sit next to their friends. I'm the odd man out. Besides Marco and Lena, I'm a stranger who has already crashed their group once. My palms are sweating and I want to leave. Just turn around and sprint out of here and stay home where I belong.

I don't realize I'm still standing until Mika is slipping her hand into mine again and pulling me onto the bench. "Going to stand there all night, or do you want to drink?" Her tone is playful, and she keeps her eyes on mine when she speaks. It's like she wants to keep me centered on the conversation, reminding me that I exist in this moment.

"What are we drinking?" I ask, gently pulling my hand from hers. Part of me wants to drop her hand quickly so she won't notice how sweaty it is, but I also don't want to offend her. And then a part of me didn't want to let go.

Fuck, why do I over think everything?

A pretty woman holds my hand, even platonically, and I'm on the verge of a breakdown. It wasn't always like this. Before Adele, I was fine around people. Mostly fine anyway. I've always been a little anxious in social situations, but once I got serious with Adele, and she started to push me out of my own life, well, it all got so much worse.

And now here I am, in a bar on a Saturday night with people who could be my friends if I let them, doing what normal twenty-somethings do on the weekend. Totally normal. I've got this.

"Not alcohol, unfortunately, for me." Lena pouts as she rubs her small baby bump.

"Yeah, but they have great mocktails, so don't let her bitching fool you, Ash," Marco says as he slides over a menu to Mika. She takes it, scoots closer to me, and holds it between us. She's not even touching me, but she's close enough I can feel the heat from her skin. She smells like strawberries and cream, and I'm suddenly overwhelmed with the desire to lick her peach skin to see if she tastes like it too.

I need to get my head out of the gutter or whatever perverted place it's gone off to. I try to focus on the menu in front of me, but Mika is too distracting. She just has to sit there, so close, and I'm left with my thoughts scattered. I don't think any woman has ever made me feel so much in so short of time.

I don't even remember what I order. I just pick one at random. The conversation flows around me with all the ease and comfort of people who have been friends for a long time. But I'm not part of this intimate group, and so I stay quiet and try not to spend the whole time staring at Mika.

I catch her a few times staring back at me, and it's like my whole body flushes under her gaze. She makes an effort to include me in the conversation as much as possible. She's just so cute and considerate.

But I'm a mess. It's only been a few months since Adele and I broke up, and after so long with one person, I don't know how to be with anyone else. I have to fix myself first since Adele broke down all that made me who I am.

Besides, Mika is so vibrant. I barely know her, yet I'm aware she needs someone who shines like she does. And that's not me. She's just being nice, which is fine, but it doesn't mean anything else.

CHAPTER 5

MIKA

[Me: Sooooo what's the deal with your cousin? Is he just shy around people? Or like shy around women?]

[Marco: He's just shy around new people. Also, yes and yes]

[Marco: Want his number?]

[Me: What? No, that would be weird.]

[Me: But also yes.]

[Marco: Lol let me send you his contact info.]

I toss my phone next to me and cover my face. *Did I really just ask for Ash's number? What am I thinking?!*

After Quinn, I told myself there was no way I would ever get involved with someone who played B&B. It would be too painful if something happened. B&B is a big part of my life, and I would never make the group choose between me and another player. Not again.

Which was one of many reasons why I always turned Nico down for a date. He's more of a brother, anyway. Kissing him would feel incestuous.

I'm just trying to be welcoming, I tell myself. Besides his family, Ash doesn't know anybody else in the District. I just want him to know he has a friend already. It's neighborly. Yeah, that's it. It's totally not because of his gorgeous eyes or his defined arms and legs, and definitely not because he's so tall I could climb him like a tree.

Definitely not.

I just need to act natural around him. I mean, I'm usually a big flirt anyway, but all my friends know that and know that's just the way I am. But Ash doesn't know me, and I don't want him to feel like I'm constantly hitting on him. I'm not trying to, I swear. I just need to be cool.

Fly casual.

What I definitely don't need to do is think about how long it's been since the last time I had sex. Or just made out with somebody. Because it has been ... a while.

Sure, I've dated plenty since Quinn and I broke up, but nothing serious, just flings that lasted a few weeks or a few one-night-stands. But something more meaningful, more lasting? Nothing. It's like I'm relationship immune. The minute someone starts to show an interest in my hobbies like B&B, and I just boot them out of my life.

I'm determined to be friendly with Ash but not too friendly and just ogle from afar. Or better yet, not ogle at all. Just passively enjoy his handsome features. But that's it. I'll help him get the hang of B&B, and the only flirting allowed is in character.

Good, that's settled then.

My phone vibrates with another text from Marco. He's sent me Ash's number.

I groan loudly. *Okay, maybe not so settled,* I think as I save the info to my contacts.

I want to rip the headphones off and throw them across the room.

It's hour ... *fuck*, hour four of this transcription project, and I swear my ears are bleeding. I'm pretty sure that I'm transcribing every single talk at this conference, and they are all literally the worst speakers. The first session's speaker was so monotone that I legit started to nod off. The one after that talked so fast, I could barely keep up. They got progressively worse after that.

That brings me to the current speaker. Her voice is just below that of a dog whistle. I swear one of my eardrums has ruptured. What's worse is that the woman rambles like crazy. It's like she only bullet pointed her notes and just riffed off that. I feel sorry for the people who actually sat through this whole thing in person.

I need to get out of here and away from this conference transcription. At least for a little bit. I have some other projects to work on, one of which is a translation. I have eleven years of Hebrew school and summers in Israel with Bubbe for this part of my work. While I enjoyed the Hebrew school part, I absolutely hated going to Israel. It's definitely not the homeland for this Jew. That would be Chevy Chase, the town in Maryland, not the actor, where I was born and raised.

My laptop gets stuffed in my bag, and I'm grabbing my bike off the rack when I have an idea. What if I invited Ash out to lunch? Strictly platonic of course. Just two adults who have recently been introduced forming a friendship. He needs friends in the city, after all. And I ... just want an excuse to hang out with a handsome guy.

Would it be weird to text him out of the blue and ask to meet up right now? Yeah, probably, especially since he doesn't have my number.

I stop and think about it for a minute. Marco said he just got out of a bad relationship. I wonder how bad he meant. Bad like me and Quinn or worse? Fuck, I can't imagine anything worse than that.

Okay, minute up, I'm going to do it. I'm going to text Ash out for a totally platonic lunch. Let him know he has another friend in the city to hang with. And who doesn't love a free meal? Because I am definitely paying for his lunch.

Before I can talk myself out of it, I pull up his contact info and shoot off a text.

[Mika: Hey, it's Mika. Marco gave me your number. I wanted to see if you would be up for lunch. My treat to welcome you to the DMV.]

I wait several minutes before he texts back, watching as the text bubbles appear and then disappear. I'm still on my porch, bike leaned against my leg. I yelp when my phone vibrates in my hand.

[Ash: Today? Now?]

[Me: Only if you're up for it. I just have to get away from work or I'm throwing my laptop out the window.]

[Ash: Okay. Then sure?]

[Me: Is that a question? You can say no if you're uncomfortable, no hard feelings.]

[Ash: Not a question. Sorry. Sure, lunch sounds great.]

[Me: 👍]

A thumbs up emoji! Seriously, I sent a thumbs up emoji?
No, this is what I wanted: keep it casual; don't make it awkward. I just want to be friends and nothing more. He just got out of a relationship, and I'm not looking for one right now. Relationships are bad news anyway. They just set you up to get hurt. But I can still hang out with a cute guy and have it be totally platonic. I can do this.

I send him the location of the restaurant, one of the Busboys & Poets locations that should be near both of us, and we set a time for an hour from now. Then he sends me back a thumbs up emoji, and I seriously want to off myself.

Yeah, there's zero chance of me playing this cool.

I get there five minutes before 1:00 p.m., which is when we agreed to meet. I plan to grab a table and then wait for him so we can order together. But when I walk in to the noisy place, he's already there, sitting on a large brown couch with a coffee table in front of him.

I wave when I spot him, and I can't help but smile when he looks at me and his cheeks turn pink. There's not a chance in hell of me resisting making him blush like that as much as I can. It's so adorable.

He stands awkwardly at my approach, and he doesn't quite meet my eyes. I place my hand on his chest and give him a light shove. "You don't have to stand up for me. I'll just shimmy around the table," I say. If I'm being honest with myself, I just wanted an excuse to touch him.

And oh fuck, there are muscles under that dark blue t-shirt he's wearing. That one small touch has me tingling all over thinking about what it would be like to take his shirt off and just stare at his body. God, I'm being such a perv thinking about this guy.

Ash flops back down on the couch, and his face is so red now that I'm worried I went too far in just that small touch. I take a seat on the couch next to him, making sure to leave a large enough space between us that I don't make him uncomfortable any more than I already have. "Thanks for meeting up with me. I had to get out of my house, or I was going to burn my laptop and then my headphones," I say with a laugh.

Ash fidgets with his fingers in his lap, and it's then that I notice his trademark bag is next to him on the floor, so he has no strap to hang onto. "I thought you said you were going to throw it out the window? In your text. You said that." He doesn't look at me when he responds, but I'm starting to get use to that. He'll make it out of his shell in his own time.

"Ah, but that comes after I set it on fire. I don't want to inhale all that toxic junk computers have in them." I laugh. We take a few minutes to order food and then sit back with glasses of water.

"So, what do you do that makes you want to destroy your things?" he asks suddenly, and I won't lie, I'm surprised he asked the first question.

I am going to coax this little turtle man out of his shell!

"I mostly do transcriptions, especially for conference videos. There's AI for that now, but they all still kind of suck, so until the robots replace me, I still have a job trying to make sense of mumblers. Sometimes I do some translation work, but that's even less exciting." I turn my body so I'm facing Ash and lean back against the arm of the couch.

While he doesn't look exactly at ease, I can see his shoulder drop a little as I get more comfortable on the couch, still giving him his space.

"You must have pretty stable work to live in place in Petworth," he says, and then he immediately starts to fidget more, and he doesn't look at me. "Fuck, I mean, that's none of my business. I'm sorry."

I want to hug this man and run my fingers through his hair and tell him he never has to apologize for saying what he's thinking. But that would be crossing like every line and probably a little patronizing, so I keep my hands to myself.

Instead, I laugh. He glances over at me out of the corner of his eye, and what he sees on my face must make him feel a little better. At least he stops fidgeting. "No, no, it's totally fine. It's steady work, but the house was my Bubbe's. She's in a senior living place up in Silver Spring, real nice place where she plays mahjong with a bunch of other catty women. She didn't want to sell it, so she gave it to me. I'm also a trust fund baby, so that helps."

Let me spill my life story to you while I'm at it, Ash. Want to hear all my most embarrassing stories from summers at Camp Louise?

"What about you? Marco said you are an artist." He doesn't exactly radiate artist energy, but I can't judge by that. There are some people you can just look at and know exactly what they do for a living. Ash is not one of those people. In his t-shirt and jeans with those solid muscles underneath, fuck, you could tell me he's a personal trainer, and I would believe it.

"Sort of. I'm a graphic designer. I work for a marketing company out of New York, but it's all remote now. I design book covers on the side, which is more fun and rewarding than my actual job. I would do it full time if I could," he says with a sheepish look. He finally turns his head again to look at me when he speaks, though he's looking past me. It's a start, so I'll take what I can get.

"Book cover designs? Like for self-published writers?" I'm curious now. I have some online friends who are writers and always looking for a new cover design.

Ash nods. "Yeah, I love working with independent writers. They have a lot of passion and a lot of faith in me to deliver their dream cover. It feels good to finish a project and know they love it."

Wow, the guy is on a roll with the words. Seems he's also passionate about his work. So, that's the secret to get him to talk. That and some roleplay at the gaming table. *Wonder if he's the kind of guy who's open to roleplay other places?* Not that I will ever find out because this is just a totally chill, no ulterior motives, hangout lunch.

"Sounds like you love it. That's admirable. Not everyone gets to do what they love and make money off it." I laugh. I don't want him to think I'm being critical.

"Do you love what you do?" he asks shyly. He's stopped fidgeting now, so that's a good sign. Before I can answer, our food arrives, and we spend a few minutes eating in silence, our plates balanced on the coffee table.

I stop to think it over for a minute. *Do I like what I do?* I never really took the time to reflect on it. I'm good at what I do. I'm quick, fulfill my deadlines ahead of schedule for the most part, and have a good professional network that keeps hiring me for more jobs. But it's a job. I have to do it to make money. I don't want to rely on my trust for everything.

Ash manages to watch me as I think it over, and I feel compelled to give him an answer quickly—which is probably why my answer surprises me. "It's okay, but not exactly what I want to do with my life. I have a master's in English, which helps with what I do, but I've always wanted to be a writer. I don't know. Maybe I feel like I'm wasting my potential."

Talk about spilling my guts to a stranger. But maybe that's what I need. Ash doesn't really know me, and there's no history between us, so his judgment doesn't matter.

He gives me a long lingering stare, like he's trying to read something on my face. "So do you write?" His face turns to mild horror. "I mean, I … didn't want to imply that you don't write, that you don't try. I just..."

I cut him off with a raised hand. "Chill out. You didn't offend me or anything, so don't apologize. I get what you mean. And yes, I do write but only for myself. I don't like to share it with anyone. Well, not anyone I know. I do post things on the internet, but it's all anonymous. The rest of the group doesn't know, and I'm not ready to share that with them." I give him a look that clearly says *This is between us.*

To my relief, Ash nods, agreeing to keep my confession to himself. I think I like him a little more for it. "Maybe one day I'll finish the novel I've been writing forever. Who knows? I might actually do something with it."

"You should," Ash says, and he looks directly at me, his eyes shining. Just let me get lost in those gorgeous eyes.

We stare at each other longer than is probably comfortable for him, but he doesn't look away and neither do I. There's still a physical distance between us, but it feels like this chat has really opened me up to knowing Ash. I want to know more about him, but this is our first time one on one, so we'll save the deep dive into pasts and wants for later.

He breaks eye contact first, and I'm a little disappointed but keep it from my face. "I should get going. I still have some projects to finish up before I call it a day. Not that I want to leave—I don't. It's nice to talk to someone who isn't family. I love Marco and Lena, don't get me wrong. It's just ... nice." He picks up his bag and starts messing with the strap again.

I nod. He's right. It has been nice. And I also need to get back to work, even though I really, really don't want to.

I pay for our meals and head back out to the street. Our bikes are locked close together, and we exchange light goodbyes before riding off to our respective homes. As much as I want to let my head drift to think about Ash while I pedal home, I force myself to focus. My bike has been clipped before by asshole drivers, and I've seen even more people hit, so I need to be vigilant.

By the time I get home, I find that I can't wait to see Ash again. Now I just need Wednesday to come a little sooner. The rest of the day is a slog through more mumbling conference talks, and it's so hard to concentrate. All I can think about are Ash's eyes staring at me, his shy smile reaching them. When he smiles, it's with his whole face. A girl could get totally lost in a smile like that, even if it does look a little like he hasn't smiled much.

Maybe that has something to do with the bad relationship he just got out of. I know when Quinn and I broke up,

I couldn't bring myself to feel anything for weeks. Months maybe. I almost forgot how to smile. If it wasn't for the gang, I think I would have stayed numb for much longer.

But they dragged me out, took me to do fun things, and kept me playing the game so I could have a channel to vent my problems. And it worked. Eventually the pain dulled, happiness returned, and I moved past the worst of it. I hope the group and I can do that for Ash. He seems so sweet and yet a little broken. But nobody is beyond helping and fixing. Not like he needs to be fixed— more liked healed.

Later that night, as I get ready for bed, my phone goes off with a text. It's from Ash.

[Ash: Thanks for lunch. I enjoyed the company.]

He enjoyed the company! How am I supposed to take that? Did he just enjoy having someone around, or did he like my specific company? *Don't overthink it.*

[Me: My pleasure. We should do it again sometime. Gets me out of the house, which I totally don't mind.]

Shit, does he think I'm asking him out? No, it was casual. Totally casual. Just someone asking a new friend out to a meal. Lunch isn't romantic. Lunch is a hang out meal. It's not like I asked him to dinner.

I agonize over my response for several minutes, and Ash doesn't text back, which makes it so much worse. Finally, my phone goes off again.

[Ash: I would like that. I stay in my apartment way too much.]

So I didn't scare him off! Score for me.

[Me: Sounds good. Just text me whenever you want.]

[Ash: Will do.]

[Mika: Goodnight, Ash.]

[Ash: Goodnight, Mika.]

I plug my phone into the charger and lay down on my bed. I fall asleep with a smile on my face.

CHAPTER 6

ASH

It's Wednesday again, and I'm standing outside Mika's house. Only this time, I don't hesitate as long to approach her door. I don't feel quite as anxious to be here as I did last week. Maybe that has something to do with the group hangout from the other night.

No, it's because of Mika. I know it's because of her. She has made me feel so welcome and comfortable. It was nice to have lunch with her the other day. She didn't push me or invade my space, even if I might have wanted it just a little. The first two times we've met, she gave me small little touches, and after going so long without that small kindness, I find myself craving it.

"Do you always need to hold my hand like you're a child? Honestly, Sebastian, grow up." Adele's voice plays in my head. It was the last time I tried to hold her hand in any intimate way. After that, I didn't bother to try. I couldn't even walk down the street holding my girl-friend's hand because she thought it was childish. But that was years ago. The only time she let me touch her

was when we had sex, and even then, that was so rare and uncomfortable for so long that there was no joy in the touches.

Fuck, I'm really messed up. My therapist says I'm suffering from c-PTSD, whatever that means, and I guess talking to someone through my issues has been helping a little in the few weeks I've been seeing him..

I bring myself back to Mika's door and knock. She's there in a second, this time in an emerald green dress with thin straps. The top part hugs her body, showing off her impressive curves while the skirt flairs out. Her gloriously pink hair is tied up into two braids, and all the blood rushes south at the sight as I imagine how I would love to wrap those braids around my hands in a compromising position.

I am really depraved. I barely know this woman, and I'm already sexualizing her like crazy all because it's been too long since anyone outside of family has shown me any affection.

She doesn't give me long to stew in my own sexual frustration. Mika quickly grabs my hand and drags me into the house, which honestly, still does nothing to alleviate my dirty thoughts. Her hand is so warm and wrapped around my own hand so perfectly.

"Oh, thank God you're here. I need to borrow your mouth," she says, her words a rush as she pulls me into the kitchen. *Shit, what does she mean she needs my mouth?* My mind immediately drops to the gutter. But I find myself willing to offer my mouth for anything she needs.

"Fuck, phrasing! I didn't mean it like that. I meant I need you to try this baklava. I've never made it before, and I don't know if it's good enough to serve to humans.

Please just be my taste tester." She's even cuter when she flustered, and her cheeks are definitely pink. I bet her cheeks feel warm too, and my hands itch to place my palms against her beautiful face.

Mika drops my hand once we reach the kitchen. She rushes over to a pan sitting on the counter and quickly returns with a sticky triangle of baklava. My mouth waters at the sight of the layered pastry. "Open," she commands, lifting the dessert to my mouth. Without thought, I obey and she gently offers me a bite.

Flavors explode on my tongue as I chew. It's amazing. But I can't take my eyes off of Mika. She's looking at me with such beautiful, big eyes, waiting for my judgment. She sucks in her bottom lip, and shit, she's actually nervous about this. Maybe not me, specifically, but she's sincerely worried the food tastes bad. I don't want to see that look on her face.

Once I swallow, I can't help the smile I give her because it's the kind of dessert that you can't help but feel happy after eating. "It's amazing! I've never had a baklava this good," I say, meaning every word. Mika is an astounding cook. I'm beginning to wonder if there's anything she can't do.

"Really? You're not just saying that? Because I have no problem with constructive criticism. You won't hurt my feelings." She looks down at the remainder of the baklava in her hand like she's unsure about it. I can't have her second guessing herself or thinking I'm not genuine.

Clearly thinking with my dick instead of my brain, I lightly grab her wrist holding the dessert, bring the piece of baklava to my mouth, and take it from her fingers. And if my mouth lingers a little long on her fingers, it's because my dick is in completely control. Her eyes grow wide, and I watch as her pupils dilate. *Is she turned on?* Because I am absolutely turned on, and this is dangerous territory.

All of my anxiety slams into me at once as I realize what I just did. My gaze drops from hers, and my hands reach for the comfort of the strap of my bag. I'm ruining this friendship before it really has a chance to start, all because a pretty girl is nice to me.

I can't tell if it's just me breathing heavy or if my actions affected her all that much, but I suddenly want to run out of her house and never come back. But I don't move, and neither does she. It feels so awkward now, I can practically feel the tension in the air.

Sexual tension, maybe? Or is that wishful thinking?

I'm saved from my fight or flight, fight definitely being kissing Mika, by the front door opening and the loud chatter of the rest of the group filling the hall. Whatever was happening between me and Mika shatters, and she steps away from me, but I manage to raise my eyes just a little to look at her. There's pink staining her cheeks, and she is breathing heavily, but her eyes dart toward the hall where everyone is quickly approaching. Her bright smile pulls up her lips, and she transforms back into bubbly and happy Mika before my eyes.

"Hope you nerds are hungry because I have enough for an army in here. Or a troop of ravenous adventurers, to be more accurate." She moves away from me to grab plates. Despite what just happened between us, she still has people to feed, and I am pretty sure she isn't going to bring up what happened to the rest of the group.

"I smell veggie lasagna!" Nico yells as he walks into the kitchen, Stella and Marco on his heels.

"And cheesy breadsticks just for you, Nico," Mika says, pulling a tray of golden-brown breadsticks out of the oven. She sets it on a trivet on the counter next to the dessert. The dangerous, sexy temptation dessert. I'll never be able to look at baklava again without thinking of Mika's fingers.

I have to get out of the warm kitchen. It's making my head fuzzy. It has to be the heat and not the lust overtaking my body. I inch out of the kitchen and head toward the dining room where we'll be playing. Nico's voice carries out of the kitchen. "Can't you just come to my house and cook for me every day?" Over my shoulder, I can see him wrap his arms around Mika from behind.

Something flares up within me. It feels like ... jealousy? Nico gets to touch her so easily, practically draping himself all over her. I can't stop myself from wondering if there's something going on between them.

Are they more than friends? Or is she just flirty with everyone, and I'm not special at all?

"Hey, you okay?" I register Marco's hand on my shoulder. I turn to look at my cousin, and he looks concerned. Hiding my emotions has always been my biggest weakness, and I'm probably an open book right now.

"Yeah, I'm fine. Great. Everything is great," I say, convincing no one. It doesn't surprise me when Marco narrows his eyes at me.

"Right, sure. Did something happen? Work? Or did she contact you?" He looks so worried, and I want to put my cousin's mind at ease. But I know who he means by *she*, and it's not Mika. Well, that wipes away the last of my anxieties about Mika. Instead, my heart plunges to my stomach, and I feel a little sick.

"No, I haven't heard anything from her since I got here. Work is great. Business as usual," I say, trying desperately to school my features. It's only sort of working.

"Then what's going on? You seem really flustered," he says, and I want to hug Marco for being so concerned for my well-being. I've tried to let him know whenever I can how much I appreciate all he's doing for me.

But then I betray myself. I can't help that my eyes flick to Mika through the open kitchen doorway. Marco doesn't miss the look, and he turns toward me with a mischievous grin. "So, you and Mika have been spending some time together, I hear."

I splutter, then find my voice. "Who told you that? We're just getting to know each other. You wanted me to like your friends."

Marco laughs and claps his free hand on my other shoulder. "Oh I do, and it seems like you are really taking that to heart." He continues to laugh a little, not at me, but at the situation. Whatever that is because I don't even really know yet.

Marco sobers quickly though, and he turns serious. "Look, Ash, Mika is a great woman, and I love her to death. I really think you two could be good together. Eventually. You just got out from under Adele's bullshit. And Mika, her last serious relationship was a disaster, and she's been messed up by it." He squeezes both of my shoulders. "I want you to be happy, okay? But give yourself some time."

I'm honestly touched by his words. Marco keeps finding ways to look out for me and have my back. And he's right. I know he is. Mika is cute, and fun, and has been nothing but kind to me. But I'm still a mess, and I don't want to put that on anyone. And if she's been hurt before and still isn't over it, then it wouldn't be right or fair for either of us to do anything more than be friends. I'm okay with just being a friend.

So, I nod. "I know. I'm just looking for friends right now. That's all I want. And Mika's nice. Besides, I don't want to upset the group dynamic or anything." Even though my heart sinks a little at my own words, I know they are the right ones.

Marco pats my right shoulder and drops his hands. "Yeah, good call. We've already had to deal with that disaster before, and like I said, it really left Mike messed up." He gives me one last pat on the shoulder and walks back into the kitchen to grab a plate.

But I'm left puzzled. I don't know what happened with Mika. Marco implied that she dated someone in the group, and it ended badly. I doubt it was Nico or Stella since they all seem to get along so well. *Was there someone else before? Someone who isn't in the group anymore?*

"Come grab some food before these ravenous monsters eat it all, Ash," Mika calls out to me. I set my bag down next to the chair I sat in last time and head back into the kitchen. Whatever happened in the past with Mika isn't my business, so it's best if I don't think on it. I should be focusing on the game we'll be starting soon. But it's really hard not to think about everything around Mika when she's standing less than five feet from me.

"Okay, Varic, you're up. Whatcha doing?" Marco asks Nico. It's his turn in combat and so far, we've been doing pretty well in taking down the group of whatever we're facing. I'm not still not sure what all the creatures are in this game. Marco said he would lend me the book on monsters later so I can get an idea.

Across the table from me, Nico ponders his character sheet for only half a second. "I think I'm going to have to make him feel bad about himself and use Mocking Word on the guy to the left of Uriel."

"Okay, and what are you telling him?" Marco prompts.

"I say, 'Hey ugly, I've got more brains in my dick than you've got in your head.'" Nico makes a V with his hands descending below the table, but we all get what he means.

Everyone at the table laughs, myself included. Nico's Mocking Word insults, while not great, have been ridiculous.

Behind the GM screen, Marco rolls a die. "Right, so he fails on his wisdom save, and now he feels even worse about his intelligence than he did before. Roll damage."

Nico rolls a pyramid die and responds with 4 damage.

Before I know it, it's my turn. "Kilris, you've got one guy beating on Uriel and another who is trying to make his way to you. What are you doing?" Marco stares at me over his screen, waiting for my action.

I stare down at my character sheet, looking for what I am able to do, when Mika leans close to me. "Try Vines. It's a good one. He'll get all tangled up and make it easier for the rest of us to hit."

She smiles at me, and I'm undone all over again. How I manage to focus back in on the game is a mystery to me. I pick up the d20, which I'm starting to realize is my most used die, and announce to Marco what I plan to do. "Which one are you aiming for?" He half stands to point out the one near Mika's character and then the one coming near to mine.

"Uh, the one near Uriel." Because of course I want to be her hero. My character, that is. My character wants to be the hero to Mika's character.

Marco shrugs, and maybe I should have gone after the one closest to me. But the other guy has a clear advantage over Mika's character. I'm helping a team member. Once again, Marco rolls behind his screen, but he lets me know what he's doing this time. "This guy has to make a strength save or else he's going to be wrapped up tight."

My cousin doesn't even consult his sheet. "And he fails. So, that guy is restrained by vines and won't be going anywhere until his next turn. He'll get another chance to make the save." Marco turns his attention to Mika. "Uriel, you're up, and you have advantage to hit on the baddie next to you."

Mika takes her d20 and says to Marco, "I'm going to stabby-stab with my rapier. And that's..." She rolls her die and then rolls it again. "Damn, twelve to hit?"

She raises her eyes expectantly at Marco. "That's your best roll?" Mika nods, looking dejected. "Well, that just barely hits. Roll damage."

When her turn passes, I turn and ask her why she rolled twice. "Since you grappled that guy, he can't do shit. So I have advantage to hit. Which means I get to roll twice and take the higher number. Pretty cool, right?" I nod because that's pretty handy. Seems I did something right with my turn.

The rest of the game progresses without any mishaps toward our characters, and before I'm quite ready, the game is ending for the night, and everyone starts packing up. "This game really sucks you in, doesn't it?" I ask Mika.

She grins at me and nods. "Yeah, it has that effect. It also helps that Marco is like the best GM out there. A good storyteller can make or break a game."

My cousin grins at us. "Please, keep talking about how great I am." He laughs, and it's easy to just laugh with everybody.

"Okay, babes, as much as I want to linger and enjoy your beautiful faces some more, I have an early fucking day tomorrow. I'm out." Stella stands from the table and comes around until she's next to Mika. "Bye, sweetie," she says, not even having to bend to give Mika a kiss on the cheek. Mika air kisses her back and then Stella is gone.

Nico follows a minute or so later, heading out the door with as much noise as possible. Nico is starting to grow on me. He's louder than anyone I have ever met in my life, and that includes members of my own family who are notoriously boisterous. But while I think he's fun and great to be around, it's probably best to be around Nico in moderation.

Part of me wants to stay at Mika's, to find any excuse to stay longer: help her with the cleanup and dishes, anything. But I think of what Marco said before dinner, and I know the best thing I can do for myself is get out of there and not be left alone with Mika again. I'll probably just embarrass myself if I do.

I give Marco a hug and haul my bag over my head. When I turn to Mika, I don't know what to do. Hugging is definitely a bad idea, and we still don't know each other that well. A handshake seems really dumb. So, I panic and do nothing but mess with the strap on my bag. "Thanks again for dinner, and the game. I'll ... uh, see you next week." I can't even look at her. I have to look past her just to get the words out because all I can think about is earlier in the kitchen before everyone showed up.

Mika gives me the biggest, warmest smile I've ever seen, and it's really time I leave before I fall to my knees before and beg for her to just keep smiling like that at me. I don't say another word, nor do I let her say anything before I'm dashing to my bike and out the door.

I'm several blocks away before I remember to breathe normally.

CHAPTER 7

MIKA

It's several weeks after whatever the hell happened in my kitchen with Ash, and I'm still thinking about it.

Like constantly.

But that was the last of the super-charged flirting we did. Since then, Ash hasn't been able to look me in the eye. Again. And I have to admit, I hate the feeling. I was so ready to jump his bones after the Baklava Incident, but Marco talked to me after Ash ran out of my house. It's not like Marco told me stay away from his cousin. More like, Ash and I should keep things friendly right now and not rush into anything romantic. Ash has been out of a toxic relationship for barely two months, and it really messed him up. Marco isn't blind; he can tell we're into each other. He's just looking out for the both of us.

I respect Marco for that because he's not just looking out for his family, he's looking out for me too. Quinn made me wary of trusting people. And relationships require trust. Sure, I think I could have a lot of fun with Ash. But I won't do that to the group because nothing just stays fun, and then things would get awkward with the group. Since Ash is Marco's actual family, I'm not sure he would pick me this time if there was a falling out. It's better for everyone if Ash and I remain friends and not even friends with benefits.

So I'm determined to keep things chill with Ash. No more one-on-one with him, even if I really want to get lunch and hang out with him. Group settings are the best way to avoid temptation. We still sit next to each other at the gaming table. Once seats are established, well, it's hard to break the habit. When we go out though, I try not to always sit next to Ash. Look, I can't entirely keep my distance. I'm only human, and I'm still very attracted to him. Still, occasionally I plant myself between Stella and Nico, just to create a buffer, and let Ash get to know the rest of the group.

And if I can't help but stare at him every now and then, well, that's a me problem. Maybe I just need to get laid and get some of this sexual frustration out of my system. Maybe it's not even Ash specifically. It could be I just need a cute person to lust after and Ash just happened to show up at my door at just peak horniness.

I make the executive decision to go out and find someone to at least make out with at a bar. Sure, it would probably be easier to download a dating app, but there's so much effort into putting together a profile, and I just don't care that much. So, I'm doing this the old-fashioned way and heading to a bar.

It's Friday night, and Nico's band is playing at the Black Cat, which isn't my usual scene, but their drinks are cheap, and I try to go to as many of Nico's shows as possible to support him.

[Me: Coming to your show tonight. Get me the VIP pass.]

[Nico: I'll buy you a rum and coke, and that's pretty much the extent of the VIP package, babe]

[Me: Works for me.]

[Nico: 😵]

I stick out a little at the Black Cat since I decided on a lilac skater dress with spaghetti straps. Maybe I could have tried to dress to the vibe of the bar, but I have to be my authentic self, and my authentic self is colorful. At least the dress has pockets, so I don't have to bother with a purse.

Nico greets me outside with a one-armed squeeze around my shoulders and a kiss against my temple. "Hey, babe. Ready to get your face rocked off? Our set is fire tonight." He drags me into the bar after paying my cover fee. Guess I'm not one of the band groupies. Truth be told, I absolutely love Nico's band. They are exactly the type of music I listen to, which tends to surprise people. But give me a hard rock band any day.

"We're up in twenty. I'll get you that drink, and then I have to set up with the rest of the gang." I can barely hear him over the noise. Not only is there a band currently on stage, but the people packed into the space are loud. Nico leads me toward the bar on the left-hand side of the room and gets my drink ordered pretty quickly. Then I'm left alone while Nico heads off to get ready.

There's a lot of black-clad people and a whole lot of studded accessories as well as hair colors more vibrant than mine. I love the energy here. I missed going to bars and concerts during lockdown. There's just something about being around people, all the hype, sweat, and general loudness of it all. The drinks here are heavy pours, and it won't take me long to get tipsy.

I'm not one to be a wallflower, so I stand toward the center of the crowd, waiting for Nico's band to take the stage. Around me is the smell of cheap beer and sweaty bodies, and I love it.

"So, which band are you with?" a husky feminine voice asks in my ear. I turn to see a gorgeous woman with short black hair, heavy eye-linered eyes, and skin-tight black jeans and shirt. She's holding a half-drunk beer in her hand.

I take a sip of my rum and coke, keeping my eyes on hers. "Just seeing my friend's band, the Cozy Cadavers. They're up next." I flash her my flirtiest smile. If I play my cards right, we could be making out in the back in no time.

She smiles back at me. "So I don't have to worry about fighting off a drummer boyfriend or something if I talk to you." I can barely hear her laugh over the noise, even with her leaning close to my ear.

"No boyfriends to worry about. I'm Mika, by the way." I have to practically shout in her ear. Nico's band is going to go on any minute, so there's limited time to get introductions out of the way.

"Simone," she responds, clinking her plastic cup against mine. Any more talking is cut off by the sound of a guitar cutting through the air as The Cozy Cadavers take the stage. I turn my attention from Simone to the band, though I make sure to stand close to her, not quite touching, but enough to be in her orbit.

Nico looks every bit the rock god he tries to be. His ginger hair is tussled just so to make it look like sex hair, but he totally spent an hour making it look that way himself. The old teal guitar he's had forever is slung low and covered with stickers, most of which I've given to him and many are B&B themed. He's the lead singer and guitarist, and he's actually really good.

"Hey, we're The Cozy Cadavers, and we're gonna play some jams for you," Nico says into the microphone to the loud cheers of the audience. The band breaks into their first song, and I'm completely lost to the music. It's loud and hard, but melodic enough that I can sway my hips in a sort of dance. Nico's voice is lovely, especially contrasted by the bassist Jason's background screams. Jason's twin Ariel is on drums, and she's the most badass drummer around. Rhythm guitarist Marshall is still a baby; the kid can't grow a beard to save his life. But he's got so much talent and is the newest member after the old guitarist left to take over the family business in like, Wisconsin or something.

I'm totally in my groove when I feel a slim hand come up to my waist. Simone has one hand attached to me, and her thigh is smashed against mine as we sway together to the music. Yeah, this is what I need, someone to just have fun with, to dance with, and hook up with without strings.

Simone and I dance together through the rest of the set. At some point, she's behind me, and we move against each other. My drink is long gone, and I could get another, but I don't move from my spot.

As the set ends, Simone guides me toward the back of the room where it's darker and less crowded. She takes the cup from my hand and gets rid of both of the empty plastic cups. Before I have time to overthink anything, she has me pressed against a wall and her lips crash against mine. Simone places one hand on my jaw and the other rests against the wall just above my head. She presses one leg between mine and pushes just enough against me that I moan into her mouth. Her tongue slides into my mouth, and I let her take whatever she wants.

It's been a while since I've done this. Not just the whole making out with someone at a bar thing, but the whole kissing in general. But here I am, pinned against a wall with a totally hot goth chick's tongue down my throat. Her thigh nudges harder against me, and yeah, I'm getting more turned on by the minute.

Hot kisses move away from my mouth and down the side of my throat, and I am definitely panting heavily now. Both of Simone's hands rest on my hips, and I'm ready to feel her palms against my bare skin.

"Do you... ughn... want to come to my place?" Words are hard right now, but I want this woman to tear my clothes off.

We break away from each other just far enough to make our way toward the exit. I spot Nico over the crowd and gesture to him so he sees me leaving with somebody. He gives me a shit-eating grin and a thumbs up. Then I focus back on Simone, and we head toward the Metro station.

We barely make it into my house before Simone is back on me, kissing me up against my door. I take her upstairs to my bedroom, and we start pulling at each other's clothes. My dress is off in a blink, and I help her shimmy her tight jeans off.

This is exactly what I needed. Some random stranger to blow off my pent-up sexual frustrations with and it's great. Simone is attentive, and wow, is her mouth amazing. Despite how good she is though, my mind is somewhere else. Well, with someone else. I can't help but think of Ash, and what it would feel like to have his shaggy, dark brown hair, a shade lighter than Simone's, between my fingers while he was between my legs. Or how he would turn that tentative smile on me while he made me come.

Simone's smile is big and arrogant as I scream through my orgasm; there's nothing shy about it. When it's my turn to pleasure her, all I can think about is how it would feel to have Ash's toned, hard body beneath me instead of Simone's wonderfully soft curves.

After a few rounds and several orgasms later, Simone falls asleep wrapped around me. But I can't sleep. I had fun, and yeah, it was great to have that many orgasms in one night. Simone is definitely skilled and an expert at what she does.

The problem is now I feel super guilty. Almost the whole time we were screwing, I was thinking about Ash. It wasn't fair to Simone; I should have been in the moment with her. I feel like a huge asshole for thinking about some random guy whom I haven't even been with while some hot girl is fucking my brains out.

Okay, so maybe hooking up with someone else while I have a crush was a bad idea. Clearly, trying to get someone out of my system by getting sex somewhere else doesn't actually help the situation, and if anything, I feel worse off than I did before. Not sexually frustrated, no, Simone took care of that part just fine. But fuck, I feel awful.

I try not to move in Simone's arms. I don't want to wake her. It's not like I'm going to kick her out in the middle of the night. She didn't do anything wrong, and it was fun in the moment.

I resign myself to not asking for her number in the morning, and finally I drift off to sleep.

When I wake up the next morning, though, I don't have to worry about saying anything to Simone because I wake up alone. The bed is cold on her side, so she's long gone. There isn't even a note with her number or anything, so that saves me from an uncomfortable moment.

I walk to my kitchen and start my coffee maker. At least there's no hangover to deal with; I barely got through one drink last night. See, I can make bad decisions without even being inebriated.

There's this ridiculous urge to text Ash and apologize. Not that I have anything to apologize for. He's not my boyfriend. He's not my anything. We've just started being friends. We still barely know each other.

The idea of moping around my house all day in lounge clothes sounds great, but it's Shabbos, and I'll schlep my lazy ass out to Chevy Chase in a few hours. Not that I don't love seeing my parents because I do. Plenty of my friends growing up had bad relationships with their parents, but mine are great. We've always been close, even when they couldn't always give me the attention I wanted.

They like it when I come home for Shabbos lunch, not that we're particularly observant Jews because we are not, but it's just a time for us to be together and shirk off the stress of the week. Dad picks Bubbe up from Silver Spring, and she dishes on all the gossip at her senior living home. My older brother David comes down from Baltimore; he's doing his residency at Johns Hopkins, the overachiever, and we just enjoy each other's company.

But if I plan to be around my family for a few hours, I should probably shower the smell of sex off my body. They don't need to know about that part of my life. When I come out of the shower, there's a string of messages in my friend group chat.

[Stella: I passed out at like 9 last night, so I need to do fun late night things tonight.]

[Nico: Ya boy has work. But you are welcome to visit me at the bar, I'll be the one pouring drinks]

[Nico: Which you will have to buy yourself]

[Marco: Lena says she'll do dinner, but she out on the bar, says it makes her sick]

[Nico: Rude! I keep my bar clean and vomit free]

[Stella: Debatable]

[Nico: I'm charging you double for all of your drinks]

[Stella: Screenshotting this for your boss]

[Nico: Go ahead, Nellie won't care. She loves me]

[Marco: Ash, you down for some dinner?]

[Ash: Sure.]

[Marco: Mike? You in?]

[Stella: omg she's dead, isn't she?]

[Nico: Oh I bet she is]

I type back quickly before Nico can say anything more. He would absolutely spill to the whole group that I went home with somebody last night, and I really don't want that. Okay, I don't want Ash to know I hooked up with somebody.

[Me: It's been like 5 minutes, I was in the shower.]

[Me: But yeah, I'm there. I'll be at my parents' for Shabbos most of the day, so just let me know]

[Stella: Oh thank God, she's alive! Wait, is your dad making brisket by any chance?]

[Me: No idea, but probably]

[Stella: Can I come?! Not that I would ever betray you when it comes to food, but your dad's brisket... I would kill a man for it]

[Nico: I want to come!]

[Marco: Okay, change of plans, Lena is having what she's calling a "barf day" so I'm out today.]

[Ash: Want me to come over and help out?]

[Marco: Nah, why don't you go with the gang to Shabbos? You don't want to miss papa Levenberg's brisket. It really is worth the hype.]

[Me: It's true. I learned all my tricks from my dad. He's the true master of the kitchen.]

[Ash: Okay.]

And just like that, I now get to spend and probably evening with Ash.
Great.
Just when I'm feeling super good about what happened last night, I'll totally be able to look him in the eye and have a conversation with him and not think about how all I wanted was him while I was getting railed by someone else last night. Yeah, this is going to be just awesome.

CHAPTER 8

ASH

Lunch with Mika's parents. What. The. Hell? Sure, it's a group setting with my other ... friends, but it's still meeting the parents of the girl I'm crushing on. Because apparently, I'm a teenager again, and a crush is a big deal.

Mika and I aren't anything other than friends. That's all we're ever going to be. Okay, that's all we're going to be for now. Marco and my therapist are right. I'm not ready for anything more than friendship. Every time I have a meaningful moment or let myself enjoy Mika's soft touches during our game, I hear Adele in my head telling me I don't deserve to be touched. I don't deserve the kindness Mika is showing me. Every horrible thing she has ever said to me comes bubbling up, and I feel awful for expecting any kind of affection from anybody. Hell, it took me weeks of being in DC with Marco and Lena before I could uncomfortably hug Lena. Adele had beaten me down so much that even hugging a family member felt like I was doing something wrong.

I'm not doing anything by going to a friend lunch at a friend's parents' house. I just have to keep telling myself and let it be okay for me to enjoy life. Even if Adele wouldn't like it. Her opinion doesn't matter in my life anymore.

Stella is the one who drives us since she's the only one with a car. It's crazy how few people have cars around here. Not that it was much different in New York. I guess I just thought that was singular to New York.

Mika is in the front seat, and I wish I could see her more clearly, but from my spot in the back behind Stella, I can only see the side of her face. There haven't been any invitations to lunch or time alone without the group since the night I made a pervy ass of myself. And that was good. It's what I wanted.

It's what I should want.

But yet, I find myself disappointed every lunch time when I don't get a text from her. I'm bummed when we all go out, and she doesn't sit next to me. Mika is a touchy person, and even if she's just chatting away, she sometimes rubs her arm against mine or places her hand on me while she's making a point.

My brain keeps telling me I need to heal and take some time to myself. But my heart, and well, probably my dick too, wants to see what could happen with Mika. Maybe find out what it's really like to be with her rather than let my imagination fill in while I'm alone in bed.

I need to get my head on straight. I'm in a car with three other people, one who is sitting right next to me, as Nico slides into the seat behind Mika. I can't go around getting a hard on now, especially since we're on our way to Mika's parents' house.

"I hope you assholes had a better night than I did. The kids gave me such a headache that I barely made it through dinner with Elise before I fell asleep. Nico, how was your show?" Stella asks, slowly taking us out of the city.

Beside me, in the backseat of the small blue Honda, Nico immediately becomes animated. "Mind blowing! The energy last night was off the charts, and I could see a lot of ladies totally vibing with me from the stage. Good turnout too, dontcha think, Mike?" He leans forward and places his hands on Mika's shoulders.

Oh, so she went out to Nico's show last night. I slump just a little in my seat. She didn't invite me. Not that I expected her to, and it wasn't like I even remembered Nico had a show, but I can't help feeling like she ditched me. She didn't, but it feels that way.

"Mmhm," Mika responds.

Nico leans back and grins. The only way I could describe the look on his face would be *devilish*. "Right, I forgot, you had your own little party to worry about. She looked cute. Invite me next time." Nico laughs, but I can barely hear it. There's a muffled sound in my ears, and my heart sinks into the pit of my stomach.

"Ooohh, you hooked up with someone! Did you get her number?" Stella's voice seems pleased. *How can she be excited about this?*

I don't want to look at Mika, but I can't stop myself. She's slumped down in her seat, and I can tell even from this angle that she's uncomfortable with the conversation. "It was just sex; she was gone before I got up. Which is fine. I just needed to get it out of my system. Can we please move on?" Her tone is curt.

Isn't this something that friends talk about? Or am I the problem here?

I'm spiraling a little. Mika hooked up with someone, and I'm falling apart hearing about it. This is ridiculous. She doesn't owe me anything—we're friends. It's not like she cheated on me because we're not together.

Yeah, well tell that to my stupid heart, which feels more like a shriveled husk in my stomach by the minute. How am I going to make it through a whole lunch around her while I feel this way?

"Fine, Mike doesn't kiss and tell. But I absolutely do." Nico starts telling us in elaborate and enthusiastic detail about his night, but I don't hear a word. He's just noise to me now. I can't look at Mika, so I just stare out the window, watching as the city slips by. DC isn't as busy as New York, yet somehow there's enough traffic around to ensure our escape to Chevy Chase takes longer than it feels like it should.

I can't focus on anything inside the car, which is probably why it takes Stella calling my name several times for me to realize the car has stopped, and everyone else is standing next to the car, parked on the street.

Pull yourself together, Ash.

I need to focus on anything other than Mika with someone else. I don't have a claim on her, and if she wants to have a random hookup, that's her business. Right now, I need to focus on not being a shitty house guest at her family's lunch.

With a deep, fortifying breath, I exit Stella's car and follow the rest of the group up a brick walkway to a large, white, three-story colonial style home. There are black shutters on the side of every window. A smaller addition on the left-hand side looks like a solarium with wide, tall-paneled windows. A small porch with columns covers the entrance to a white-washed door. The whole street is treelined, and the yard at the Levenberg home is no exception. It is an extravagant home on a street full of extravagant homes. Mika really wasn't joking when she said she is a trust fund baby.

The front door opens wide, and a tiny woman with brown hair with a large gray streak at the front stands smiling brightly. She looks exactly like Mika if she were pocket-sized. This has to be Mika's mom.

"Hi sweetie!" she says brightly to her daughter, who bends way down to hug her mom as she makes it up to the door. Then the older woman's attention snags on the rest of them. "And the gang's all here. Wait, no, you seem to have swapped out Marco for a handsome, younger version. Not that I don't love Marco." She actually winks at me. So that's where Mika gets her flirty nature. It runs in the family.

"Marco is my cousin, ma'am. I'm Sebastian. Ash. Thank you for having us at your home, Mrs. Levenberg." My manners kick-in automatically. Abuela would be proud of me.

I find myself being pulled into a hug I was not prepared for, and I stiffen immediately. Mrs. Levenberg doesn't seem to mind though. "Oh, I like this one. So polite. Take notes, Nico," she says, drawing away from me to pull Nico into her arms. I watch as Nico's smile takes over his whole face, and he practically melts into the older woman's arms.

Stella is pulled in next, and the women are nearly the same height with Stella's wedge platforms giving only an extra inch or two over Mika's mom.

"But please, call me Esther. Mrs. Levenberg was my mother-in-law. May her memory be a blessing. I don't want to be compared to that cantankerous old shrew," Esther says, a laugh following as she leads us all into the house.

"Mom!" Mika responds. Then she laughs too. She leans over and whispers to me—no, to the group. "It's true though. That woman hated everything and everyone."

We're ushered through the house, which is both tastefully decorated and comfortably cluttered. This house is well lived in and well loved. Exactly the kind of place I expected Mika to grow up in.

Esther leads us to the kitchen, where a tall, broad man with a full head of stark white hair stands at the stove. He turns around, and that smile is all Mika. He's wearing an apron over his button-down shirt with a minimalist image of what seems to be Uncle Fester holding the charred remains of a pot roast from the Addams Family movie.

"What a sight for sore eyes! If it isn't my daughter and her merry band of adventurers, sans Marco. I'm sending you home with leftovers for Lena. That girl needs to eat more if she's going to be having my little nibling soon." He leaves the stove to give everyone a bear hug, myself included, before he introduces himself.

"Mort Levenberg. You must be the cousin Marco has told me all about. Welcome to our home and to your first Shabbos meal in the Levenberg house. You won't have another one like it—trust me. If you leave my house anything under five pounds heavier than you entered it, I've failed."

I like this man immediately. He's everything a dad should be. I bet my dad was like him. I hope he was. It's no wonder everyone jumped at coming over for Shabbos lunch. The Levenbergs have a way of making a stranger feel like family immediately.

Mika is the perfect combination of her parents, not just in looks, but in demeanor as well. "Bubbe is in the family room, probably watching her murder shows, if I had to guess. And David just texted to say he's ten minutes out. That boy never thinks of the traffic on the Beltway, ever," Esther says, her phone still in her hands, relaying the information from the text.

"Is that my Mikey, I hear?" a voice calls from the hall. A moment later, an old, willowy woman enters the room. She's not much more than skin and bones, so wrinkled from a life well lived. Her white hair is cut short, and a small silver Hamsa hangs around her neck. When she smiles, I can see where Mika gets it from.

Mika walks into her grandmother's arms, and they cling to each other tightly. I feel a small pang of home sickness. Not for my home with Adele in Brooklyn. I would be happy to never set foot in the borough again.

No, I feel the loss of the Bronx in my heart. Back there, in Van Nest, I have a whole loud as hell family. My brothers and sister, my mom, abuela, and abuelo still living in the same house I grew up in. All my cousins, aunties, and uncles live nearby, some actually related to us, some that just came as part of the package of living around other Puerto Ricans. There is always food and people no matter whose house you are at, and it's been so long since I've had that. Adele hated my family. She hated the Bronx as a whole and refused to step foot in it. And she hated me going anywhere without her. So, I stopped going.

But as I stand here in Mika's childhood home with her Bubbe approaching me for a hug, I realize that I've missed having a family. More people have hugged me in the last ten minutes than in the last several years combined.

"This one is handsome, and he has strong arms. Mikey, dear, you should marry this one. Wait, are you Jewish?" she asks me, holding me away from her as if to scan me head to toe for any signs of Judaism. Her grip is surprisingly strong on my biceps.

"No, ma'am. I was raised Catholic." I try to keep my voice strong, but I would be lying if I don't admit that Mika's Bubbe kind of intimidates me.

She gives me another look over. "You call me Yael, not ma'am. I'm not old enough for that. Now, do you want to become Jewish? Mika needs a nice Jewish man..." She pauses and thinks for second. "Or nice Jewish woman. You come to my temple, and we'll talk to Rabbi Magat about some Torah study." Yael pats my cheek and lets me go, turning her attention to Stella next.

Mika is at my side suddenly. "God, I am so sorry about her. She's a bit much. You are not going to Torah study, and if she tries to invite you a Rosh Hashanah service, for the love of fuck, say no. Please just ignore her. She's been trying to marry me off since the minute I was bat mitzva'd."

I'm not into the idea of marrying someone I barely know, but if it means keeping Yael happy, I'm open to reconsidering. The woman has this air about her that makes my spine go straight and my urge to please skyrocket.

My gaze goes toward Mika, but I can't look at her yet. It's dramatic to say that my heart is broken a bit, but

I'm feeling dramatic at the moment. She can sleep with whomever she wants. I just thought that person was me. That's not fair to her. I can't just say, *Hey, I know we really want to sleep together, but could you be celibate for however long it takes me to work through my hang ups?*

Yeah, not fair to either of us. I'll just have to work through this. Shabbos lunch isn't exactly the place I would have chosen to address my issues, so I push my feelings aside as we sit down at a huge table with a white tablecloth with lace trim. The table is completely covered in food; the promised brisket centerpiece, sliced and steaming, exudes such a delicious smell that my mouth immediately starts to water.

I'm seated between Mika and her Bubbe, a dangerous place to be really. Mort sits at the head of the table, his wife to his right and Yael to the left. Stella is across from me with Nico next to her. "Where the hell is David? I'm starving. Look at me. I'm wasting away to nothing," Yael says next to me, grabbing her flat stomach.

"Mom, he'll be here in like—" but whatever Mort was going to say was cut off by the slam of the front door. David walks into the dining room, and it's like he's the exact opposite of Mika. He is stupidly tall, probably the tallest person I've ever seen and basically all arms and legs. His skin is a shade darker than his sister's, and his eyes are much darker. I don't know Mika's natural hair color, but David's is dirty blond with a single teal streak at the front. The only resemblance to his younger sister is the large smile that graces his face as he takes in the room.

"Full house today! Nothing makes Shabbos better than people to share it with." David is all exuberance; the peppy energy must be a Levenberg trait. He moves around the table to stand behind Nico. "Hey, Nicky, move over so I can sit next to my wifey." He pats Nico on the shoulder, and without complaint, Nico slides over to the next chair. David sits and slings an arm behind Stella's chair.

"Hello, darling. It's been too long since I've seen your beautiful face," he says, giving Stella a kiss on the temple.

She playfully pushes against his chest. "Literally just saw you last week. And no, I'm not leaving Elise to marry you. You're going to have to Thunderdome with her for my hand."

"As is proper, of course. Oh, hey, new face. One of Marco's relations? You look like him, just not so grizzled." David turns his attention on me. Why are all the Levenbergs so charming? I can't help but love everyone in this family.

"Ash, and yeah, I'm Marco's cousin. I just moved here from New York a few months ago." I would hold out my hand, but there is too much space between us.

David nods. "Cool. I absolutely hate that city. It's good you got out and moved to a better place."

"Enough chitchat, I'm dying of starvation over here," Yael says, wasting no more time in reaching for the brisket and placing a heaping serving on my plate. Rather than fill her own plate, she piles a little bit of everything on my plate before she starts on herself. Beside me, Mika is laughing to herself, and when that smile spreads across her face, I feel my heart beat just a little faster.

The chitchat does cease for only a few minutes while we all tuck into our meal. That doesn't last long as Yael starts to speak again. "So, Sebastian, you're a New Yorker. Born there?"

I wipe my mouth with a cloth napkin. "Yes, born and raised in the Bronx. My mom grew up there, but my grandparents moved there in the 70s from Puerto Rico and my dad was from Puerto Rico."

"You said was. I take it he is no longer with us." Seems Yael doesn't miss a thing.

I know there should be feeling of loss when it comes to my dad, but really, I was too young when he died to remember him. "Yes, he died when I was two. It was cancer. They caught it too late. I don't really remember him, but he was a writer, so I have his books." I look down at my plate. I don't really want to talk about my dad, mostly because I just wish I had him around.

Yael picks up on this. "I know how that feels. My mother was the only one to make it out of the old country, pregnant and alone. I never knew my father or anyone else in my family. But look at what I've built here. Now I have a full table of family. Some I made myself and others that found us." The mood lightens considerably at her words, though I can see the sadness linger in Yael's eyes.

"So, Ash, what brings you to the District? And are you sleeping with my sister?" David looks at me with a huge grin on his face. If it's possible, I can actually see the red glow coming off my face.

"Oh my god, David! Seriously?! This is Shabbos lunch; you can't just ask people that!" Mika screeches at her brother across the table, but David's grin doesn't waver.

"That's not an answer, Mikey." He raises his eyebrows in a suggestive manner.

Luckily, we're all saved from this whole embarrassing scene by Esther jumping in with a new topic. Meanwhile, the siblings stare each other down across the table for the rest of the meal: Mika glaring, David grinning.

My face is warm and probably red the rest of the meal, and I don't make eye contact with anyone as we leave. Not even Yael as she pats my cheek and promises to send information about Torah study over to Mika for me.

I can never come here again, I decide.

CHAPTER 9

MIKA

I can never look at Ash again. Thanks to my family, I am so thoroughly embarrassed that any guilt I felt about sleeping with someone else has vanished into the cloud of sheer mortification at the things my Bubbe and brother said at the Shabbos table. He's never going to speak to me again. This will probably drive him away from the B&B table too. The whole group will be mad at me because my family made Ash uncomfortable.

This is all David's fault.

After Stella drops me off, and I basically sprint into my house so I don't have to say anything to anyone ever again, I start texting my brother in earnest. Of course, he doesn't take me seriously. He thinks it's all hilarious and that he's "just looking out" for me.

Like hell he is!

And it's not like this is the first time he's done it. I should know better, but I just thought it wouldn't be a problem because Ash and I are totally not dating. When I brought Quinn home the first time for Shabbos, David did the same thing. Quinn, though, was more brazen and proudly said *yes*, which dropped the grin from David's face, even as he turned it into a loud laugh.

But, oh my god, poor Ash! I thought he was going to combust with how red he got. I could practically feel the heat of embarrassment radiating off his body. I had to fight every instinct to reach out and touch him, comfort him, because that would have added fuel to David's shitty older brother fire.

After the text fight with my brother goes nowhere, I debate whether I should text Ash and apologize again. I don't feel like I did enough of that at my parent's house. Mostly because I could barely speak to him after that. I couldn't even look at him, which seemed to go both ways.

No, Ash is my friend, and I owe him a thousand apologies. Time to be an adult and get this over with, so hopefully we can go back to being slightly less awkward friends.

[Me: I am so so sorry for my family. I should have warned you about David. He's an ass. And I totally understand if you never want to speak to me again. Today was not fair to you.]

I stare at my phone, willing Ash to text back right away. He's usually pretty quick about responding. Unlike most of my friends, he doesn't leave me hanging for long.

So, after thirty minutes have passed and still nothing, I'm worried everything with Ash is totally fucked up. Then another thirty minutes pass, and I'm wearing a hole in my bedroom floor with my pacing. Maybe I should just call him. Or maybe he doesn't want to talk to me ever again.

Not only did my family embarrass him, but Nico did announce to the whole car that I had slept with somebody, and I didn't miss the way Ash looked at the news. I did hurt him, and then, thanks to my big brother, I've completely humiliated him.

I am the worst!

Just as I start to spiral into full-blown self-loathing, convinced that Ash will never speak to me again, my phone vibrates with a text. I throw myself toward the phone, like actually lunge for it.

[Ash: It wasn't your fault. Not the first awkward family conversation I've had to endure. Don't worry about it.]

Yeah, fat chance of that. I'm going to worry about this for the rest of my life.

[Me: It was still really rude of David to ask that. And I'm sorry about my grandma, she's just very eager.]

[Ash: I liked her a lot. I hope I'm half as cool as her when I grow up.]

[Ash: Seriously, Mika, don't apologize. You didn't do anything wrong. I liked your family.]

[Me: I like them too. Most days. Excluding David. He's awful. I'm never speaking to him again. I hope the harbor swallows him up one day.]

[Ash: Lol]

[Ash: If it makes you feel any better, my siblings did the same thing to my last girlfriend. She never went back.]

[Ash: Not that I don't want to go back to your family's house. I would.]

[Ash: Not that I expect you to invite me back. I'm just saying. I like your family. I like you.]

And my heart has stopped in my chest. He likes me. *But wait, does he mean he likes me* likes me, *or is it just he likes me? Fuck, why am I suddenly thinking like a middle schooler?*

[Me: My family likes you too. I like you. Which is why you are going to let me treat you to lunch or coffee sometime this week so I can continue to grovel for the sins of my family.]

Fly casual, Mika. Don't push too hard or he'll bolt. And again, this is just a friendly hangout. We can totally do that without it getting weird. We are two adults who enjoy each other's company but don't want anything more than that.
For now.

[Ash: I would like that. Monday?]

[Me: Monday sounds good.]

I'm sitting on a well-worn leather brown couch at Tryst in Adams Morgan, trying to talk myself out of ordering a bourbon chai for some liquid courage. But it's not even eleven in the morning, and it probably wouldn't do much to help anyway.

I made sure to arrive earlier than I normally would just so I could beat Ash to our coffee date. Nope, not a date. Our coffee meetup. It's the first time we've seen each other since Saturday, which admittedly, was like two days ago, but still. It seems so much longer after how Saturday afternoon went down.

I'm considering ordering a coffee or something when Ash walks through the door. I wave him over, letting my smile do the work for me. If I look at ease, maybe he'll be chill too. He comes toward my spot with a small smile on his own lips, and yeah, I'm calling this a win. Ash only smiles when he's comfortable. Well, not exactly comfortable but less likely to bolt.

I stand to greet him, and somehow find myself giving him a hug. My head doesn't think that one through, but clearly other parts of me are in charge for a moment. I just want to touch him, and this seems right.

I expect him to be stiff in my arms like he is when anyone hugs him or touches him for too long. But he isn't. His hands actually leave his bag, and he wraps his arms around my back, returning my embrace. I could die right now, and I would be happy. He's hard and warm beneath his shirt, and my head fits perfectly against his chest, nestled under his chin. We stay like that for longer than necessary, but I can't find a reason to care.

"Have I mentioned how sorry I am about my family?" I mumble against his chest. Surprising me, he laughs, and his chest rumbles against my ear. It's officially my favorite sound.

Ash pulls away from me, and I stop myself from snuggling back into his embrace. "Don't worry about it, Mika.

Your family is really great, and they are just looking out for you. Now, let's forget about it and get some coffee. I need the caffeine boost."

I laugh and he joins me. Yeah, caffeine is exactly what I need. The tension that was there on Saturday is gone now, dissipated with a hug. We order our lattes and head back to the brown couch once the barista hands them over in ceramic cups.

"So, are you excited for Wednesday? It's your first Big Bad fight. It's kind of a big deal," I say, resting my back against the arm of the couch so I can angle the rest of my body toward Ash.

"Is it? What makes it different from our other encounters? Do I need more dice?" He matches my position, lounging against the side of the couch. We're not touching, which is fine; at least this way I get to look at him.

My laugh is loud, but it's lost in the din of the crowded place. "Yeah, it kind of is. Our other encounters had small enemies; combat doesn't take that long. But with a Big Bad, like the whole session will probably be just taken on that guy. We'll do less roleplay and more fighting. As for the dice, I will always say yes. You should always get more dice." He nudges my foot while he laughs with me.

This is nice; it's easy. Ash is really great to talk to once he passes his awkward phase. And I can talk about B&B with literally anyone, anytime, but I especially like talking about it with him.

"You know, when you first started playing with us, I thought you might have hated it and ditched us. You just seemed so freaked out by the whole thing. I'm surprised you stayed, but like, also really glad you did." My brain is clearly slower than my mouth today because I wasn't planning on saying any of that to Ash. I mean, it's all true, but I didn't need to say it to him.

The blush creeps up on his cheeks, and I'm congratulating my brain for letting my mouth take over because that look of his makes me melt. "I'm glad I did too. I didn't realize how much I needed something like B&B. I was isolated and alone for so long, I kind of forgot what it was like to just hang around with other people with no expectations other than to just have fun. I... I really don't know how I would have gotten through the last few months without it." The red darkens on his cheeks, and his voice gets quieter.

There's something clouding the look on his face just a little. God, what has this poor man gone through? I sit up and reach out to touch his hand, the one he has resting on the couch cushion. "She really fucked you up, didn't she?" I don't know who the *she* actually is. I just know that she took a wonderful man and broke him down until there was barely anything left.

I want him to look at me, but that's pushing it for Ash. Instead, he stares at our hands, mine still crossed over his. I keep my hand there, and he doesn't move his from under mine. My hope is that it helps him feel grounded to this moment, and that the warmth from my hand on top and the softness of the leather below his palm keep him here with me in Adams Morgan and not floating back to a black hole in New York.

"She did. I forgot who I was when I was with Adele. She made my personality for me," he says, and his voice is so low I can barely hear him. I scoot closer while still keeping my hand where it is.

"You don't have to talk about it. This is supposed to be a relaxing coffee break." Now I slide my fingers under his and give him a comforting squeeze. I want to lean my head against his shoulder, so I let myself. A second later, he rests his check on the top of my head, and we're quiet.

There doesn't need to be words between us. I want Ash to just be who he is. He doesn't need to fill the silences with words because he fills them up enough by just being here with me, taking up all the space he wants.

"Thank you, Mika," he whispers into my hair. "I want to tell you some day, just not today." I nod gently because I am okay with that. Ash will tell me his whole story one day, but only when he's ready. And I can wait. I will wait. Because Ash needs more people in his corner.

I could honestly spend the rest of the day just sitting like this, leaning against Ash like we have nothing in the world to worry about. But that's not realistic since we are both adults with jobs that we've probably been away from too long.

With a huge amount of reluctance, I pull away and sit up straight. "Okay, well, you are too comfortable. I was about ready to just fall asleep on you. We should get back to work or whatever the kids are doing these days for money."

Ash's attention is on our hands, which are still joined on the couch. "Yeah, I have a few projects to finish up today and then a cover to finish this evening." He looks up at me, finally, and his face is open and earnest when he continues, "Thank you for today. I ... I'm really glad I've gotten to know you, Mika. I needed a friend, and I couldn't have asked for a better one in you."

Then he smiles, and it's one I've never seen before. It's big and reaches his eyes. And oh fuck, he has dimples. Plural! I literally feel my heart beating out of my chest at the sight of him. I'm so absolutely screwed when it comes to this guy.

All I can do is smile back, my best and brightest smile, because he deserves that from me. "I'm glad too." I squeeze his hand again before letting go so we can stand and leave.

I smile the whole ride home, wishing my time with Ash could have lasted a little longer, even though I know I'll see him again in two days. It's just not enough. I want more time with him. I want to spend all my time with him.

I'm in serious trouble.

When Wednesday rolls around, I find myself excited not just for the game, but to see Ash. I feel like we've had a turning point in our friendship and find myself happier when he's around. We could be entering best friend territory. Better let Stella know she has competition.

It's been a busy first half of the week since I'm working on one large conference transcription project, and I'm transcribing lectures for one of Stella's colleagues. It's not as time consuming as the conferences and has a been a good break from the monotony of business presentations. But that means there was little time to prepare a meal large enough for five, so I opt to order pizza. Dessert was made last night after I picked up beer from the store. This time it's just a ton of chocolate chip cookies with an extra plate set aside for Lena, who has the biggest sweet tooth, even if she throws it up immediately after.

The pizza arrives just before the gang does. I already have paper plates set out on the table and a bottle of beer next to each. It's nothing fancy, but I also don't feel like doing dishes. Nobody is going to fault me phoning it in every once in a while.

"The food of the gods!" Nico proclaims when he sees the pizza boxes on the table. "Babe, I love your cooking, but pizza will always be my first love." He gives me a hug, then bee lines it for the boxes.

"I'm telling your mom," Stella says as she drops her leather messenger bag on the floor so she can take off her sky-high shoes.

Nico doesn't wait for the rest of us to dig in. "Joke's on you. My mom loves pizza more than me. She gets it." He talks around a mouthful of food. This guy won't let anything stop him from shoving as much food as possible into his face.

"Your mom seriously loves pizza more than you?" Ash grabs his own plate from his spot next to me and starts to fill it up.

This time Nico swallows before responding. "Dude, my grandparents are from Sicily. My whole family takes pizza seriously. Now this New York style is great and all, but my Nona's pizza is the most magical thing in the world."

"I thought your last name was McLeod. That's not very Sicilian." Marco is already through a slice, and I didn't even see him sit down.

Nico's well into his second slice now. "Dad is the McLeod. Mom is so Sicilian, it hurts."

"How can one be so Italian it hurts, exactly, Nic?" Stella asks. She immediately goes for the beer. The kids must have been a handful today.

Using his pizza to point toward Stella's face, he says, "Don't let anyone in my family hear you call them Italian. We're *Sicilian*. There's a difference." Stella just rolls her eyes and keeps drinking.

"Okay, do we want to eat then play or play and eat? Because this is going to get crazy—fair warning." Marco is already pulling his things out of his bag, getting ready to set up his GM screen.

The thrum of excitement grips me. There's nothing better than the anticipation of an exciting game ahead. Will we all survive and save the day? Will we lose one of our own to the king lich we're about to fight? We're about to find out.

Marco posed it as a question, even though we all know we are going to play and eat. A lull in pizza face stuffing happens as each of us begins to pull our dice and sheets out. "You did get a new set!" I squeal happily as Ash pulls out a beautiful set of dice that are orange and yellow. There's just a bit of glitter to them, giving the dice a fire effect. They are perfect for Ash.

He smiles sheepishly at me. "Yeah, well, you told me I should for my first Big Bad." And there it is, the stain of pink on his cheeks. I live for that. When I look away to focus on pulling out my own things, Marco catches my eye. He gives me a knowing look, his gaze flicking over to Ash for just a second. It's not a warning look, exactly, more like a reminder. Ash isn't ready for anything more with anybody, and I need to remember that.

I flash Marco a smile, and he nods. Nothing needs to be said between us, and that's what I love about Marco. We can have a whole conversation without words.

My dice are arranged just so next to my character sheet, my dice tray perfectly aligned next to my sheet, and I'm just about ready to go when the sound of Stella yelling makes me jump and my things move just off center. "I'm ready to bring the motherfucking pain!" She slams her small fist down on the table, causing a few beer bottles to slosh around.

I'll kill her myself if she ruins my table.

Then Nico joins in with the table pounding, and it's looking to be a double homicide. If Ash decides to do it too, I'm going to have to find a new friend group if they don't put me in jail first. Thankfully he doesn't, and Marco manages to get the upstarts in line so we can start the game.

"Alright you chucklefucks, the Bone Brigade is having one last drink in the Rainbow Bovine before heading out to fight Agondo, the Lich King. You can pick up any gear you need before heading out to his lair. All shops are open, and the apothecary is stocked up on health potions. Where do you want to go first?"

Our merry band makes our way around the city, grabbing up the health potions Marco mentioned and more crossbow bolts for my character. Varic, Nico's bard, finds the Bagpipes of Heavy Breath in one of the shops. In classic Varic fashion, he doesn't have enough coin for it because he insists on buying rounds for everyone in the tavern wherever we go and has to borrow a bit from each of us. But at least now he has a +2 to his charisma, and that'll boost his spells.

"Bone Brigade, are you ready to face the Lich King?" Marco asks ominously. I'm practically buzzing with excitement in my seat. Final battles are tense, high energy, and can get downright wacky, so fuck yeah, I'm ready.

I turn to Ash, who is rolling his new d20 in his hand anxiously. I can't quite tell if he's excited or nervous.

Maybe a bit of both. I place my hand on his forearm; his bare skin is so warm under my palm. "You ready for this?" I ask with a huge smile.

He nods but doesn't say anything, though he does put the die back on the table.

"You approach the crumbling tower that is Agondo's lair. The courtyard is quiet and devoid of life. Before you sits the heavy front door. The iron handles look heavy and are tarnished black. Are you marching up to the door and going in, or is there anything you want to do in the courtyard?"

"Oh, I want to check for traps on the door. Bet that fucker booby trapped the thing." Marco prompts me to make a check to see if I can find anything. "I rolled a seventeen."

Marco checks his notes. "Okay, you notice a tiny rune etched toward the bottom of the threshold. Since you are an arcane thief, you know this is the symbol for a fireball spell. How are you getting through the door?"

"I'm not wasting one of my spell slots on a Dissipating Magic. I find the biggest rock in the courtyard and chuck it at the door as hard as I can," Nico says, mimicking throwing a rock.

"Give a strength check," Marco responds, threading his fingers together under this chin.

Nico rolls, groans, and drops the die into his dice jail. "Eight," he whines.

"Dude, you have the strength score of a toddler with a negative modifier. Leave the throwing to Tamotur." Stella elbows Nico in the arm, and he feigns injury.

Marco smiles, and it's evil. "Varic tosses a rock toward the door, but because he has weak noddle arms, it doesn't quite reach the door and falls just short of the rune."

"Ugh, puny man, this is not a job for weak soft hands. Allow Tamotur to defeat the door." Stella puts on a thick accent, like she really is a gruff barbarian orc. Stella lives for the roleplay, and she's really good. She rolls her strength check. "And that's a crit for me! Always at the beginning of the game. Why does this keep happening?" Nico pats her on the back, but it's more patronizing.

"Alright, so Tamotur hefts what is essentially a small boulder, yeets it at the door, and hits right at the handles. The heavy wood shatters into thousands of shards a second before the fireball rune detonates. The door is now a charred, splintered mess, and what's left is hanging off the hinges."

"Dope. I'm hefting my great axe and charging in," Stella says. Of course our resident barbarian just heads straight into danger without thinking. You play the role you make.

We're lucky there's nothing waiting for us in the first hall. As we make our way up the level of the death trap castle though, we're not so lucky. This place is crawling with hordes of the Lich King's underlings and traps.

By the second level, my rogue Uriel is feeling a bit woozy from blood loss. I have Ash's druid Kilris beside me in beast mode deflecting some of the blows, but I'm going full blown with my rapier since everyone is too close for ranged weapons.

"Alright, who's not dead? Sound off," Nico says after we finish level three. We're hurting, that's for sure. Tamotur is on the verge of being unconscious, Kilris is at half health, and Uriel is barely hanging on. Only Varic is doing alright, and that was only through a series of successful charm rolls.

"Can we take a short rest, GM?" I ask Marco. I mean in game, though a quick pee break might be in order too; we're a few beers in.

Marco gives me a wicked smile. "I don't know. Can you?"

"Don't fuck with me, Marco. I have one hit point, and I'm about to piss myself," Stella says, not bothering to wait for Marco's response before she dashes off to my downstairs bathroom.

"You know that up the next flight of stairs you will face Agondo, so yeah, you can take a rest without being disturbed," Marco concedes. We take some time out of the game to use the bathroom, eat some more pizza, which by now is cold, and stretch out a bit.

"I feel like I drank a pot of coffee in like five minutes. Is this normal?" Ash asks me as he stands and stretches his arms above his head. His shirt rides up, exposing a bit of his toned stomach, which is right at eye level for my still-seated self. I swear, my brain short circuits at seeing just that small bit of skin.

"What?" My dumb brain finally remembers he asked a question. I tear my eyes away from his body and take a long drink from what's left of my beer. When I look back over at Ash, he's no longer stretching, and that delicious bit of skin is hidden away again. What's not hidden is the smirk on his face. His cheeks are pink, but if I didn't know any better, I would say Ash looks a little smug. My temporary lapse in brain function did not go unnoticed or unappreciated.

The words finally catch up with me, and I remember to answer the question Ash asked. "Uh, oh yeah, totally normal. It's the anticipation of battle," I say too brightly. There's no way he's going to buy my fumbled recovery.

Ash isn't the only one to notice my drooling. Stella shoots me a look over the table. It's part confusion, part *I see and I understand.* Guess I'm going to have to prepare to dish to Stella, if not tonight, then over drinks tomorrow. And she'll have me spilling my guts with ease; it's one of her superpowers.

"Alright, settle down, kids. It's time to kill a lich king. You can use your hit dice to shore up some health points since this is a short rest. Last chance to do what you need to do," Marco announces to the table as he pulls out the Big Bad Dice from his bag. They are not exactly special in any way, just black dice with red numbers. It's the story behind them that makes them legendary. A few years ago, we went to a B&B convention in Baltimore, and Marco signed up to GM one of the epic games, which are like a whole day thing. He bought those at one of the vendors right before the game and ended up TPKing his whole table at the end of the epic. It's still talked about in some B&B circles.

"I'm going to do a Restful Song for everyone, so add a d6 to your hit point rolls," Nico says, though he doesn't have any health points to recover.

"What are you playing for this rest?" Marco asks. Nico doesn't have to provide a song; it's all for the flavor.

"Uh duh, the song of the universe: 'Tom Sawyer.'" It should have been obvious since Nico almost always plays a bard, and when he does, every final battle he insists on using "Tom Sawyer" by Rush as his Restful Song. And every time, he also finds a cover to actually play at the table, depending on the instrument his bard uses.

So, of course, the minute he says it, the first few ear-splitting notes start from his phone, which he then sets on the table. "What is happening?" Ash leans as close as he can to me so I can hear him whisper over the noise.

"It's the Song of the Universe," I say with a laugh. Ash pulls away just enough that I can see he's giving me a look like he has no idea what that's supposed to mean. "Have you ever watched *Chuck*?"

Ash shakes his head and leans closer again. "No. Is that a movie?"

"TV show from a few years ago. You should watch it. This," I gesture toward Nico, who is now full on head-banging to bagpipes, "still won't make much sense because it's Nico, but if you watch it, you might understand why it's called that."

He sits back and nods, but he doesn't seem convinced. I loved that show. I used to watch it with Quinn all the time. But ever since all that happened, I can't bring myself to watch it anymore.

"And that's enough of that," Marco says, making a motion against his throat to clearly signal it's time to shut it off. Any more bagpipes and I think we would all go a little crazy. "Now." We watch as Marco transforms himself into the ominous GM, ready to wipe us all out through the Lich King Agondo.

He sets the scene for our final showdown, and then he says the three most exciting words: "Let's roll initiative."

"So, I'm like super dead," Stella says at the end of the battle. We're all standing around the table at this point. Agondo the Lich King is dead, but then, so is Tamotur.

That's the hazards of playing the tank—you take the most damage.

"We'll get you resurrected back in the city at one of the temples. No bigs," I say, though I know it's going to cost a ton of gold to do that. It's better than Stella having to build a whole new character, even though she definitely already has one ready.

"Anyone up for a drink or something? I'm too wired to just go home," Nico asks, bouncing on the balls of his feet. I understand that feeling. Something about imaginary battle just gets you hyped up. I know I won't be sleeping any time soon. I will just lay in bed thinking about the whole thing all over again, replaying every action in my head.

Still, I'm not really feeling going out. I'm buzzing, but not in the go out and dance kind of way. "I'm not really feeling going out. But you all are welcome to stay and hang if you want," I say instead. If I know Nico, he'll decline. He'll be on the hunt for someone to take home, and he won't get that here. Marco will want to get home to Lena. So that will leave Stella and Ash.

"If I stay, can we make out?" Nico asks, a playful smile on his face. He's so predictable.

"No," I say, trying not to grin back at him.

He shrugs. "Sorry, Mikey, I just can't go unsmooched tonight."

"And Lena wants some of these cookies as soon as possible." Marco grabs the plastic container I packed up especially for Lena. I nod because it's not surprising, nor would I ever hold it against Marco.

"I'll hang for a bit. Elise is at work anyway, so it's just our lonely place, and I wasn't planning to sleep anytime soon," Stella says, setting her bag on the table.

I turn to Ash, hoping he'll stay but not voicing it aloud. "I'll stay. I don't think I can sleep either." He surprises me with a small smile, and there's a lightness in my chest, like I expected him to say no, and that weight is suddenly lifted because he's staying.

Nico and Marco leave with much fanfare from Nico. Stella, Ash, and I make our way to my living room with fresh drinks. "Movie?" I ask, picking up the remote.

"Is it going to be *The Mummy*?" Stella asks, like she doesn't know the answer. She takes a seat on one end of my couch and settles in.

"What other movie would it be?" I laugh, flipping through until I find the movie. I sit down on the middle cushion so I'm next to Stella, leaving Ash the option to sit on the other end of the couch or on the chair.

"Are we talking about the Tom Cruise movie? Because that one is awful," Ash says, sitting down next to me, much to my delight.

"Please, only the 1999 *Mummy* has my heart. Pretty sure it was my bisexual awakening." I laugh as I start the movie.

"It's such a horny movie. I don't even go for men, and even I'm attracted to every character. It's Mika's favorite movie, so we do a lot of lusting." Stella's not wrong; it is my favorite movie of all time. It's also true that everyone in the movie is insanely hot.

"You have good taste." Ash settles against the couch, spreading his arms over the back of the couch, including one behind my head. I have to force myself to breathe normally and focus on the movie starting rather than how close he is to me.

Less than thirty minutes into the movie, things change quickly. "Shit, I gotta run. I totally forgot I have an early meeting with the dean, and I have some shit to present to him. Sorry, Mike." Stella sits up abruptly and rushes into the dining room to grab her stuff. I would say that Stella was just trying to give me and Ash space, like a good wingman, but one, Stella is not that smooth, and two, I remember her telling me at Monday drinks that she had this meeting and the presentation she was putting together.

Stella is gone within seconds and that leaves me and Ash on the couch. I pause the movie while Stella packs up, so I turn to Ash. "Do you want to continue, or are you heading out too?"

Please say you'll stay. Please. Please. Please.

Ash looks both comfortable on my couch, and like he's ready to bolt. "I'll ... stay. I love this movie."

So, we settle back into the movie. I don't move from my spot, preferring to stay near Ash, even if we're not touching at all. As the movie progresses, I start to feel more exhausted. The thrill of the game has waned, and the weight of the day is finally catching up to me. I should tell Ash I'm ready to tap out and just go to bed. When I look over though, his head is leaned back against my couch, and he's breathing softly. He's already asleep.

Rationally, I know I should wake him or at least make him comfortable so he can sleep on my couch. But I'm not feeling super rational; I'm feeling super tired. Just for a minute, I'm just going to let us rest on the couch for just a minute. Okay, just until the end of the movie. When it's over, I'll wake him, and I can go to bed.

I wake with my face pressed against something warm. There's a heavy weight on my hip and top of my head, and something is poking me in the chest. I snuggle a little further into the warmth, pulling it closer to me as I have my arms wrapped around it.

Then consciousness finally kicks in, and I realize several things at once. First is that the warm thing I'm burrowing into is Ash's stomach. He has one hand resting on my hip, and one tangled in my hair. And the thing poking me in the chest? Yeah, that's definitely his morning wood. And holy shit, is it impressive. I must have moved because suddenly Ash jerks awake. I look up, unmoved from my position laying across his lap, hugging him around the middle.

His eyes catch mine, and for a moment, there's a tenderness there. Like he's just as comfortable as I am waking up like this. But then reality must hit him too, and his face goes the darkest shade of red I've ever seen on a person. With me still draped across his lap, he jumps up, and I roll gracelessly onto the floor.

"Oh my god, Mika, I'm so sorry!" Ash is in full on panic. He starts to crouch to help me, but then seems to remember he still has a raging hard on, and one hand goes to cover himself through his jeans, and the other to help me up. All the while, his face gets impossibly redder, and he looks ready to spontaneously combust.

"I didn't mean... it wasn't intentional. The floor... I didn't mean... Fuck, just kill me now." He buries his face in his hands once I'm standing upright again. At first, I'm dazed, having gone from being snug and happy on him to face planting on the floor. I don't want to embarrass Ash further; the poor guy might never look me in the eye again at this rate.

"Ash, honey, you're fine. It's totally natural and not the first time I've woken up with a dick on me. I'm sorry if I made you feel uncomfortable." I want him to know there's nothing to be ashamed of, especially because, besides the falling on my face part, I really enjoyed waking up like that—with him.

But my words do little to comfort him, and he keeps his face in his hands. I keep my eyes above the belt, though I'm dying to see if that impressive part of him is still flying. "You probably think I'm a huge pervert. Fuck, Mika, I'm so sorry. I should go. You probably never want to see my face again. I won't bother you ever again. I'll never come back. I'm moving back to New York." He frantically moves away to the couch and runs to the door. It doesn't seem to matter that he's forgotten his bag, and his bike is still hanging on my wall.

I can't just let him leave like this, embarrassed and promising to never return. I quickly follow him to the door and wrap my arms around him from behind, my hands resting on his flat stomach, pulling him back to me before he can touch the doorknob. I rest my cheek against his back and soak up the warmth there. I'm addicted to touching this man.

"Ash, seriously, you're fine. I don't want you to leave and never come back. You're not a pervert, and I don't think that of you. You freaked out. It's not a big deal. My nose is fine. You don't need to be embarrassed. Besides, you are like a really good pillow. I haven't slept that well in a long time." I rub the tip of my nose back and forth against the spot where his neck meets his shoulders, the highest place my face can reach, and let my hands latch a little tighter on his front.

He tentatively places one palm over my hand. "I liked being your pillow," he whispers, and I almost don't catch it. "I should go. Just to my apartment. Not like leave the whole District. Just... I'm sorry."

I squeeze his body tight to mine. "Seriously, Ash. You're fine. I'm not at all mad at you or anything. Just promise me you'll come back and you won't stop being my friend."

Ash's body sags in my arms just a little. "I promise," he whispers, and he lets me hold him just a little longer.

I stand on the porch a few minutes later, watching him pedal down my road. He didn't look at me while he gathered his stuff and took his bike from the wall. But just before he started off, he strapped on his helmet and turned to face me. His cheeks were a little pink, nothing like the atomic red they had been, and the barest hint of a smile graced his full lips.

Now I'm standing here in last night's rumpled clothes, watching Ash disappear down the street, already missing the warmth from his body.

CHAPTER 10

ASH

"**W**hat do you mean you haven't been to the Smithsonian? Like any of them?" Mika asks me incredulously. She looks like she's personally offended that I haven't gone to any of the museums in DC. It's not that I'm anti-museum or anything; I love museums. It's just weird to go out on my own.

"I've been busy. And it's weird to go by myself. Isn't that something you do with other people?" I answer, though I know it's a ridiculous thing to say. I went out all the time by myself before I met Adele. It's just I got so used to going everywhere with her, never having time on my own, that even the idea of going to a museum by myself, or hell, sitting at a coffee shop to work alone feels uncomfortable.

Mika isn't buying my excuse. "Since I know you set your own hours, I know that's bullshit. We're going this weekend. You pick the museum, and we'll enjoy a fun-filled day, and I'll even buy you overpriced museum food." I can't say no. I've really wanted to check out the museums in DC, and there's no excuse now since Mika is offering to go with me.

"Native American History, then. I've heard it's great." It's actually my top pick anyway. And I honestly wouldn't mind spending more time with Mika. Things have been a little awkward, at least on my end, since the morning I woke up on her couch with her sleeping in my lap. Just when I thought we were getting to a comfortable spot in our friendship, I have to shove my dick into her chest as a good morning.

Mika hasn't been awkward toward me though. She wanted to make sure I know that she wasn't weirded out by it at all, but that does nothing for how I feel. For the last two weeks, I've barely been able to look her in the eye. I don't know if it's because I'm worried she'll think I'm a pervert, or more likely, that any show of physical attention, even unintentional, would have gotten me screamed at by Adele.

Mika isn't Adele. I just have to keep reminding my brain of that fact. Mika won't hold any of this against me. She won't make me feel small for just being me. It's just my trauma brain telling me to just wait until the other shoe drops, and Mika's kind façade disappears. Even now, after months of therapy, I still can't seem to call myself a victim, even though that's exactly what I am. I want to trust Mika more; I want to trust all my new friends more.

I just can't.

Not yet anyway.

"Oooo, good choice. The exhibits there are fantastic. And the tamales in the food court are awesome! Sunday, ten o'clock. We'll meet outside. Okay?" Mika looks so excited that I can't say no.

I nod. "Yeah, sounds good." We leave the restaurant soon after. I don't meet up with her for lunch often, but she texted me that morning, and I just want to see her.

I head back home to continue working, contemplating if I should invite Marco and Lena to join us on Sunday. No, that would feel too much like a double date, and it's definitely not a date at all. It's two friends hanging out. Maybe I should text Stella or Nico and ask if they want to go. But a museum seems like the last place Nico would end up, and Stella likes to spend her Sunday afternoons with Elise since it's usually the one full day they get together.

The rest of the work day is grueling. I'm working on some marketing materials for an upcoming event, and it's uninspiring. I have a few book covers to work on later, and I'm more looking forward to those. Two are sci-fi, which is always fun, and one is a fantasy. I'm picturing a lot of forest green on that cover since it's set in an enchanted forest.

Before I know it, I'm sitting at Marco's dinner table with what seems like dozens of Chinese takeout containers on the table in front of me. It's one of the few things that doesn't make Lena sick at the sight of, so they've been eating a lot of Chinese lately.

"How's work?" I ask Lena.

She rubs her baby bump affectionately. "Oh, you know, asshole opposing counsels think they can steamroll me because they think I'm a hormonal woman, and therefore that makes me incapable of doing my job. Joke's on them. I'm a hormonal attorney who can still kick their asses in court. Offloading my case load for maternity leave is going to be a bitch, though."

Lena Perez, divorce attorney extraordinaire. She is literally the only lawyer I like. The rest are all bastards. Adele made sure my opinion of attorneys was permanently tainted. She's so obsessed with power and climbing in her own law firm that it's made her a heartless monster.

Lena's not like that at all. She actually gives a shit about who she represents, and her courtroom reputation is so good that she can be picky about her clients. She made partner two years ago, and I wanted to be there for her party. Marco invited me, but Adele didn't want to travel to DC because she had plans with her friends that weekend, so I stayed home by myself. I remember looking at the pictures on social media after the fact, wishing I had been there and hating Adele for making me miss out on yet another family event.

I won't be missing any more. Not the holidays with my mom and siblings. Not any special event in my nieces' and nephews' lives. And especially not the birth of my new cousin. With distance from Adele, and a whole lot of therapy, I've realized how much I've missed out on the last four years. Fuck, I even missed the birth of my youngest niece because Adele had just taken off her makeup and wouldn't go without a full face. Which meant I couldn't go either. I had to wait two weeks before Adele was gone long enough that I could sneak out and see little Rosie.

How fucked is that, that I had to sneak out of my own home to see my niece? My sister still hasn't let me hear the end of that. We'll be old and sitting in the nursing home together, and she'll still yell at me for missing Rosie's birth and "letting that bitch, Adele, come between me and the people who matter." There's no greater humbling experience than telling your younger sister she was right. Another thing that Regina will never let me live down.

"I would ask how work is for you, but you did send me like a million texts showing off your latest cover designs. Which are amazing, by the way. Instead, I'll ask how B&B is going for you. I get the whole play-by-play from Marco, but are you enjoying yourself? You don't have to let Marco strongarm you into playing if it's not your thing." Lena takes a bite of cookie from a plate I recognize as Mika's. She must have sent some home with Marco last night after the game.

"I love it. Honestly, I never would have played if it wasn't for Marco. I always thought it was a super nerd thing. But it's great, and I don't know, maybe exactly what I needed after everything." I wave my hand as if to indicate basically the last four years of my life. Lena gets it though.

Lena nods her head, though her focus is still on the cookie. "I guess I figured you would hate it. It's such a social thing to do. Plus, Marco says you keep making googly eyes at Mika. I think it's cute you're sweet on her."

I can feel my face heat up. "Who talks like that anymore? What are you, eighty? I'm not *sweet* on anyone. Mika has been a great friend. I'm really glad to have met her. We're going to the Native American History Museum this weekend." Lena gives me a raised eyebrow and a knowing look. "As friends!" I say, though my tone is defensive.

Lena nods again, though it's much more exaggerated than before. "Sure, hon, you're just friends. And friends totally put their dicks on their friends while cuddling together."

I groan loudly and bury my face in my hands. "I'm never telling you or Marco anything every again!" She pats my head and then grabs another cookie.

"You'll tell me everything in your life, like you always do, because you know there's no real judgment here. I love Mika to pieces, and you two would be cute together. She definitely isn't a crazy bitch like your last girlfriend." Lena goes on chewing on the cookie, oblivious to the thoughts in my head, which are all on Mika. She's nothing like Adele, the complete opposite, actually. As much as I would like to try something with Mika, she's too good for me. I'm not trying to put myself down, but I know I'm still a mess—broken. And I won't be a project for anyone. I have to fix myself before I even think about being with anyone else.

"You're right, Lena. I can't keep a secret from you." I smile.

"Damn straight." Her laughter fills the room. "Marco should be just about done recording. I should stop eating all these cookies if I'm going to have room for the actual dinner we ordered."

I look down the hallway of their condo. Marco has a recording studio set up in one of the back rooms, and there's a red light above the door for when he's recording. As I look, the light switches from on to off, and a few seconds later, Marco emerges from the room.

"I need to eat! I could not get a single take right. It's like I've forgotten how to speak English. Maybe I should have just done the whole thing in Spanish. Most of my listeners probably wouldn't understand anyway, right?" Marco drops heavily into his chair and reaches for the first container in front of him.

Lena pats his arm. "Yeah, hon, they would." Marco huffs loudly, but then he focuses on his food, and the three of us finally begin dinner. I'm split between the chatter of Marco and Lena and thinking of my upcoming Sunday with Mika.

It's not a date. It's just two friends hanging out at a museum.

So why am I so nervous?

For once, I actually beat Mika to our meetup. But that's only because I arrived twenty minutes early. I don't know why, because I'm usually a right on time kind of guy, but Mika is habitually fifteen minutes early, and I wanted time to calm myself down about the day.

I forced myself to leave my bag at home. It's become too much of a crutch, and I'm wearing out the strap from all the intense clutching. I shove my hands deep in my pockets to keep myself from reaching for the non-existent bag. What I need is one of those fidget blocks or whatever they're called. Something to keep my hands and mind occupied.

I look like a totally sketchy person standing in front of the museum, hands in pockets, crazy eyes looking every which way for Mika to appear. I'm surprised they haven't called security on me yet.

Just before I make the decision to bolt away from the doors, Mika rounds the corner. She's in a pale pink sundress, a shade or two lighter than her hair, which is thrown up in a braided crown, and has white, strappy sandals on her feet. God, she's so fucking cute.

"And here I thought I was too early." She laughs as she walks up to me. She gives me a one arm hug, and I stiffly return it, trying to remember how to breathe. This is a friend hang out, and friends go to museums in the middle of the day to do friend things.

"Hey, you ready to go in?" she asks, breaking through my mental pep talk. I nod and we head through the doors, side-by-side. There's no more than a foot of space between us, which is fine. I should probably step a little farther away because this is totally platonic. Part of me though, wants to reach out, grab her hand, and let her pull me through the museum.

We work our way around the first floor. Mika wasn't exaggerating when she described how amazing the museum collections were. Each section is divided by tribe and location. There are so many colors, and the craftmanship in the artifacts is nothing short of amazing. As we climb the levels of the museum, it's easy to see the differences in art from tribe to tribe. It's not something I appreciate in my daily life since it's not part of my iden-tity, but seeing it here, displayed so carefully, it's easy to acknowledge the beauty in another group.

Mika points out different exhibits that she loves. It's clear she's been here many times. By the time we make it back down to the café, I'm starving. There is so much food from different regions, and I quickly find that I could eat my weight in fry bread and bison dishes.

"So, what did you think? Good choice for your first Smithsonian?" Mika asks, grabbing more of the fry bread we agreed to split.

I don't even have to think about it. "While I think New York has the best museums, DC is still impressive." I smile at the faux indignant look Mika throws my way.

She points a piece of fry bread in my face. "Now see here: New York has nothing on DC. I mean, there are twenty-one museums in the Smithsonian alone, which are all free. Then there are the other museums around the Mall that sure you have to pay for, but are awesome. Not to mention all the monuments that are just open to the public. You don't come into my city and say such blasphemous things."

"Guess you'll just have to take me to more places to convince me," I say, and holy shit, I think I'm flirting.

Mika bats her lashes at me, and yeah, it's not going to take much to change my mind if she keeps looking at me like that. "I guess I will." My heart thuds in my chest, and I try to school my face into a pleasant smile. But my stupid face is heating up. How is it that this woman can make me blush as easily as she takes a breath?

This not date is over too soon. Before I'm ready, we're walking out of the museum, stomachs full, and yet I'm still full of energy. I'm not ready to go home to my apartment, so I do something that is probably extremely dumb. "You want to hit up another one? I have nothing else going on today."

Mika smiles so brightly, the sun should take notes. "Absolutely! Let's hit up the American History Museum. It's like on the other side of the Mall, but it's one of my favorites. And it's not really that far."

It's really not that far; everything on the Mall is incredibly walkable. It's a sunny day, and the weather is muggy and hot. There's no shade on the walkway, and sunglasses are only a small reprieve. But the company makes it worth the discomfort, and Mika does a good job of distracting from the heat.

The blast of cold air as we enter the museum is welcome. The museum is huge and full of enough people that there's constant chatter around us, but not enough that we have to wait to see anything.

"Why is it so large?" I ask after we round the corner of the escalator to stand in front of a huge statue of George Washington styled in the Roman fashion.

"I have no idea," Mika responds, staring. "And what's with the toga? Like Washington never wore a toga."

"That we know of." I laugh.

Mika laughs loudly, snorting through her nose. I love how unabashed she is about her joy. "Don't kink shame George Washington," she says through her laughter. A group of middle-aged women give us judgmental looks as they pass, like how dare we have fun in a museum. Mike doesn't seem to care, and we continue on our way through the rest of the museum.

I have forgotten how much fun just hanging out with another person can be, especially not having to worry about doing something wrong. There's no expectation with Mika. We're just enjoying being where we are with each other. I don't feel guilty for making jokes or laughing at certain exhibits or feel like I have to experience everything with solemnity like I would with Adele. Mika's zest for life is infectious, and I feel like I can finally really breathe in the world around me.

As we make our way through the museum, we talk about work and life. Mika tells me about some of her weirdest transcription jobs, the best being a lecture series on human sexuality through the ages. "I lost count of the number of times I had to write dildo and erect. Good thing I'm not squeamish about sexy things, or it would have been a really awkward job."

She asks me about the book covers I design. That's a lot easier to talk about than my actual day job. I show her some examples, including a few of my favorites I designed for a husband and wife duo who write sci-fi romantic erotica. "They pretty much let me go wild with my design, and they are both wonderful people. I'd read their books even if they weren't paying me to design their covers," I tell Mika as we head toward the full display of Julia Child's set kitchen.

"Have you done all their covers?" she asks me, and I'm grateful that she's actually showing an interest in what I do. Adele always hated that I worked on book covers for self-published authors. She thought it was a waste of time since, in her opinion, they would never sell anyway. And she especially hated that I designed covers for what she called "trashy books." But rather than give that up, like I knew she wanted, I just stopped telling her. That was one thing I kept for myself because not only did it make me feel a sense of accomplishment, but I also loved the feeling when the authors gushed over my work.

"Most of them. I know occasionally they use some other artist, but I don't hold that against them since it's good to have some diversity in cover art. But I would absolutely make all their covers if they asked me. You get some people who are super picky about what they want, which I understand, a book is like their baby, but most are pretty chill and trust my judgment. Not everyone does it, but I read a copy of every book I design so I can get a full idea of what the cover should convey." I know I'm probably rambling, but Mika nods her head alone with my words, actively listening to everything I say. It's such a small thing, but after years of feeling like the person I was closest to didn't hear a word I said, and didn't care to hear it, this is really refreshing. It's actually making me feel better about myself and my work.

When we finally leave the American History Museum, it's hotter than it was when we went in. It's midafternoon, and the Mall is crawling with tourists and people just enjoying the sunshine.

"Have you spent any time with Abey Baby?" Mika asks me, sliding on her mirrored aviator sunglasses. I stare at myself in them as I turn to face her.

"Abey Baby?" I raise an eyebrow, though I have a pretty good idea what she means.

She points ahead of us, but all I can see in that direction is the Washington Monument. "The Lincoln Memorial. My bestie Abey Baby hangs out there. It's the best place to people watch. If you're still up for adventuring. The walk down the Reflecting Pool is actually super shady, so we won't bake the whole way.

"Sure, I haven't been yet." We start off in the direction Mika pointed. After a few steps she threads her arm through mine without breaking stride. It's too hot to be walking this close together, but I find that I don't care. I like the feel of her arm in mine, even if it overheats me a little.

As we walk, Mika tells me about growing up in Chevy Chase and going to Petworth to spend weekends with her grandma. She learned to cook during her time there, and she helped her dad in the kitchen when she was home. I tell her about my life growing up in the Bronx with a single mom and the rest of my extended family all around me.

In a way, our upbringings are similar. Food is a huge part of my family. It's a way to connect to where we're from and brings us all together at least once a day. I miss those dinners with my family. It was always loud, everyone talked over one another and it was damn near impossible to get a word in when a heated debated started. I tell Mika all of this. She laughs at all the right places, and her smile stays on her face.

"I wish I had that growing up. But my great-grandma came to this country alone and pregnant and never remarried, so it's just Bubbe. My mom had a younger brother, but he died before I was born, so I don't have any cousins on that side. My dad is from California orig inally, but came to DC for college and never left. All his family is still out there, so we only see them maybe once a year, if that. I do have cousins out there though." I can tell there's a bit of wistfulness there, like she wished she'd had more growing up. I can't imagine what that's like, to know you could have more family around, but either distance or a horrible tragedy kept that from happening.

Guilt floods me. Because I have a huge family, both from my mom and my dad's side. I grew up with them all around me and took that for granted. I missed out on so much when I was with Adele. Time I should have had with them all. I know my family loves me and forgives me, because at the heart of it, I was a victim and a hostage in my home. But that doesn't change that I let Adele alienate me from them. And now I'm alienating myself by moving so far away. True, I Facetime my mom weekly, if not more, and I talk to my siblings nearly as much. It's just not the same as being there.

"So I get wanting to get away after a breakup, by why DC? You're super close with your family, and New York is huge, why not stay there?" Mika asks, like she can read my thoughts.

I stare ahead and we walk in silence for a few moments while I think of an answer. "New York is a big place, and there was no way Adele would ever come to the Bronx, she hated it. But it didn't seem far enough, you know." She nods her head, and I keep going. "I was making up for lost time with my family. I barely saw them in the years Adele and I were together, but it got to the point where I felt smothered. Then I felt bad because I felt that way when my family was only trying to help me. Things were really bad after I moved back in with my mom. She wanted to help me but didn't know how. I thought distance would make things better, allow me to be better."

"Is it working?" She asks, and there's no judgment in her tone. She doesn't expect me to be cured from whatever harm Adele caused me, not that she knows the extent of it, in just the few months I've been here.

I stop, and since we're still attached at the arm, so does Mika. I look at her, wishing I could see her eyes behind the sunglasses. "It's starting to," I say, with as much conviction in my voice as I can muster. I'm sure my face is pink, but I'll blame the sun for that. Mika rewards my confession with her megawatt smile, and we continue on to the Lincoln Memorial arm in arm. I feel lighter after telling Mika some of my truth.

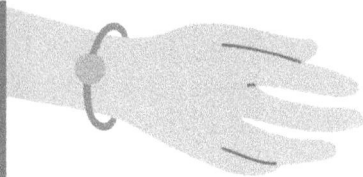

CHAPTER 11

MIKA

*A*fter our first museum day, Ash and I make a habit of going to a new museum every week. Sometimes we just hit up the monuments or parks. But we always make sure to go during the day. I insist without actually insisting. I'm worried that if we do anything in the evening, it'll feel too much like a date, and I don't want to put any unnecessary pressure on our friendship. Because I really enjoy what I have with Ash. He's a really good friend. I feel like I can talk to him about things I don't want to talk to Stella about. Not that I don't tell Stella just about everything in my life, but it's refreshing to share my secrets with someone who hasn't known me for years, who hasn't seen my lowest points yet.

Wednesday finally rolls around. Ash and I have spent the last month spending every Sunday together, and it's been great. Sometimes we just spend the time enjoying what the exhibits have to offer with superficial talk about our week and general life things. Other times we spend our excursions deep diving into each other's thoughts.

I like being there for Ash. It's clear he needs a friend, someone who doesn't have any history from his time in New York.

Tonight I've made chicken salad sandwiches. I don't usually make a lot of meat dishes for game nights, but Stella, our resident vegetarian is eating with Elise before game time, so I get to make a crowd favorite. I have an array of chip flavors out to go with it, and a small veggie tray I put together in like five minutes sits next to them on the counter. I also made lemon bars for dessert. Two pitchers of margaritas are chilling in the refrigerator, waiting for everyone's arrival. Seems like the perfect summer spread.

I'm surprised when Nico is the first one to walk through my door. Nico is never the first one here, not once in the years I've known him. "Alright, Nico doppelganger, who are you, and where is the real Nico?" I laugh as he walks into the kitchen.

"Har har, Mikey. I had an afternoon shift at the bar and got let out early. It was easier to come here than head home. Can I shower real quick? I smell like I am the bar." He adjusts the backpack on his shoulder to sniff his shirt.

"Sure, clean towels are in the closet. You need anything to wear?" Nico isn't a big guy; he's worn my t-shirts and shorts plenty of times when he's hung out here after work.

He shakes his head. "Nah, I have stuff in here." He pats his backpack like I don't know what he means. "You know, in case a fine lady wants to take me home, I don't want to be doing the walk of shame in last night's clothes."

I laugh as he leaves the room and heads upstairs to my bathroom. At least I don't have to worry about him using all my hot water. Nico showers in five minutes or less.

Literally seconds after Nico turns on the water, my front door opens, and I hear Marco and Ash coming down the hall. "Hey Mike!" Marco's voice booms throughout the kitchen. The two of them enter, and Ash gives me a small wave.

We chat for a few minutes, munching on veggies from the tray. "Twenty-five thousand subscribers, Mike! Can you believe it? Twenty-five thousand people actually want to listen to me talk about dumb 80s shit. Ten years of work is finally paying off. I'm just over the moon. You up for celebrating this weekend? I feel like this is a big milestone." Marco is absolutely buzzing with energy. As he should be. He's put so much effort into *Be Kind, Rewind*, he deserves to celebrate such a big milestone.

"Absolutely, this is huge!" I give him a full body hug. Marco is a lot bigger than me, so when he wraps me up in his arms, I'm completely smothered. There's no better way to be hugged in my opinion.

When he pulls away, he swings an arm out and drags Ash to him by his shoulders. "And the art this guy has been doing for the podcast has really made an impact on my numbers. My social looks amazing, and the thumbnails are so good." Ash's smile is soft and embarrassed and just ridiculously cute.

The moment is broken up by a damp Nico reappearing. "Hey gang, how's it hanging?"

Ash gives Nico a once over. "How long have you been here?" Because yes, we're all surprised Nico showed up early!

Nico, being Nico, walks around the counter and slips his arm around my waist. "Oh, I just got out of the shower.. I was just too sweaty after spending some time with Mika," he says in a sultry voice. Nico is all flirt, and he knows it annoys me.

I watch as Ash's eyes grow big, and then for a moment, he looks almost ... sad? Disappointed? No, that can't be right. For one, he knows I would never with Nico. And two, we're just friends anyway, so why would he look like that?

I give Nico a playful shove in the ribs and move away from him. "Ew, gross. You came in smelling like a bar. The only sweaty person here was you, and that was from slinging booze." I make sure to direct this toward Ash, to make him see that Nico is just being a dork, and I would never, ever do anything with Nico.

"Ha, Nic, everyone knows Mika wouldn't touch you with a ten-foot pole. You'll just fall in love with her, and she'll never be rid of you." Marco is laughing again, and Ash, well, he doesn't smile, but he looks more at ease. Good, I don't want our friendship to get weird because he thinks I'm banging Nico.

"Grab some food, guys. Stella will be here soon. Nico, veggies first, then lemon bars," I say as I watch Nico bee-line for the sweets. I'm pretty sure that man wouldn't eat a single green thing if I didn't practically shove it down his throat each week. He's like a tall toddler sometimes.

I'm just pouring out glasses of margarita when Stella bursts through the door.

Literally bursts.

The door flies open so hard and fast, it bounces off the bikes hanging on the wall, and then I hear a second bang when Stella assumably kicks it back closed again. "Everything okay, Stella?" I call from the dining room, even as I'm standing up to greet her down the hall.

"Fine! My bag slipped as I was opening the door, and it was either use the foot or drop my leftovers and like hell, I'm dropping those." She meets me halfway, and she hands over a takeout bag so she can shift the large bag full of her class materials and B&B stuff.

Stella makes quick work of getting herself situated at the table and we begin.

"Let's recap. Last time on the Bone Brigade, Anglehert Viskna has contracted you to clear out his ancestral home, which he intends to reclaim and take up his title and dominion over these lands. So far, you have managed to clear out most of the vermin living within the estate grounds. We stopped just as you reached the front door." Marco goes through this part like he's recapping an episode of one of the shows he podcasts; it's his storyteller voice, the one he uses to set the scene.

"Just a reminder, not that I think you need it, but you haven't taken a rest yet, so keep that in mind as you head into the manor proper." This he says in his GM voice, not his storyteller voice.

"Ooo, can we take a rest?" Nico asks because of course he does. Marco allows it, though only Nico really needs it since last week he decided to try his hand at being a barbarian without having any skills or adequate armor rating. He went rushing through the hedge maze without waiting for anyone else and got his ass kicked.

"Restful Song for you bitches. And I start playing the Song of the Universe on penny whistle." Nico smirks at all of us. And then it happens: a penny whistle version of "Tom Sawyer" starts playing through his phone, and it's honestly worse than the bagpipes. It's horrible.

"Turn it off, or I'm banning you from playing bards from now on," Marco says, covering his ears. The look of panic on Nico's face as he scrambles to turn off the music is hilarious. Nico only plays bards, and I think it has more to do with the fact he's comfortable with the class and doesn't want to learn another one than it is about keeping with his rockstar image.

"Fine, you win. No more penny whistle," he says with mock glumness.

"Moving on," Marco says, and it's back to storyteller Marco. "The door stands in front of you. It's nothing special, just a front door. I don't want to waste time on a door again, so I will tell you that it's not trapped, and it's not locked. It's just a simple door."

"A likely story. Never trust a door!" Stella yells. "I charge the door, full speed. But I'm not raging, just FYI."

Marco pinches the bridge of his nose, closes his eyes, and sighs deeply. "Make a strength check." He sounds so defeated.

"Balls! Nine," Stella says, glaring daggers at her d20.

Another deep sigh comes from Marco. It's not like he hasn't been through a door ordeal before, and it definitely won't be the last one. "Tamotur rams the door; it flies open. The door remains intact, the lock unbroken, and there were no traps."

The main level of the mansion is all goblins. Angry, mean, smelly goblins. "I'm aiming for the one attacking Varic." I point toward the miniature goblins on the board set into the table. The mini I'm indicating is closer to Marco, so he points at one. "No, the other one on Varic." I point again, and Marco moves his finger toward the other goblin currently beating on Nico's character. I roll my d20 and check the number with my attack bonus. "Thirteen total. Does that hit?"

Marco levels a look at me. "He's a goblin; of course it hits. Roll damage."

My six damage is enough to take out the goblin attacking Varic. "Thank you, my lady Uriel. Your aim is true as ever. Your demonic spark burns a fire in my heart." Nico lays it on thick in character. It's like he's playing an only slightly exaggerated version of himself.

"Unless you are giving me some inspiration, shut it, bard," I snap back in character. Marco encourages us to roleplay, so long as it doesn't slow down combat.

"Kilris, you're up," Marco says, turning his attention toward Ash.

Ash looks at his character sheet and then over at the book he has open next to him. "Um, okay. Well I'm going to use beast form and go into tiger mode. Is that a bonus action or action?"

"Action, but I'll let you use a bonus action to change, and you can take an attack action after that." Marco is a diplomatic GM, and hey, he's the game god. We're all just his pawns.

Ash contemplates the board for a second and then points to the other goblin on Varic. "Okay, so I turn into a tiger and claw at that one." He rolls without prompting, totally in his element in this game now. "Shit! A natural twenty!" Ash gapes at his dice. Then he raises his head and punches the air.

We all cheer so loudly that I'm pretty sure my neighbors can hear us. Ash has worse luck than Stella with natural twenties. He's only rolled a few since he started playing, and almost all of them were on minor checks or initiative.

"Woooo, go get 'em, tiger. Kilris is next to me. Can I give him a slap on the ass for good luck while I say that?"

I mimic smacking a backside while I direct my question at Marco. Everyone is laughing now, and I know if I turn to look at him, Ash will be beet red.

"Ash, is it okay if your party member sexually harasses your character?" Marco laughs.

I turn my head so I can see Ash, and yup, he's atomic red. "Uh ... harass away," he manages to finally say.

"Okay, Uriel is going to slap Kilris' little tiger booty. It won't give you any bonus or anything, but you'll feel good about yourself," I say to Ash. He looks intently down at his character sheet, and the effort to not look at me seems to be his main focus. I decide to leave the poor guy alone before he passes out from all the blushing.

Hours later, when the game finishes, I ask around if anyone wants to stay and hang again or go out. I can afford to start later tomorrow, and I'm not ready for the night to end. Maybe, just maybe, I'm secretly hoping it'll just be me and Ash again, and if cuddles happen on the couch, then hey, cuddles happen on the couch, and it's totally cool.

But I'm disappointed immediately. "I can't. I have an early appointment, and a day full of meetings tomorrow. Sorry, Mika." And he really does look sorry. It might just be wishful thinking, but he's giving me this longing look, like he wishes he could stay.

Stella stands from the table and starts packing her stuff. Nico follows suit. "Can't tonight, babe. Elise's parents are heading into town tomorrow, so I still need get the house in order. Though why they are showing up on a Thursday afternoon is beyond me," Stella says, shoving her binder into her bag with a little more force than necessary. She likes her in-laws, and they love her, they just

... tend to wear out their welcome at Stella and Elise's place way too long.

"I could always hang around and shower again. Maybe this time you could join me, Mikey." Nico waggles his eyes brows and makes kissy faces at me. I roll my eyes.

"Pass. Besides, you probably hog all the water when you share the shower," I respond as I start to clear up my area.

"It's true, I do. Anyway, I'm actually totally beat, and for once in my life, sleep before 1:00 a.m. sounds pretty nice." He follows this up with a huge yawn that, on anyone else, would look wildly exaggerated. But I know Nico, and that yawn tells me he didn't sleep last night.

I don't need to hear Marco's answer to know he won't be hanging out. I don't hold it against him at all. B&B is the one thing he allows himself to have lately without Lena, and even then, I have a suspicion that Lena pushed him to keep playing through her pregnancy. He doesn't like leaving her alone.

"Guess it's just me tonight. When did we all get to be so adult and responsible on weekday nights?" I laugh. I'm bummed, but it's not like I don't understand that we all have lives. I just happen to have a lighter load tomorrow. That doesn't mean everyone else does.

"Some of us have already been adults. I'm nearly forty and about to be a dad." Marco chuckles, and he already has a dad laugh. It's loud, and mirthy, and great.

I wave him off. "Yeah, yeah, I get it. I'm the baby. But I will also enjoy this last year of my twenties while you are all closer to rotting in the ground since it's all thirty and flirty with the Grim Reaper with the rest of you."

"Hush, child. It's past your bedtime," Nico says with a grin. Nico is exactly nine months older than me and just turned thirty a few weeks ago. He doesn't remember the day though or the weekend. There wasn't a sober moment for his birthday extravaganza, though the stacked hangover days lasted nearly a week.

Sucks to get older.

Everyone heads for the exit, and I walk my friends to the door. "If we don't get together this weekend, I'll see you all on Wednesday. Open invite to Shabbos on Saturday," I remind them. My dad will always make too much food, whether people come or not.

We don't make concrete plans, but that's okay. Most of our plans are spur of the moment anyway with all our schedules constantly changing. I wave to the gang from my porch as, one by one, they disappear down my street.

When I trudge back inside, I try not to feel down. I love my friends, and they love me. That doesn't mean they have to stop their lives just to keep me company. That's what Netflix and leftovers are for.

I shower and put on my pajamas, which is just an old t-shirt from Nico's band and underwear. Who needs pants when I'm home alone anyway? I fix myself another chicken salad sandwich and head to my living room. It would be better if a friend was curled up with me on the couch, but I'm okay with being alone.

Just as I settle in for some binge watching, my phone vibrates with a text.

[Ash: Sorry I couldn't stay. Please don't think I'm ditching you.]

[Me: No worries. I know you're not. You have shit to do.]

[Ash: Yeah. Early morning therapy appointment. It was the only slot I could get this time.]

[Me: Nothing like pouring your trauma out first thing in the morning. Goes right up there with coffee.]

[Ash: Lol. Yeah, I get to do this once a week. It's great fun.]

[Ash: Want to do dinner tomorrow instead?]

[Me: Sounds good.]

We make plans to meet up, and I feel lighter. I never thought Ash was ditching me. I respect his time. But it's still nice to know he thought of me and didn't want to hurt my feelings. I'm really lucky to have met Ash and that he's in my life. We're becoming really good friends, and I hope we have a lot more adventures together, not just playing B&B, but in real life too.

CHAPTER 12

ASH

"I feel like I might be ready to start dating again," I announce to my therapist.

"There's a lot to that statement. Why do you feel like you might be ready?" Danny the therapist asks. I've been seeing him since the week after I moved to DC, and in the last several months, he has been exactly the type of help I needed. It feels less like therapy and more like a conversation, which is honestly a lot easier.

I shrug. "I don't know. I just think it might be time. It's been almost six months since I left Adele. I can't let what she did to me hold me back forever, can't let her hold me back forever." Because it's true: I don't want Adele to continue to have power over me.

Danny levels me with a knowing look. "This conclusion wouldn't be because of a certain pink-haired nerd girl, would it?" Naturally, I've told Danny all about my new friends and hobby. And if I've talked a little more thoroughly about Mika, that's only because we've become really close.

"No, it's not about Mika. She's like my best friend. Even after I totally embarrassed myself a month ago, she still wants to be around me. She... I don't know, gets me out of my own head." It's not that I think I'm ready to date because of Mika. No, that's not it.

Danny looks at me over the rim of his wire frame glasses, which I'm almost completely sure he doesn't actually need. "You want to date her?" he asks like he already knows the answer.

"No, it's not like that," I say, but my response sounds feeble even to my own ears.

Danny leans forward in his seat, clutching the top of his legal pad. "Listen, Sebastian. You can lie to yourself all day, but you can't lie to me." He gives me that knowing look again, and he's right. I am lying to myself.

"She's just so cute and confident. There's just no way she would go for a guy like me. I'm ... chronically awkward." I throw my hands into the air, exasperated with myself.

Danny finally leans back and smiles. "Ash, she told you she enjoyed having you as her pillow after she accidentally had a face full of your penis. I think she likes you."

Great, now my therapist is embarrassing me. "It was her chest, not her face, and you make me sound like a huge perv. Isn't therapy supposed to make me feel better, not worse?"

Danny writes something down, then touches the tip of his pen to his mouth. "Hm, nope. It's supposed to make you examine shitty things and figure out how you're going to handle it all. And then take your money."

"You're a shitty therapist, Danny," I grumble, though I don't actually mean it.

Danny points his pen at me. "I'm the best damn therapist you've ever had."

He's right of course. I didn't start therapy until I moved out of the apartment I shared with Adele and went home to the Bronx. My first therapist there knew my grandma and didn't exactly keep doctor/patient confidentiality when it came to my family. The first therapist in DC spent the entire session eating his dinner and within five minutes of meeting me said that I needed to be on an anxiety drug. I know I'm fucked up, but I don't think I'm so fucked up that someone would decide I need medication within the first five minutes of meeting me. So, he was out. The second therapist here, and one before Danny, was entirely too touchy feely. I had a sense she might actual enjoy sleeping with her patients, so I noped out of that entire practice.

I lucked out with Danny, finally. He was younger, probably only a few years older than I am. He got my personality and humor, and he didn't let me get away with any bullshit. Talking to Danny was like talking to a friend. Just one I paid over a hundred bucks an hour to listen to me.

At least insurance covers most of it.

"Listen, Ash, I can't tell you if you're ready to start putting yourself out there again. Only you can do that. What I can tell you is that you've been making great progress over the last several months, and I'm happy with how you are healing. If part of that healing means asking out the cute girl you've been crushing on, then go for it. But if that means just being her best friend for a while longer, that's great too. The main thing is that you are happy, and your relationships, romantic or otherwise, are healthy." Danny's eye dart to the little clock on the side table. "And that's about it for us this week."

He's not dismissing my feelings. I know that. That's just how therapy works. We exchange parting pleasantries, and then I'm riding back to my apartment, feeling a little lighter than I did before. If I had known therapy would be this good for me, I would have started years ago. Probably wouldn't have stayed in an emotionally abusive relationship for years if I had just taken care of myself, but I can't think about that.

What I can think about is if I plan to actually do anything about Mika.

In the month since the movie incident, she's never said a word about it. Another reason I like her so much. She didn't want me to feel embarrassed then, and she won't let me feel it now. It didn't change our dynamic. Mika, as always, is affectionate, touchy, and flirty. She still helps me through B&B nights when I run into issues, which are becoming less frequent since I've become more familiar with the rules and just lose myself in the game.

Sometimes, when she's not touching me, I find I want to touch her. Or sit next to her when we all go out.

Wasn't it just a few months ago that I was trying to put distance between us? Hasn't she been doing the same?

Movie nights after the game were a no go. I think we both realized that was dangerous territory. But on non-game days, when we can start sooner in the evening, I started going over to her house so she could show me *Chuck*, and we sit on opposite ends of the couch.

Just as I enter my apartment, my phone pings with a text.

[Mika: I can't decide between Indian or Thai tonight. On the one hand, I want to eat my weight in garlic naan. But then there's noodles. Lots of tasty noodles.]

I can't help by smile at her text. Mika is such a food girl, and I love that. She can make just about anything, and it's always amazing. But then she gets on one of these kicks where she wants something she doesn't normally cook, and everything sounds good to her.

She's not directly asking me to come over, but that's not how Mika works. She's asking my opinion on food, which she then intends for me to come over and help her eat.

[Me: You want Indian tonight. And if there happens to be samosas, I can take one for the team and eat them.]

[Mika: Bold of you to think I'll share my samosas.]

[Me: You are nothing if not generous, Mike.]

[Mika: Keep saying more nice things to me, babe, and there might be an extra mango lassi waiting at my house.]

[Me: I'll pick up cupcakes from that bakery you like on my way over.]

[Mika: OMG marry me. Not a question. I'm calling my Bubbe right now. I'm sure she has the rabbi on speed dial to get us in quickly.]

[Me: Can we eat first? I love your grandma, but I can't face Yael on an empty stomach.]

[Mika: Fair point. Food first, then marriage, then cupcakes. Our life is planned.]

[Me: L'chaim!]

I'm smiling as I set my phone down and head to my room to take a shower. Flirty banter with Mika is the easiest thing in the world. She really is my best friend, and she makes it so effortless. I don't have to worry about the things I say might set her off. I don't have to worry about going out or staying out too late. I go to Shabbos lunches with her family and not always with the whole gang anymore; sometimes it's just the two of us showing up. Danny said something about healthy relationships, and outside of my own family, Mika is the healthiest relationship I have.

Part of me wants more than what we already have. Don't get me wrong—what we have is beautiful, and I love having her as my best friend. But I'm still attracted to her. I still want to do ... more than friend things with her. The other part of me knows that it's risky to want that. Because what if it doesn't work out? It'll cause a split in the group, and all of these new friends I just made will be gone. Marco will feel forced to pick a side, and even though I know he'll want to keep the whole group, he'll pick me just because I'm family. Then I'll have to live with the guilt that not only did I break up a group of friends because I couldn't keep my dick in my pants, but I'll feel even more guilt over fucking up my cousin's friendships.

I'm overthinking and spiraling again. As the hot water sluices over me, I try to draw my thoughts away from the worst-case scenario. Look at the facts: Mika and I are attracted to each other. We both clearly want something more. Not even I am dense enough not to notice. I know Mika had a thing with someone else in the group and they got kicked out when it ended. I don't know many details, but I do know she's worried about it happening again. And I know I'm worried about breaking up the group if something goes wrong. It's just—I know myself and I know Mika. Even if things end, they would end amicably. Someone might get their heart broken, but I know neither of us would cheat or do something heinous like that. I trust that I know her and myself well enough to know that we could stay cordial, if not friends, in the case of a split.

I think it might be a good idea to talk to Marco before I make any move though. My cousin has known Mika for longer. He was there for her when everything went down before, and I trust his judgment. The big question though, is if I'll listen to him if he tells me what I don't want to hear. I don't know the answer to that.

I'm changing into clean clothes, something I can lounge around Mika's place in, when my phone starts to ring. Mika doesn't usually call, but maybe she's having trouble picking what to order and wants to do it fast. I accept the call without looking.

"Mike, you're going to get the saag paneer. I don't know why—"

"Hi, Sebastian," a soft voice says on the other end of the line.

My whole body reacts to that voice. I go rigid and immediately break out into a cold sweat. I'm flooded in fear, and I don't know what to do. I should hang up, but I don't. I can't.

"How did you get my number, Adele?" It's the only thing I can think to say. I had my number changed after I moved out and blocked her on everything. I didn't want her to contact me. And then when I moved to DC, I tried to make sure she couldn't find me.

"I have my ways. Besides, I'm your girlfriend. I should have your number." I once thought she had a lovely voice. It's soft yet husky, feminine yet dominating. Now, she sounds like a snake. Like her voice is dripping with poison trying to infiltrate my brain.

"You're not my girlfriend anymore, Adele. You haven't been for a while now." I keep my tone harsh; I can't give her an inch. I try to remember some of the techniques Danny taught me. We planned for a scenario like this when I first started with him.

I already broke the first step: don't answer.

Second step: keep it brief. Give no information.

"Hm, a technicality for now. But we're just taking a break." There she is, creating her own narrative.

"What do you want, Adele?" *Just make your point and leave me alone forever.*

"You're touchy today, Sebastian. But then, you've always had an attitude, haven't you? Whatever. You'll get over it. Anyway, I'm going to be in DC in a few weeks for a fundraiser. It's a big thing being hosted by a senator. And since you're in the neighborhood now, I want you to be my date." First the barb, and then the sweetness. Like she's doing me a favor by inviting me.

"How do you know where I live?" *Just give it all away, why don't you, Ash?!*

There's a small chuckle on her end. "I said I have my ways. It's on the twenty-third. Wear a suit. You do own one of those, right?"

"I have plans," I say automatically because it doesn't matter if I have plans or not. I'm not going anywhere with Adele Stevens. Not again.

Again, that small patronizing chuckle. "I doubt that. You'll pick me up at 7:00 p.m. I'll send you my address when I arrive in the city."

So fucking self-assured, like how could she not possibly get what she wants? "I said I'm busy." I'm gritting my teeth so hard it feels like they are going to break.

"Just do as you're told, Sebastian. Don't be difficult. It's unbecoming." And God help me, I can hear the fake disappointment in her voice. Because, of course, it's fake. She would have to care first for any of it to be real.

"Find someone else to take you, Adele. Goodbye." And before she can respond, and before I can talk myself out of it, I hang up.

But now my whole body feels numb, and I'm still sweating and shaking. I'm a mess. Months of therapy blown open from one five-minute phone call. I feel like I'm right back where I started.

My phone pings in my hand, and I nearly drop it out of fear. When I look at the screen, though, it's just a text from Mika.

[Mika: Hey are you leaving soon? I haven't heard from you. I can't eat all this food by myself!]

I don't know what to say to her. I want to continue my plans with Mika. I want this to be a normal night and forget that Adele ever called me. Just forget Adele altogether.

But I can't. Fuck, I can't even move from this spot.

Somehow though, my fingers know something my brain doesn't, and my thumbs fly across the screen seemingly of their own accord.

[Me: I need you. Please.]

There's barely a second between my text and her response.

[Mika: I'm on my way. Just stay put, honey.]

There's a knock on my apartment door. It's too soon for it to be Mika, even if she pedaled full speed here. I freeze in my living room. Immediately my brain tells me it's Adele come to fuck with me in person.

No, Adele is still in New York. She said she was going to be here soon, not that she was already here.

Another knock on the door.

"Ash, honey, it's me. Let me in." Mika's voice floats through the door, and I almost cry in relief. Everything will be okay now that she's here.

I open the door and there she is, all bright colors, beautiful expressive eyes, and a look of pure concern on her face. I'm so struck by her, by how she seems to calm all my anxieties just by looking at her, that it takes me a minute to realize she has her arms full of plastic bags. Our Indian food by the smell of it.

Mika doesn't wait for me to explain anything. She just sets the bags down inside the door and pulls me tightly to her. My arms wrap around her middle, letting the warmth of her body ground me. I bury my face in her bubblegum curls. Despite the color, her hair smells like cinnamon. It's my new favorite scent.

She keeps her arms tight around my shoulders, and she just holds me. Minutes go by and we still don't pull away or say anything. I could die right here, held in Mika's arms. To me, Mika is starlight personified, burning bright in a sea of darkness. Her smile can turn a whole day around. Her laugh can quell any bad mood. And her embrace, well, that can jumpstart a numb heart and make it feel again.

I'm not saying I'm in love with Mika because I'm not sure I know what love really is. But I could love her one day.

When I'm ready.

"How did you get here so fast?" I mumble into the side of her neck and asking the most important question. Her shoulders shake with a small laugh.

"They have these things called cars. I took a Lyft. You can't just text me you need me and not expect me to not pay for an overcharged taxi ride just to get to you as soon as possible." She pulls away just enough to look me in the eye, but not enough to actually break contact. She clearly doesn't want me to go far, and I don't want to. I need to stay tangled up with her a little longer.

Mika studies my face like she's trying to discern all my problems first and then ask questions. "What's going on, Ash? What happened?"

Part of me just wants to brush it off, tell her it was nothing. Not that she would believe that, and since she's Mika, she definitely wouldn't let me get away with that. *If I can't lay bare my soul to my best friend, who can I?*

I steel my nerves and my grip around her waist tightens a little. "Adele called me. She's coming to DC for some fundraiser in a few weeks and wants me to take her. I don't even know how she got my number or how she knew where I was." There are so many emotions swirling within me that I would cry if I could. But Adele ruined that, too. Any emotional reaction from me, and she would break me down, tell me I wasn't being a man.

There's no judgment from Mika. She just keeps hanging onto me. "Want me to kick her ass? I've never thrown a punch in my life, but I'll do it. For you."

Though I laugh, her face is serious. Yeah, she absolutely would fight for me because she's amazing. "No offense, Mike, but Adele has been a blackbelt in Tang Soo Do. I'm pretty sure the only ass kicked would be yours."

This time she laughs. "It's the thought that counts. I would absolutely take a beat down for you." Her face turns serious again, the laughter fading from her eyes. "You're not going with her, are you?"

Mika doesn't know the whole story with Adele. She just knows it was a bad breakup, and I had to get away. I have the urge to tell her everything; it's time she knows. I don't answer right away. Instead, I pull her toward my couch and we sit.

"No, there's no way I'm going anywhere with Adele again. I can't be around her. I never told you this, but I trust you more than just about anyone else—aside from family. So I feel like you need to know." Mika doesn't interrupt me; instead, she holds my hand and looks at me with a level gaze. I take a deep breath and tell my truth.

"Adele never was physical with me, but she spent years abusing me. Emotionally and mentally. She made me seek her affection, and when I didn't live up to her standards, she used that against me. I let her isolate me from my family, from my friends, all because she said she didn't like them. And I always had an excuse for why I didn't leave. I didn't see her as a project I could fix. No, she made me feel like I was the broken one, and she was fixing me. What she was doing instead was breaking me down and making sure I was under her control."

Mika remains quiet. She won't interrupt me, and I'm grateful for that. Even though I trust her completely, this is still hard to say. It's hard to admit to anyone that you're a victim, especially as a guy. Nobody wants to believe a woman could abuse a man in any way.

"My family tried to convince me to leave. They saw what she was doing to me. My friends, well, they stopped trying to get through because I just wouldn't listen. We were together for four years, and I knew halfway in that I didn't love her, but she wouldn't let me go. Until finally, one day we had a stupid argument. She wanted to go to a party at her friend's, but I was sick. I felt fucking miserable and could barely get out of bed. Adele didn't care. She thought it was all a ploy to get her out of the house so I could have another woman over or something like that. I have never cheated in my life. But I got dressed anyway because it was what she wanted and went to the party. I was so sick, I passed out right in the middle of the living room within thirty minutes of being there." I stop and my mind immediately pictures that night. I was barely conscious on the floor; everything was fuzzy, and I felt like I was burning alive.

Mika starts to rub her thumb against my knuckles, and I let it soothe me back into my story. "Someone took me to the hospital. Turns out I had a really severe case of Covid and was dehydrated. Adele didn't even come visit me in the hospital, even though I was allowed a visitor. My mom was the one to come see me right away. She took me home after that. After a week, Adele came to my mom's house. She never came to the Bronx. She screamed at me that I embarrassed her at the party, and I should have just sucked it up for her sake. That I didn't love her enough because I went to a party when I had Covid. It didn't matter that I didn't want to go. That I told her how sick I was. She twisted it back on me and made it my fault. She didn't even text me the whole week I was gone. And it finally clicked. She didn't love me, and I was putting up with her bullshit for nothing."

"So you left," Mika says softly, giving my hand a gently squeeze.

147

I nod. "So I left. I stayed with mom for a few weeks, and then Marco invited me to move to DC. I lived with him and Lena for a week before I found this place. Changed my number and blocked Adele on everything so she couldn't find me and made sure she would never get my address. And until now, I haven't heard anything from her."

Telling Mika all this hollows me out but in a way I need. I feel exhausted but better somehow. I've told all this to my family, Marco and Lena, my therapist. But telling it to Mika, my best friend, somehow feels more cathartic. Especially since she's hearing this in a very vulnerable moment for me.

Mika scoots closer to me and pulls her hand from mine so she can wrap her arm around my shoulders. She leans her head against my shoulder and just holds me. I ease into her body and rest my hand on her bare knee. Any other time I would probably blush and concentrate too much on touching her skin, but right now, it's comforting. It makes me feel close to another person. Because I'm allowed to feel close to people.

"Offer still stands: I will kick her ass. I'll find a way. I'm scrappy like that." She's not trying to make light of anything, but I can tell she doesn't want this heaviness weighing on me.

I press a kiss to her temple, chaste and friendly, and close my eyes, savoring her closeness. "You can be my white knight any day," I say.

CHAPTER 13

MIKA

I pull the vegetarian lasagna out of the oven just as my friends walk in for B&B night. I congratulate myself for prepping dinner first thing this morning because work ended up being super consuming, and then I worked on my own special project, a novel I started several weeks back. I've always loved writing, but it wasn't until Ash came into my life that I felt I could really do something with it.

My kitchen is warm and smells amazing. Lasagna may be too heavy for the weather today, but it just sounded perfect. It's been super-hot, even though it's midway through September. I'm ready for cold weather already, but that won't be happening any time soon.

The whole gang is loud as they walk into the kitchen. I give the food time to cool a little before I cut into it, setting aside enough for Lena and then the rest of the vultures can descend.

"Just a heads up, everyone. This is probably going to be my last game for a bit. Lena is due any minute, so I'll be in full dad mode. The Bone Brigade is going to take a break, and everyone is going to take turns at the GM helm. No shenanigans while I'm gone." Marco leans over his chair, ready to dig in as he delivers his little speech.

It's going to be weird without Marco around, but Baby Perez takes precedence. I'm already planning to make a ton of meals for them so neither of them has to worry about cooking. They have a good support network for the baby. Besides us, Lena's mom is already down from Baltimore staying with them for a few weeks. Marco's family are coming in from New York for a bit, but opted to stay in a hotel. Lena was worried about being crowded by people, and luckily her in-laws respected that. It helped that it wasn't the first grandchild on the Perez side, so they didn't feel so overbearing.

"Won't be the same without you. And there will be shenanigans. You can't stop that, Marco," Stella says, and the first part is said sincerely. She's not wrong about the second part though. We're full of shenanigans, especially when Nico is in charge.

"There's going to be a harem of succubi again, isn't there?" Marco deadpans, looking directly at Nico. Guess we were all thinking it.

Nico sighs dramatically. "No, Dad, no more succubi harems. I promise."

"Do I want to know?" Ash asks the table.

"Absolutely not," I say. "Just so you know, my mod will be all doors. Nothing else, just doors. You're all going to die of starvation by door two." We all laugh. It's a truth universally acknowledged that a simple wooden door is the greatest enemy in B&B. They don't even have to be locked.

We spend a few minutes eating, eager to get to the game, so talk dies down a little. I totally outdid myself with the lasagna, and it's gratifying to see the pan cleared out by my friends.

"I ate too much," Stella says, holding her stomach. She may be tiny, but the woman can put away food like a professional eater. It's pretty impressive actually.

"Oh good, means more dessert for me," Nico says, and I know he's dying for a piece of the German chocolate cake I made last night. But he'll have to wait. Dessert is for break time tonight.

As Marco sets up his screen, Ash collects plates while the rest of us pull out our gaming stuff. We're starting off in the tavern again, which seems to be our base of operations in the city. "Now that the Bone Brigade has a bit of a reputation in the city, you all are being recruited for jobs. You received a note that morning asking for a meeting at the Rainbow Bovine about a lucrative job. The note is from someone named Thom, but none of you know who that is, so you're sitting around waiting for someone to approach you. You see—hang on, sorry, my phone is going off. Nobody calls me unless it's important." Marco stops abruptly and pulls his phone from his bag.

We sit and wait for Marco. We don't usually allow phones, but Marco gets a pass for family reasons.

"Hey Shazi. What?! Now! Oh shit! Oh shit! Yeah, I'm on my way!" Marco ends the call and starts immediately tearing down his screen and shoving things into his bag. "That was Lena's mom. It's go time! I need to get to the hospital. I'm meeting them there. Holy shit, this is happening." Half of his stuff doesn't make it into his bag; he's frantic and shaking.

Not that any of us have actually prepared for this moment, but suddenly we're all jumping up and getting ready to go. I go over to Marco and help him pack up his things. He won't need them, but I know it will drive him nuts if he leaves them at my house.

"My car is out front. Thank fuck I drove today," Stella says, fishing her keys out of her bag. There's a lot of frantic movements and running as we make our way to the car as a group. I don't know about anyone else, but the only thing I can focus on is getting Marco to the hospital.

I end up stuck between Nico and Ash on the bench seat in the back of the car. I smile at Ash as he slides in beside me and buckles up. His gaze shifts from me to look at the other side of the car. I turn my head to follow his gaze. "Nico, did you bring the cake?!" I only ask because sitting in his lap, clutched between both hands is my covered cake stand with the cake inside.

Nico looks down. "I feel like all important moments need cake. As my Nona always says to me, *Nico, you can't ruin a good thing if your face is stuffed with cake.*"

"I don't think she meant that as a good thing, Nic," Stella says from the front. She's already gunning the car into gear. Beside her in the passenger seat, Marco bounces his knees, which keep hitting the dashboard. His phone is out, and he's texting like crazy. Probably to alert the whole family.

If Stella didn't know her way around the city so well, it would have taken us forever to reach the hospital, but traffic laws are just a suggestion to her when she's on a mission. Marco doesn't seem to notice, but in the back of the car, Ash is gripping onto the handle for dear life, I'm gripping onto Ash because if I'm dying today, I'm doing it wrapped around a handsome man. And Nico, well, I'm pretty sure that cake is in the safest position in the car, considering he has his body wrapped around it.

We arrive at the hospital in record time. Stella drops us all off at the front and then speeds off to park the car. I have to jog to keep up with Marco, who is nearly sprinting to the desk and then up to Labor and Delivery.

Marco is led back to Nina's room while the rest of us are left in the waiting area with Lena and Marco's dads. It's a full house with the rest of us there. Twenty minutes later, Stella joins us and flops into a chair. "There was literally no parking at all. I'm like in a back corner in a spot that is definitely for a compact. Any news yet?"

I shake my head. "Nothing yet. I'm sure it's going to be a while. Marco will probably text us when something happens." I plop down on a two-seater couch next to Ash and throw my arm around his shoulders. "New cousin on the way. The family just keeps getting bigger."

Ash chuckles. "There have been five Perez babies in the last four years. I'm used to them. Although, this is my first time hanging out for the birth." He presses his thigh into mine, and we all settle in for a long wait.

Two hours pass before we hear anything. Marco walks out, looking a little worn around the edges. "Hey gang, it's going to be a while. She's barely dilated. You can go home. We're in for the long haul. Lena is doing great, making jokes and playing Animal Crossing, and baby is looking good."

The dads opt to stay, but the rest of us still have to work the next day, so we say our goodbyes, and Marco promises to let us know when it's show time. Because, yeah, fuck work. Our nibling is being born.

"I don't know how I'm going to sleep or get anything done in the morning. Stel, you willing to drive again? Or I can totally Lyft it. I know you have the kids tomorrow," I ask from the passenger seat. I don't care how much that car costs. I am going to be here for Lena and Marco.

"Fuck those kids. I'm driving everyone. Nico, make sure you put your phone on ring, so you actually hear it when it's go time." Stella laughs.

"Yeah, yeah, I will," Nico responds, the cake back in his lap.

Stella glares at him through the rearview mirror. "Do it now because you'll forget."

Nico grumbles from the back seat, but I turn and see him follow instructions. At least I know he'll actually answer it because Nico has two settings on his phone: vibrate and siren. For real, his ring tone is a siren, but only because Stella set it to that after he slept through it so many times and missed a bunch of stuff.

Nico is dropped off first, and that asshole takes the whole cake with him. I swear, he loves the cakes more than anyone else in his life. When we get to my house, I turn around in my seat to face Ash. "You want to work from my house in the morning? WIFI is good and that way it saves Stella a stop when we need to jet."

I tell myself it's just practical and not at all that I just want to spend more time with Ash. But then again, I'm clearly a liar, especially to myself.

"That's probably a good idea. Yeah, I'll come over first thing. Want me to bring breakfast?" Ash is seriously the best person I have ever met.

"Yes, do that. I'll see you guys tomorrow. Hopefully there'll be a baby to see soon." I shut the door and head up to my house, realizing as I'm opening my door that

I'm exhausted. It's not super late since we left for the hospital around 6:30 p.m., but it's basically 10:00 p.m., and I'm beat.

I force myself to clean up from dinner since there wasn't time before we left, and then make my way up to bed. I make sure my own phone is set to ring before sliding between the sheets and passing out within minutes.

Ash arrives at my house just after 9:00 a.m. the next day, a bag of bagels in one hand and two coffees balanced in a cup tray in the other. We still haven't heard from Marco yet. Seems like poor Lena is in for the really long haul on this birthing thing.

I usually work at my desk in my spare room/office, but since Ash is hanging with his laptop, we set up a combined work station at the table. Normally, I would tuck my phone away so it won't distract me from work, but today I leave it sitting next to my laptop, and I notice Ash does the same.

"Okay, I'm not ignoring you, I'm just going to put on my headphones so I can hear this lecture." I'm sure Ash gets it. I mean, I transcribe for a living, so of course I wear headphones ninety percent of the time.

"Figured. Mind if I do the same? I don't need it for my job. I just like listening to music while I work. I need some kind of noise." I nod, and he puts in his earbuds. I pull my large purple headphones over my ear and drown out the rest of the world with the monotone of a man describing Aristotle. The headphones were a bit of a splurge, but they are amazingly comfortable and noise cancelling, not to mention I got to write them off as a business expense. I just can't do earbuds. They agitate my ears, and the left one always seems to fall out.

After the first thirty minutes, I set down my headphones and stand up to walk around and grab a drink. Ash's eyes flit up to me for a half second and then back down to his computer and drawing tablet.

"You should move for a few minutes," I say, hoping I'm not totally breaking his flow.

Ash removes his earbuds and looks at me. "What was that?"

"I said you should move for a few minutes. It's recommended that you stand and move for a few minutes every thirty minutes. And you look like the kind of guy who will sit at his desk until compelled to move for either food or bathroom breaks." I used to be the same way. Sometimes I would even ignore the need to eat to keep working. But that left me aching and exhausted all the time, so now I make sure to stand and walk around periodically.

The tiny grin on Ash's face tells me I've nailed it. "You might be right. I tend to get sucked in and forget to do everything else." He stands and stretches his arms above his head, and I don't stand a chance. His shirt rides up, and I'm greeted by the sight of part of his toned stomach. The expanse of smooth skin is tan, and there's a trail of fine dark hair leading down into the waistband of his jeans. I have to stop myself from drooling, even as the beautiful sight is once again hidden from me when he lowers his arms, and his shirt resumes its normal place.

But then I look up into his face, and his cheeks are pink as he looks at me.

Oh no.
Oh shit.

He totally caught me staring at his body. Like there's no way to hide that was exactly what I was doing. I was so entranced, I didn't even try to be covert about it. Rookie move. I'm supposed to be a professional.

I've noticed Ash check me out on more than one occasion. And if sometimes I bend over a little farther when I'm wearing one of my low-cut dresses, well that's neither here nor there. I can toe the line between good friends and being sexually attracted. Though by the way Ash is looking at me now, pink cheeks and sultry eyes, I'm not so sure he can.

Would I like to see what kissing Ash would be like? *Yes, a thousand times yes.*

Do I know it would be a terrible idea? Also, yes because that could really ruin the group dynamic, and no relationship is ever guaranteed, and then everything will be ruined in the group, and it'll be my fault again.

Because I know Ash would be a relationship type of guy. He doesn't seem the kind to just want something casual. And honestly, I don't know what I want. I haven't been in a relationship since Quinn, and that was five years ago. There's been nothing serious since then, and I've been fine with that. Happy even.

Until now.

With Ash here in front of me looking like a whole, slightly rumpled snack, I'm starting to think my Bubbe is onto something with that whole marriage thing.

"Mika, I wanted to—" he starts, holding my eyes captive with his own. I don't know what he's going to say next, but I'm eager to find out.

But I'll never know because right at that moment he's cut off from finishing whatever he's going to say by our phones going off. Eye contact breaks, and we dash to our phones. It's Marco on the group chat.

[Marco: It's show time!]

[Stella: I'm already driving over to Mika's. Nico, how fast can you get there?]

[Nico: I'm already out the door, babe]

I quickly tap out my excitement and then Ash and I are in scramble mode. The charged moment we just had is forgotten or at least put on hold while we shove our work into bags. I get the bag of snacks I had prepared and put that in after my laptop.

We head to the porch to wait for Stella, and I lock the door behind me. Ash and I don't say anything to each other while we wait, but both of us are buzzing with energy. This is such a big day for our little nerd family, and it's hard not to be completely focused on getting to the hospital.

In classic Stella fashion, it takes only half the time it should before I see her car careen down the road. Nico arrived less than five minutes before Stella's car showed up. It's like Nico turned thirty and suddenly got responsible. He doesn't look like he just rolled out of bed or still hungover.

We call that growth.

Before I can think on that more, Stella is pulling over for more of a rolling stop than an actual stop. I watch as Nico literally dives hands and head first into the back seat after Ash gets the door open. I hop into the front, and before any of us can fully fasten our seatbelts, Stella is zooming off again.

"Stell, I love you, but it's like 10:30 a.m. on Thursday, and I've heard the cops are actually out at this time." I'm holding onto the handle for dear life. At least I got my seatbelt clicked quickly.

Stella weaves around an SUV that is clearly going the speed limit, but at least her eyes don't deviate from the road. "Fuck the police. We have a baby coming," she yells way too loudly, gunning it through a yellow light.

"Isn't your dad a cop?" Nico asks, bracing himself on the back of Stella's seat. He looks pale, and I hope he doesn't puke while we're all in the car.

The next turn is so sharp, I swear we go up on two wheels. "I said what I said," is her only response.

When we arrive at the hospital, we do the same routine as last night; Stella drops us at the door and heads to find a parking spot while the rest of us make our way upstairs. Lena and Marco's dads are still there, though by the change of clothes and clean-shaven faces, I'm guessing they went home at some point. Marco's mom sits in a chair by the window scrolling through her phone.

"Any updates?" I ask as we make it to the small group of family.

"She started pushing about twenty minutes ago. Shazi says the baby keeps popping back in after every other push," Rosa, Marco's mom says in her thick accent. The phone pings in her hand, and she reads the text quickly. "Oh, seems Lena might have dislocated one of Marco's fingers. Eh, she's a strong woman, and Marco has nine other fingers."

I love Marco's mom. Nothing fazes the woman. And she treats all of her kids the same, even those of us who are not actually her kids, but she's claimed us anyway. I've been to enough Perez family events now that my figure has definitely filled out more because of how much food Mama Rosa has forced on me.

There's no news even as Stella joins us again thirty minutes later. Seems the parking lot is never empty around here. "I nearly beat this guy's ass when he tried to take my parking spot. I swear I was two seconds from getting out of my car to punch him through his window. I don't care if he was like a hundred years old. I had been waiting for that spot for ten minutes." She paces around the waiting area, her wedges making clomping sounds as she stomps around.

"Shazi says Lena's making some progress. Baby has stopped playing peek-a-boo," Rosa informs us, her fingers flying over her screen as she probably disseminates the information over a family group chat.

I'm too nervous to sit. Who knew it would be so stressful for someone else to have a baby? Because even though Lena is in good hands, and everything has gone perfectly with her pregnancy, besides the extreme morning sickness, there's still that worry.

A warm arm slides around my shoulders. For a moment, I think it's Nico. He's as touchy feely as I am. But it's not Nico. I look up into Ash's face, and I see the same worry. "Hey, everything is okay. Lena and the baby are going to be fine. They'll be home before you know it, and we'll get to spoil them both." The squeeze against my shoulder pushes me a little closer to his chest, and it's so reassuring. Did I mention how warm he is?

Fifteen minutes later, Marco busts through the door, tears streaming down his face and the biggest smile I've ever seen on a person. "It's a girl! And she's so perfect. Lena is doing great. She's a gorgeous goddess." He collapses into his mom's arms, and then both dads are wrapping their arms around mother and son. There are so many tears from everyone.

When he disentangles from his family, the rest of us make our way to Marco and pile in for our own group hug. "You're a dad now," I say through my own happy tears.

"I'm a dad. Holy shit, I'm a dad!" Marco's tears start afresh.

"What's her name?" Stella asks.

Marco wipes his face. "Maria Avoinne Emmanuella Perez. She's so perfect. I can't wait for you to meet her."

Nico starts singing. "The most beautiful sound I've ever heard."

"No West Side Story today, Nic." Stella elbows him in the ribs, cutting off the rest of the song. One of Nico's biggest secrets is that he's a total theater nerd. He was lead in all his high school musicals.

After that, Marco slips back into L&D to rejoin Lena and baby Maria. We're informed that we can visit in about thirty minutes, once they get mom and baby all settled, and after Maria has a chance to try to nurse. They do allow Rosa and the dads, or should I say, grandpas to head back right away.

While we wait some more, Ash once again puts his arm around my shoulders. This time I don't think it's for my benefit as much as it is for his. "I can't believe she did it. I mean, I can believe it—Lena is a total boss. I just can't believe she's really here," he says with pure awe in his tone.

I slip my arm around his waist like it's the most natural thing in the world to do, though we never touch like this. "I know. It's crazy. I mean, she created a little human."

Nico comes over to where Ash and I are standing locked together and slides his arm around me, resting his hand on my hip. "I thought it was an open invitation for some cuddling. Mind if I join?" He gives my hip a squeeze. I love Nico to death, but his isn't the arm I want around me right now.

I disentangle myself from both men's arms but toss a smile toward Nico. "Totally mind." I laugh. I'm saved from saying anything more by the appearance of Rosa beckoning us back to Lena's room.

She's laying on the hospital bed looking tired as hell but extremely happy. The tiny body resting face down on her chest has light brown skin and a smattering of black curls plastered to her head. Her tiny fists rest next to her head against her mom's bare shoulders. She's also exhausted because her eyes are closed, and she's breathing deeply. Being born is tiring work.

We don't stay long, wanting to give everyone a chance to rest. I leave with promises to bring over food to stock their freezer and kisses for both Lena and Marco, though baby Maria isn't ready for a stranger's kisses.

Stella drives us home with less manic speed. She lets Nico off at work first. He's early, but it's easier than going home and then right back out. I ask Ash if he wants to come back to mine and continue work, and I admit I feel a surge of delight when he agrees. We had a good flow going earlier, and it's kind of nice to have another person around, if only for the company.

It's definitely not because I specifically want Ash's company around.

CHAPTER 14

ASH

I spent the next few days at Mika's helping her prep several meals and snacks for Lena and Marco. All things that can easily be frozen and reheated and little snack boxes full of savory and sweet snacks.

On Saturday evening, after I spent Shabbos with Mika and her family, we take the giant tote of food over to Marco and Lena's place. The hospital released Lena and the baby earlier Saturday morning, and by the time we get there, the baby is asleep in a small bassinette next to Lena on the couch, where she is also sleeping.

"Hey, I brought some food for you guys. Let me know if you need more. I'm more than happy to cook as often as you want." Mika keeps her voice a whisper so as not to disturb mom and baby. We help Marco pack it all into the freezer and cabinets, but then decide it's best not to linger. They are going to need all the rest they can get. Shazi is out picking up pizza for the family since Lena asked specifically for it. Between Shazi and Rosa, the trio should be set.

We leave after only a few minutes and stand outside Marco's place. "So now what? You want to hit up a bar or something? I have zero plans for tonight, and we're already out," Mika asks, with a hopeful look on her face. I really like being around her, and I think she likes being around me too.

I agree to head to a bar nearby. It's still early in the night, so it's not completely packed, but it'll really fill up within the hour. We order drinks at the bar before finding a table. The décor is mostly dark colors. Mika is definitely the brightest thing in the room with her pink braids and lavender dress. The music is loud, and it's hard to think with the constant bass, but I keep my attention on her. We sip on our Cuba Libre's, which is Mika's go to drink that I've sort of adopted as my own.

In the time we spend talking, the bar gets progressively more crowded. The dance floor becomes the central focus. I sit there listening to Mika talk and think about asking her to dance, but I keep chickening out. It's easier to just sit here in her aura and drink her favorite drink with her.

When I notice her glass is empty, I offer to get us another. "Sure, then I think I'm done. I'm not feeling getting trashed tonight." I lean close so she can speak into my ear, but even then, she has to raise her voice. I nod and walk back to the bar.

It takes longer than I liked to get our next round of drinks. There are so many people grouped around ordering their own drinks. When I turn back toward our table, I see a tall guy with slicked back hair and a fake tan leaning against the table talking to Mika. She's not smiling, instead giving the guy a tight-lipped look while he talks at her.

A jolt of possessiveness flares up within me, and I stomp back over to our table. I'm not a jealous person, but seeing some other guy hitting on Mika is activating some caveman part of my brain that says someone is coming after what's mine—which is ridiculous because Mika isn't mine. We're just friends, and even if we were more, I know Mika wouldn't appreciate me coming in to white knight for her.

But that doesn't stop me from glaring daggers at the guy as I make my way to the table. "Hey man, this seat's taken," asshole guy says to me as I set my drink down.

"Yeah, by me. Here, Mika," I say, sparing the guy a brief glare and then focusing my attention back on her as I hand over her drink. She takes it, a grateful smile on her lips. So my caveman brain takes over completely, and I stake out what's mine. I slide around the table and slip my arm around her waist, pulling her close to me. She immediately does the same, giving us a united front.

Asshole takes the hint and walks away without another word. Mika keeps her hand against my side. "God, that guy just would not listen. You were gone like what, five minutes, and I told him three times I was with someone. Why is it guys will only take the hint when another guy is around, but when I'm standing here saying no, it's like a challenge?"

"Men are stupid," I respond, looking down at her and smiling. It feels right to have her pressed against me, and neither of us is pulling away yet.

"Here, here," she says, clinking her glass against mine. "Present company excluded. You're the best." Her mega-watt smile sears straight into my heart, and all I want to do is kiss those perfect lips.

Maybe it's still the activated possessive brain I have going on that makes me lean close to her, my intention clear that I want to kiss her. I really don't know what makes me do it, but I go for it anyway.

Just as our lips are about to touch, she jerks back from me. My heart instantly drops into my stomach, and I'm flooded with embarrassment. I've ruined this. I've ruined a great friendship because clearly, I misread things between us. I want more, and she obviously doesn't. I can never look her in the eye again. I'll have to quit B&B and hide in a hole forever.

But before I can totally spiral, Mika grabs my chin and forces me to look at her. We are already standing close together, but she still invades my space. She stares at me for what feels like forever, then she tugs my face down until she can speak in my ear. "I don't want our first kiss to be in a fucking bar after you go all Macho Man Randy Savage. I want to kiss you somewhere we won't have to stop." She kisses my ear, and it's like all the blood flow heads straight to my dick.

I don't have any expectations when it comes to having sex with Mika. She doesn't owe me that, but kissing her? That's happening tonight. As soon as possible. But she's right—I don't want our first kiss to be in some random bar after some random guy was hitting on her.

I'm not the overly romantic type. I used to be, but Adele made sure to stamp that out. Right now, though, I'm all about the romance. Because that's what Mika deserves.

It doesn't matter that our drinks are still half full. I grab her hand and pull her out of the crowded bar and into the night. She follows willingly, a smile on her face, which is probably a match to mine.

We don't bother with the Metro; this is an occasion to spring for a rideshare. Our hands are clasped tightly together the whole ride, and it's taking all my effort to not just lean over and kiss her in the back of this random Prius. I suddenly feel like a teenager again, shy and unsure about my own body. I've been half hard since we left the bar, and I have to take deep breaths to keep myself from going full attention in my jeans.

We don't say anything the whole ride over. I have no idea what I wouldn't say. Instead, we just steal glances at each other and grin like two idiots. The ride back to Mika's seems to take twice as long, and we barely let the car stop before we're clambering out to get to Mika's door.

My head is reeling. This is happening. After thinking about it for so long, I'm finally going to kiss Mika. And more, if she'll let me.

Mika makes quick work of the front lock and pulls me inside. I don't know what's going to happen once we're inside. Lucky for me, Mika doesn't make me wait at all. As the door slams shut behind me, she crowds my space, pushing me up against the door. Her hands splay across my chest, and my heart thunders under palms.

"Is this okay?" she whispers, and I can feel her warm breath against my mouth.

Fuck, it's more than okay. My brain short-circuits, and I can't even imagine what the use of words are anymore. I'm able to croak out a small "Yeah," which is all the invitation Mika needs. She tangles her fingers in my shirt and pulls me down to kiss her. When our lips finally touch for the first time, it's like fireworks explode in my head. I close my eyes as her mouth moves against mine. The kiss is gentle with just a hint of urgency. She wants more already, but she's testing me out first.

My hands find her hips after hanging limply at my side for longer than I intended. Mika is the one in control though. My back is flat against the door, and she keeps me pinned there with her mouth and a firm push against my chest. There's no space between our bodies. We're chest to chest, and there's no way she can miss how excited my body is from her touch.

She licks at my lips, I open for her, and our tongues tangle together. She tastes sweet, like spice rum and sugar. It's intoxicating. Her lips are pillow soft, her kisses turning more demanding by the second. This is better than I imagined. And I've imagined it a lot.

Mika is a take charge kind of woman. Her hands slide from my chest, down my sides and around my back. She gently pulls me forward so my body isn't so pressed against the door, then she slips her hands down to grab my ass. This woman is going to have me cumming in my pants in seconds if she keeps this up.

I would say I'm a submissive guy. The women I've been with before Adele let me take charge of our sexual encounters. Even Adele did at the start of our relationship. But as we got more serious and she turned more abusive, sex was for her pleasure only. She would stroke me until I was hard, use my body for her needs, and then accuse me of not enjoying it enough.

With Mika leading, pulling and pushing me the way she wants, it doesn't feel like I'm being used. It feels like she's trying to make sure I'm enjoying it as much as she is. And I'm really, really enjoying it.

"You can touch me, Ash," she says in a husky voice between kisses. I don't wait to be told twice. One hand moves up between us, and I palm one of her generous breasts. The weight of it in my hand is perfect. My thumb brushes over her covered nipple, and I feel her whole body shudder beneath my hand. She moans into my mouth, and I didn't think it was possible to get harder than I already was, but here we are. My dick is rock hard, and I'm dying to cum.

Her lips move from my mouth, and she trails kisses down the side of my jaw and down the side of my neck, sucking lightly at my pulse point. "Mika, I'm dying here. Please." I'm pleading and I don't even care. I'm unravelling against her.

I can feel the smile against my skin. "Please, what, Ash?" She really is going to make me beg. I'll gladly do it. She sucks on my neck again, and I moan so loudly it echoes around the room.

"Please let me fuck you," I say, barely able to get the words out around the nonsensical noises I'm making. This is what I need, someone to take care of me, someone who will make me assert my desires and help me find my pleasure in sex again. I don't want this to feel like I'm using Mika to get over my issues with sex. Because that's not what this is. I feel safe with her. I know she's not going to use me or hurt me. She's my friend first and foremost, and my trust in her is absolute.

"Bedroom. Now." Mika uses a commanding tone. Her eyes are dark with lust, and I can't get up the stairs fast enough. She's right behind me. I don't actually know which door is her room, but she's there, grabbing my hand and leading me to the door on the left.

Her room is neat, and there's so much color. The walls are covered in art of all styles, some that are clearly fantasy and probably B&B related. I see several artistically styled Star Wars prints, including a series of the various characters from all the movies in pin-up style positions.

The bed is huge, especially since she's the only one who sleeps in it. It's covered in pillows and piled with blankets in shades of dark green. All of the furniture in her room looks to be well crafted antiques, and it's all so Mika.

This is her temple, and I plan to worship her in it as long as possible.

Mika squeezes my hand and my attention snaps to her. "Ash, I want you to be comfortable. Are you okay with this?" Her eyes hold a touch of concern. She's so fucking amazing, thinking about my comfort level before she does anything. If I'm not careful, I'm going to fall hard for this woman. Not that I think I would actually mind that.

"I want this. And I trust you, Mika. Tell me what you want me to do, and I'll do it." This my moment of truth, and I can't imagine sharing it with anyone else.

She nods. "Okay, but if it gets to be too much, you'll tell me. We'll use the stoplight. Green for go, yellow for slow down, and red for stop. I want us both to want this." For a flash second, I feel like I don't deserve her. She's so kind and considerate. But I know that's just Adele talking, and I push those fears aside and nod to her.

Her smile is wide and bright. "Good. Now, undress me." The commanding voice is back, and I have a desire to call her mistress. I don't know if she'd be into that though, so I keep my mouth shut. She turns in place and presents her back to me. I grab the zipper and begin to slowly unzip her from the lavender dress. With that done, she spins back to me and places my hands on the small straps holding the dress up. I slide my fingers under the straps and push them down, forcing myself to slow down so I don't just rip the clothes from her body. I really want to, but this time we're going to take it slow.

I push the dress down and over her breasts and holy shit, I'm presented with the most gorgeous sight. Her strapless bra is pale pink lace and so delicate. I can see her rosy nipples through the fabric, and I can't stop the groan that escapes me.

With a little shimmy, I get her dress over her full hips, and it puddles on the floor. Her underwear doesn't match; instead, they are a simple pair of gray cotton panties, and somehow that makes it even sexier. My hand finds their way back to her breasts, and I knead them through the thin fabric. I feel as her nipples quickly turn into tight peaks, and I rub my thumbs over them. Her eyes close and she moans softly, letting her head loll back.

After a moment of fondling, Mika's eyes snap open. Her hands are at the bottom of my shirt, and in one fluid motion, she lifts it up and over my head. Whereas I undressed her slowly, Mika is not so patient, and my jeans are already unbuttoned seconds after my shirt hits the floor. My cock bobs straight up as she pulls my jeans off, rock solid and leaking already.

She peels my pants and boxer briefs down my legs, kneeling as she follows them to the ground until finally my pants are off, and she's eye level with my dick. She tilts her head to look up at me, and there's mischief in her eyes. But she's also asking permission with her stare. My last brain cell escapes, and all I can do is nod.

Mika leans forward, takes just the tip into her mouth, and I have to force myself not to lose it right this second. She doesn't break eye contact as she takes more of me into her mouth. I'm not huge, but I'm also not small either. I feel it when I hit the back of her throat, but she doesn't gag. My eyes roll back, and my hand reaches out of its own accord to fist in her silky pink hair, tangling my fingers in it.

She pulls her mouth off me with a pop, and she stands. With a gentle push, she backs me up until the back of my knees hit the edge of the bed. I fall back and move until I'm lying in the center of her plush bed.

"Tell me your color," she demands before she makes any move to get on the bed.

It's fucking green all around. "Green," I manage to say, though words are hard. She smiles, and then pulls up a drawer on her bedside table. She pulls out a condom, makes quick work of the wrapper, and climbs onto the bed.

One leg is thrown over my hips, and she straddles me. My dick is nestled just in front of her center, and with such tender care, she rolls the condom onto me. In an instant, she's lifting her hips and with agonizing slowness, she lowers herself onto me. We both moan as we connect, and I feel her tighten around me.

"Fuck, I'm close to cumming already," she says, her voice cracking. Mika plants one hand on my chest. The other hand grabs mine and pulls it toward where we're joined. Guiding my hand, she shows me how she likes to be touched. Only then does she start to move, setting the rhythm slow and languorous. It's excruciating and amazing.

Mika is in full control, riding me at her own pace, and I have to stop myself from bucking up into her. She removes her hand from mine, and I keep up my movements against her, drawing out breathy moans from her beautiful lips. She slumps over me, her hair falling like a curtain around her face as she picks up speed riding me.

It's too much and not enough all at once, and I double my efforts on that bundle of nerves between us.

"Ash, I'm going to cum soon," she breathes, and I'm right there with her. As much as I want her to go first, I can't help myself when she slams down on me, clenching tight against my shaft. I explode, and I swear to fucking God, my vision whites out, and I see stars. The noise that comes out of me is somewhere between a roar and a sob; it's inhuman, but the release is so good. Mika has unmade me and built me back up again with just one orgasm.

My empty brain still remembers it's supposed to be taking care of Mika as well, and my hand doesn't stop the work between her legs. Her scream as she climaxes is my favorite sound, and the way her lips contort into a wide O is the sweetest sight in the world. Her hips slow and then stop, and she rests atop me, barely keeping herself balanced with both hands on my chest. My hands move to her waist, and she slowly lifts herself off me and rolls to the side.

I quickly take care of the condom with Mika's direction to the bathroom to dispose of it, and then I'm back in her room. But I don't get on the bed. I stand next to it, completely naked, unsure of what to do. Adele never liked to hold each other afterward and wouldn't let me touch her after she finished. Mika doesn't seem like that, but I don't know.

Mika lifts herself up on her elbows and crooks her finger at me. "Get the fuck back on this bed and cuddle me." And I fall in line so easily at her command. I lie down, and in half a second, she's pulling me close, pressing my head against her chest as she wraps her arms around me and throwing a leg over my mine.

I put my arms around her waist, and we just hold each other, her breathing against the top of my head and my lips pressed against her sternum. This is more intimate than the sex we just had. Hell, this is the most intimate moment of my life. Our breathing starts to even out as the sheen of sweat on our bodies starts to cool and dry. I should feel uncomfortable, but I don't. I'm more relaxed and happier than I've been in so long. I could die right now and be totally okay with that.

"How are you feeling? Are you okay?" I have to ask myself how someone can be so caring after sex. I know Adele did a number on me, but was this what I was missing the whole time I was with her? *Are partners supposed to be like this?*

"I feel amazing," I say, completely honest, and yet the word doesn't seem like enough to describe how I feel.

She laughs against my hair. "Yeah, I know the feeling." She shifts away from me just a little and moves my chin up so I can see her face. "Thank you for trusting me. Not a lot of guys are cool with letting the woman lead. You were amazing." And then she smiles and fuck, she could tell me to do anything and I would without question.

I preen under her praise. I want to hear more of it from her. It's a new high for me to chase. "You can lead anytime you want, Mika," I say, and I roll my hips against her. I'm half hard already just being wrapped around her.

She laughs. "Insatiable, aren't you?" She lightly slaps my thigh. "First though, I need to feed you." We reluctantly disentangle ourselves, and she heaves herself from the bed. I think she'll reach for her clothes, but she surprises me by walking out of her room completely naked. I debate whether or not to put on my own clothes, or at least my boxers, but I decide to follow Mika's lead, and I leave the room just as naked as she is.

And that's how I find myself in Mika's kitchen, having a makeshift dinner and leaning against each other wearing absolutely nothing. It's erotic and intimate all at the same time. Mika is not shy about her body, and that's one of things I love about her. While we eat, she casually touches me. It's nothing sexual. It's clear she just wants to be close to me, and I soak up every touch, every caress of her fingers against my skin. I'm already addicted to the feeling.

"Guess we should talk about what this means now," Mika says, her face turning more serious, though she keeps herself plastered to my side.

I don't know whether I should be nervous or excited, so I'm both. Does she think this was just a onetime thing and that we got it out of our system? Because there's no way I've gotten her out of my system. I need repeats of our time together.

"I guess so." And I try not to sound dejected. But Mika is attuned to me, and she picks up on it.

She nudges me in the ribs. "Hey, don't do that. Listen, I'm going to be straight with you. I haven't been in a relationship since my ex cheated on me five years ago. It was awful. She really fucked me up. Quinn was the one who brought me into B&B and the group. They picked me over her, and I'm just worried that something could happen, and it would force the gang into that position again." She looks down at her bare feet and frowns. I never want to see her frown. I know she's worried things will go sideways, and it'll impact the game. It means a lot to her, and I would never jeopardize her place.

Mika sharing her fears spurs me to share with her. If we're going to be something more than just friends, I want her to know what she's getting into with me. I grab her hand and thread our fingers together. "I don't want that to ever happen to you again. I don't want to think about us not working, but just know, I would stop playing if it came to that. You love B&B, and I'm new to it, so I would never take that away from you." She smiles at me, and I know this is the right thing to do.

So I stand there, naked in her kitchen, and bare my soul. "Mika, I like you. I want more than just to be friends with you. You already know how bad things were back in New York." I take a deep breath because after this, after she knows the truth, she's either going to accept me or reject me, and I don't know which it's going to be.

"It wasn't just bad; I've told you it was abusive. Not physically. Adele could have easily kicked my ass, but she didn't operate like that. She spent four years torturing me mentally, breaking me down until I was a shell of myself. I didn't see my family because she didn't like them. I barely left my house because she said I would cheat. She dictated my life, and I let her." All this Mika already knew or suspected. But there's more I need to tell her, and it feels the like the worst part to say aloud.

"When it came to sex, I was just a body for her to use. She didn't care if I was in the mood or even willing. I couldn't say no to her. She wouldn't let me. After she took what she wanted, she would make me feel like I wasn't giving enough. Like how dare I not enjoy it. She made me feel disgusting if I somehow got off. That's why I moved to DC, to put as much space as I could from her. I didn't want her to find me again." I think I'm shaking, but I try to take deep breaths and just get through it. Because

I know what Adele did to me has a name. I'm just not ready to think about it like that. I don't know if I ever will.

Mika squeezes my hand, and when I look at her, there are tears in her eyes. "Oh Ash, I'm so sorry. If I ever meet that bitch, I'm going to kick her fucking ass. I can't believe anyone would treat someone as wonderful as you like that." She lets go of my hand, stands, and just engulfs me into her arms. And fuck, if this isn't what I needed most, someone to just hold me without judgment.

"I'll understand if you're not ready for anything yet. I'm still your friend, Ash, first and foremost. I don't want to push you into something more if you're not ready," she says, but she doesn't let go of me.

God, I'm about ready to drop to my knees and beg this woman to marry me. How is she so perfect? I squeeze her close to me—no way I can let go of her. "I do want this. I've talked it over with my therapist, and I'm ready. Because I really like you Mika, and I want to see where this goes."

She pulls back enough so she can kiss me, and it's so sweet and so gentle that I melt against her. When she breaks the kiss, we rest our foreheads together. "I want that too," she says. I'm smiling because finally something is going right in my life. I kiss her again, and we stand there in her kitchen, completely naked and wrapped around each other, and I can feel myself falling hard for Mika Levenberg.

CHAPTER 15

MIKA

I f I thought things were going to monumentally change once I was officially with Ash, I would have been seriously wrong. It isn't like I was suddenly healed from my trust issues with relationships because in reality, spending all that time with Ash as friends had already been slowly helping me. I just didn't realize it until now.

We still go on our Sunday afternoon outings, only now we hold hands while we walk around. And maybe find a hidden corner to make out a little. That is my favorite part of the day.

On Monday after Ash and I become official, we meet up with Stella and Nico at a place on U Street. Before we meet with them, Ash and I discuss how we're going to break it to the group. Because there's no hiding this from them, not that either of us want to. We'll just be upfront that we're dating now and share our contingency if anything happens just to put their minds at ease.

I arrive first, which isn't out of the ordinary. Ash texted to say he had a meeting running over and would be there as soon as it was over. Stella arrives a few minutes after me, and Nico is not too far behind, but still early by Nico time. I'm really surprised how on top of his shit he's been lately.

We order drinks and chat. It's weird not having Marco or Lena here. Marco especially is the heart of our little group, and without him, it just feels kind of empty. But he's a dad now, and has to do dad things. I'm listening to Stella talk about some of the dumb stuff the kids were saying in class today when Ash finally arrives. It's like I'm honed in to his presence because my eyes are glued to his as he makes his way through the crowd to our table.

"Hey," I say to him with a huge grin on my face as he takes the seat across from me, the only open spot.

"Hey," he responds with his own shy smile.

From the corner of my eye, I see Stella staring at me. "I need to pee. Mika come with," Stella says, though she's not asking me. She's telling me. I shoot Ash a look, and then I follow her to the ladies' room.

Once the door shuts behind us, Stella whirls on me. "Oh my god, you're fucking him, aren't you?" I honestly can't tell what she's feeling because her eyes are wide, but her tone is accusing.

I fidget beneath her glare, which is impressive considering she's like half a foot shorter than me. "I... yes?" I say it likes it's a question, though I've never been surer about a relationship in my life.

"Mika!" she screeches. I'm going to get my ass kicked in a bar bathroom, that's what's going to happen. Have it handed to me by a five-foot nothing Filipino powerhouse. Maybe I deserve this, just a bit. I am upsetting the group balance again.

"It's not just fucking. We're, you know, a thing. But," I hold up a finger to stop her from responding right away, "we have agreed that if things don't work out, there's no hard feelings, and Ash said he would stop playing B&B. Neither of us want another Quinn situation."

Stella's face then does something I wasn't expecting; it breaks out into a huge grin. "God, finally! Do you know how weird game night has been? Like for months! Your sexual tension was getting so palpable that even Nico was picking up on it. And you know Nico is terminally dense."

I'm seriously confused now. "You're okay with us then?" If anything, I expected Stella to lay into me about this. She was with me through the whole breakup with Quinn. It was Stella who came immediately to my house after I kicked Quinn out. She saw all my ugly crying, and she hid my phone so many times so I wouldn't drunkenly text Quinn. She was the one who picked me back up after I fell apart.

"Girl, you haven't dated anyone since the She Bitch. Ash is a good guy, and he's been through some shit too. I'm not saying you two won't have baggage to work through, but you actually did this the right way. Having a solid friendship foundation is the best way to start a relationship. Elise was my best friend since we were in middle school. She was the first person I came out to. She's the love of my life, but more than that, she's my best friend. And even if we decided tomorrow our relationship had run its course, she will always be my best friend. So yeah, I'm totally cool with it." Here we are, in a public bathroom, and I burst into tears at my friend's speech.

I would say I don't deserve her friendship, but that's a lie. I totally deserve to have someone who is so firmly in my corner that she will back up my happiness in a second. I know with certainty how Nico and Marco will take the news, but I was unsure about Stella. She's fiercely protective of her own, and while Ash is definitely making his way into her inner circle, he's still the new guy.

Stella reaches up and wipes the tears from my cheeks. "Good thing you wore the waterproof mascara today!" She laughs, and I make a snorting laugh noise, which is probably the most undignified noise I've ever made in my life.

"Come on. Let's get back to the boys and get our drink on while you break the news gently to Nico." Stella hooks her arm with mine, and we walk out of the bathroom.

"He's still totally going to offer to be our third, you know that," I say, letting Stella lead us toward the table.

"Without a doubt." She laughs.

"You two look happy. Were you making out in there? Because if you were, you could have asked me to watch," Nico says, waggling his eyebrows at us.

"You're such a pig, Nico," Stella responds, though there's no heat in it. We all know Nico is joking. He doesn't actually mean a word of it. From the times I've been around his girlfriends and even some hookups, Nico is actually a perfect gentleman and very respectful. It was Nico who was the most furious when I told the group Quinn was cheating on me. He may be varied in his sexual partners, but one thing Nico isn't, is a cheater.

"Nah, the only person I'll be making out with is Ash from now on," I say, taking the seat Stella had vacated so I can sit next to Ash. He takes my hand, and we twine our hands together on the table. It's more for show; we're not going to be that couple. At least not so blatantly. But right now it serves a purpose.

Nico looks to our hands, then to our faces. It takes a minute, and then the lightbulb goes off. "Why is it never Nico?" he says with a whine, throwing up his hands like he is long suffering.

"Don't worry, Nic. You're still my contingency." I reach over and pat his hand once he brings his arms back down to the table. He places a hand over mine and winks.

"I better be." And just like that, it's back to business as usual. Well, not totally—our merry band is still missing its leader. Maybe when Lena's up to it, we can all go together to see baby Maria.

We're trying not to overwhelm them with visitors since their family will be doing that enough. It helps that Marco has sent pictures on the group chat of every move Maria makes. And more than a few spit up and poopy diapers. That's babies, I guess. Everything they do is a goddamn miracle.

My brain starts to wander as we talk. I think about if Ash and I will make it far enough in this relationship to talk babies. I've never been in a relationship serious enough to plan for a future. Even with Quinn, we were just having fun. Even though it gutted me when we broke up, I never saw anything long term with her. And before her, my college boyfriend Evan was nice and all, but when he started talking about getting married once we graduated, I dumped him.

I'm not saying I'm ready to plan my future with Ash with a chuppah and then a crib. What I am thinking is that I can see longevity with Ash. I can see us talking about those things in the future. Not now. This is literally brand new. But someday.

At the end of the night, part of me wants to invite Ash back to my place. It's nice having him there, and I'm already getting used to the idea of him being there all the time. But I stop myself, and we kiss goodnight at the Metro station. We'll see each other on Wednesday, anyway.

Once I'm home, I head up to my room and prepare for bed. Once I've done that, and I'm lying in my bed staring up at my ceiling, I can finally reflect on my thoughts. Not just the ones at the bar, but also why I wanted Ash to come home with me.

I'm sure it's just new relationship excitement, but it feels a little like I'm rushing myself. Sure, it's been five years since I've seriously dated anyone, and maybe I'm just starved for the intimacy that comes with a relationship. Still, I spent a part of the evening with him thinking about a future when our present has only just begun. Maybe it's different because Ash is my friend, a really good friend, maybe even in the running for best friend. I've never had a relationship where we were friends first.

I could easily look at the relationships around me. Stella and Elise had years of friendship before it ever became something more, and now Stella is ring shopping so she can propose. Marco and Lena only knew each other six months before he proposed when Lena was still in law school. They got married six months later.

My parents' love story is my favorite though. They met while their families were vacationing in Rehoboth Beach in Delaware. Mom's grandparents had retired there, which is really a strange place to retire to, if you ask me. Bubbe had friends who owned a beach house and let them stay for a week every summer. They were kids when they met, and every year, they met up again for one week at the beach. They first kissed the summer mom was going into her senior year of high school. Dad was only a junior. Then mom got into George Washington

University, and they dated all four years she was there. But when mom got into Yale for law school, they broke up and thought that was the end.

Until they ended up working for the same senator. And then that was it. They realized the universe kept pushing them together, so they might as well listen. Then they had David and me, and the rest is history.

I want a love like they have. I always have, even with the last five years being a total bust on the relationship front. My parents have been married for forty years and are still so stupidly in love. They have their problems, every couple does, but they always work them out together. If there's one thing my parents taught me about what it means to be in a partnership, it's that communication is the most important part of making it work. And that's why my trust in relationships fell apart after Quinn. Because she didn't communicate with me. She wasn't open and honest with me like I was with her.

I shared my insecurities with Ash, my whole past with Quinn and how much that hurt me. And in return, he bared his soul to me. It's not easy for anyone to admit they were abused, but the world is not kind to men who are victims of abuse. He trusted me with his truth, and I hope I responded the right way. I want Ash to trust me, to be open and honest with me. And if we fight, which I'm sure we will once we're past this honeymoon phase, I want him to challenge me, communicate with me, and want to make it work with me.

I have to do what I've done with him in the course of our friendship: take things slow and make sure he's comfortable with everything before pushing for more. Obviously, sex is absolutely on the table. And holy hell were we good at it. I already plan to ask him to stay after the game on Wednesday. Dates are happening, mainly because they were already happening even though we didn't label them that way. So, I guess we go from there. I want to discuss this all with him as we go along because I want to be upfront with him.

I'm all in if he is.

Have I mentioned how weird it's been already without Marco around? Well, it's like ten times weirder on Wednesday night for B&B. While he gone, we arranged for each of us to GM sessions while we put the main campaign on hold.

Everyone made an extra character, or in Stella's case, picked one of the myriad she had already created and shoved into her binder. We'll just play one-shot mods until Marco comes back.

Stella is GMing this week, and by the wicked smile on her face, I know it's going to be challenging, and she's going to be merciless. She's a puzzle heavy GM, and she delights in stumping us.

Tonight's meal is grilled cheese with the fancy cheeses I picked up at Whole Foods and tomato soup, which I did make from scratch. I was feeling nostalgic and wanted some comfort food. "Are those homemade Dunkaroos?!" Nico yells, running across my kitchen to where I have set up a tray of fun shaped cookies surrounding a bowl of cream cheese dip with sprinkles. Like I said, I was feeling nostalgic. I did add fruit around the tray too, you know, for the grown-up touch.

"This is the greatest day of my life!" Nico declares, and I swear there are tears in his eyes. I have to watch him, otherwise I'll end up losing that tray, just like I've lost the cake stand. I had hoped he would return it tonight because I know that cake is long gone, but no such luck.

When Ash arrives, I feel my heart flutter. It feels like thousands of butterflies have burst in my chest and can't find a way out, so they just fly around tickling my insides. I've never been giddy with a partner before, but I guess there's a first time for everything.

I'm still not sure how we're supposed to greet each other in this setting. Do we just do the *hey*? Or like a quick kiss or something? Because, honestly, the only way I want to greet him is by throwing myself at him and making out with him against the kitchen counter. Inappropriate? Maybe. But it sounds like a delicious idea to me. But I suppose I'll have to wait for that until after Stella and Nico leave.

Instead, I opt for somewhere in the middle. I cross the room, hug him, and plant a quick kiss on his cheek. When I move to step away, he rests his hands on my hips and keeps me close. "I missed you," he whispers, and his cheeks turn pink. I feel flushed because I totally missed him too.

"For fuck's sake, it's been two days. You two are gross," Stella says, pushing past us to get into the kitchen. Ash and I laugh as we pull apart, and I swear I feel a tingle in my hips where his fingers rested.

"Eat up, bitches. We're about to have a fun night," Stella announces while loading up a plate and bowl. Dinner goes down quickly, and I notice the tray of Dunkaroos has somehow taken up permanent residence right next to Nico's arm. It's already half gone. The guy is in for one hell of a sugar high.

Stella sets up her area. It's not nearly as impressive as Marco's. He has this custom black walnut screen. He keeps his notes tapped up for easy access, and he has a tablet set up for monster stats and ambient music.

Stella, on the other hand, has a cardboard screen with official art from B&B. She has exactly one notebook and only one set of dice out. This does not bode well. "Alright, adventurers, let's get this going. Now, like all good quests, you start off in a tavern. You've each responded to a job posting in the city center. The posting said there is a large reward for completing the job." She steeples her fingers and looks us all over in turn.

"Each of you receives a slip of paper when you arrive. It tells you the table to sit at and that a drink will be delivered to you. After some time, the three of you are all seated at the assigned table, ale in hand. An old gnome approaches your table. And like, this guy is ancient. He has maybe four teeth total, is more wrinkles than flat skin, and is adorned with layers of clothing and jewelry, all of the cheap variety. He introduces himself as Hobnick, and he wants you to head to an old temple ruin outside of town to retrieve an item of great importance."

"What is the item we're to seek?" Nico asks with his flowery bard voice because of course even his backup character is a bard.

"Hobnick tells you that you will know it when you see it, for it radiates magic and is solid gold. That's all the information he will give you. What do you guys want to do? Head to the temple now or fuck around in town?" Stella asks, waiting for our response.

We opt to get straight to it and head to the temple. Nico's bard insists on playing us music while my cleric and Ash's fighter follow along behind. At the table, Nico just plays "Toxic" by Britney Spears.

"You enter the ruins of the temple. Ahead there is a large door, probably about seven feet tall. The door is solid wood, and as you draw closer, it appears to open down the middle. The whole surface of the door is covered in hobnails, and four wooden rectangles align down the center of the door, just to the right of the seam. There are no visible doorhandles." Stella smirks behind her GM screen.

I look at her incredulously. "It's going to take us half the session to get this fucking door open, isn't it?"

She bats her lashes at me. "No, it won't."

And she's right, it doesn't take half the session to get the door open.

It takes the whole session.

Hours of trying to find where the keys are hidden, how to reveal the keyholes, which direction to turn them, which hobnail needs to be removed and which size lock pick to trigger the mechanisms to move the key further. Not to mention trying to figure out in which order we're supposed to turn the keys. Four hours to open one door! Well, three and a half, but close enough.

"Alright, the door is open. You can head in," Stella says, but a satisfied smile is on her face, so nothing good is on the other side of the door. "Ash, you're closest to the door. Make an investigation check."

Ash looks at Stella glumly. The poor guy got so fed up with the door that he spent half an hour trying to convince Nico to fireball the thing. Nico eventually burned the spell slot, but nothing happened to the evil door. "Do I have to?" Stella's smile just grows wider, and Ash groans as he rolls.

"Okay, +3, that's twenty-one," he says hopefully. He's been rolling garbage all night, so I can tell he's excited to finally get something out of this game.

"Perfect. You head into the temple. There's ample light shining through the door for you to see, and you find..." She pauses for dramatic effect. "Nothing. The temple is completely empty."

The three of us sit in stunned silence, and we just stare at Stella. And oh my fucking god, the bitch is smirking at us.

"What the fuck?" Ash says. Then his voice gets louder. "What the fuck?!"

"Stell, baby, you are evil." Nico laughs, pouring the huge pile of dice in his dice jail back into his bag.

"You return back to town empty-handed and make your way to the tavern from which you started. You find the old gnome sitting at the bar. When he sees you, he starts cackling. 'You figured out my door,' he says. From his stool, he tosses you each a bag with a hundred gold inside each, and then he continues to laugh until he falls off his barstool. As he hits the ground, the gnome disappears in a puff of smoke. And that's the end." Stella looks smug as she folds her GM screen down, threads her fingers together, and rests her chin on them.

"Okay, seriously, what the fuck?" Ash says again. It's his first Stella game. I should have warned him ahead of time. I don't think he's even registered his standing up and looming over the table. It doesn't faze Stella one bit as she languishes in her amusement.

"I probably should have told you that Stella is pure evil and her GM style is psychological torture," I say, resting my hand on his forearm. He looks down to where I'm touching him, and that at least seems to calm him down. He takes his seat again but doesn't make a move to pack up his stuff. Instead, he sits in stunned silence.

"Don't worry, Ashy. You'll get used to Stella playing mind games while she GMs. We got off easy with this one. The last time Stella ran a game, we encountered the Red Queen. You know, like from *Alice in Wonderland*? But like the book one, not the Disney movie. We got stuck running in a loop to stay in place, and we all got like three levels of exhaustion. I think Marco's character actually died because we couldn't break the loop." Nico claps Ash on the shoulder as he passes by.

Nico says his goodbyes quickly and is out the door. "Does anybody else think Nico is acting strange?" I ask, my question directed more at Stella.

She shrugs. "Yeah, definitely. Something is going on, but I figured he would tell us when he's ready." Stella packs up her things and gives me a hug. "Don't forget the extra box of condoms under your bathroom sink," she whispers to me, her eyes darting to Ash for a second. How she knows about those, I don't even want to know. I practically shove her out the door after that comment.

And now, Ash and I are finally alone. "You're staying, right?" I ask, hopeful.

Ash sets his bag on his chair. "Only if you want me to. I don't want you to feel like I'm taking up all your time and space." He's seen me naked, yet his cheeks still brighten with color.

"Ash, honey, you can take up all my time and space." That's all the waiting I can do. I'm on him in a second, wrapping my arms around his neck to pull him close while I press my lips firmly against his. Ash doesn't hesitate to bring his arms around me, resting on my lower back, pulling me tight against his body.

Ash deepens the kiss with a swipe of his tongue against my lips with an eagerness that is totally intoxicating. It really turns me on that he's leading things. I've aways been assertive in bed, but it's nice to let someone else take the lead occasionally, and Ash is rising to the challenge.

Before I can gasp for breath, he pulling my shirt over my head, and my jeans are already unbuttoned. We are wasting no time tonight. Whereas our first time together was languid and gentle, there's nothing gentle about the way we are tearing off each other's clothes. We come together for greedy, feral kisses, and break apart again to remove more layers until there's not a scrap of cloth between us.

I bite his bottom lip, and he groans into my mouth. His hands slide down to my backside, and he lifts me up into his arms. I wrap my legs around his middle, never breaking our kiss as he walks us toward my couch. Ash doesn't know the layout well enough with his eyes closed, and he is distracted by kissing because he nearly drops me when he runs into the side of one of the chairs. He lets out a loud *oomph* as he rights himself and me, and I use his shoulder to steady myself.

We laugh between kisses as he finally finds the couch, and with me still wrapped around him, he sits down heavily. I scramble to straddle his lap properly on the couch, resting my knees on the soft cushions on either side of his hips. His hardness presses against my stomach between us, and I have to make the decision if I want to stop kissing to ride him, or keep kissing and touching him until neither of us can stand it anymore.

Ash makes the decision for me when he keeps our kiss going while one of his hands slides between us to cup me between my thighs, and I lose my head. Ash has magic fingers. They know exactly where to touch. They give just the right amount of pressure. And Ash listens to my body for what I like best.

How could someone waste natural sexual talent like Ash? I don't want to think about his ex because as far as I'm concerned, she's a raging bitch who deserves every bad thing to happen to her. She could have had this, but instead she chose to make Ash feel worthless and undesirable.

Her loss, my gain, and I'm never giving this up. The orgasm he coaxes out of me comes faster than I expected. I'm not prepared, and it slams into me like a huge wave. I'm carried below the surface, writhing in the undertow. He's not even inside me yet, and I'm already breathing heavy from just his hands.

"Mika," Ash says in a ragged voice, and God, my name coming from him in that tone, it's the best sound in the world.

"Tell me what you want. I'll do anything." My own voice is breathy and way huskier than it usually is. This man is driving me absolutely wild with lust.

"I... I want you to ride me," he says, and he keeps his eyes on mine. This is good. Better than good. He's telling me what he wants, he's leading this, and I hope in some way, it's healing for him.

I lean over him toward the side table next to the couch and pull out a condom from the small drawer. Okay, so I *may* have stashed condoms in various spots around the house for such incidents like this one. It's called planning ahead, and I'm very grateful for past Mika for thinking of it.

"You were prepared for this? Or do you always keep condoms lying around?" Ash asks as I slide the condom on him.

I kiss him with a smile on my lips. "I am prepared to take my guy in every room of this house. So, I stashed a box just about everywhere this morning. We'll have to try each room for you to figure out where they all are."

He bites his bottom lip and turns out that is my kryptonite. As I lean forward to kiss him again, I lift my hips up enough to line up my center with his rigid member. It's an easy glide in since he gave me the orgasm to end all orgasms already, and I slowly slide down onto him until he's fully nestled within me, my legs resting firmly against his hips.

Still keeping us locked in the kiss, I place my hands on his shoulders and leverage myself up, pulling myself off him just a little before slamming back down. He moans into my mouth. Maybe that's my favorite sound. Actually, all of Ash's sounds are my favorite.

Ash's hands rest on my hips, and he sets the pace, lifting me up and back down to ride him. We start off slow, so agonizingly slow. I want more, but I don't push for it. This is Ash's show, and I'll follow him.

He doesn't make me wait long before the pace picks up, up and down, faster and more frantic, his hips bucking up beneath me as he slams me down, impaling me on his dick. Words are too hard now, and all I can do is moan loudly, cycling between kissing him deeply and throwing my head back as another orgasm builds.

He doesn't say anything, but he is loud, moaning and groaning and letting me know how much he enjoys this.

I like that. Some people talk too much in bed, but this feels more primal, more raw.

I move my hands from his shoulders and just wrap my arms around his neck, pushing myself up against him until there is no room left between us. And it still doesn't feel close enough. I want to crawl inside him, feel him inside and out, and let this moment consume me completely.

His thrusts up become more frantic and erratic; he's close. Sweat coats our skin, and I feel like I'm burning up from the inside. Ash's movements stutter, and then he's gripping me so tight to him as he moans loudly through his orgasm. I pull back to look at his face as he loses himself to the feeling, and I see pure bliss on his features.

When he stops shuddering, I rest my forehead against his, placing a soft kiss on his lips. He's breathing heavily, and I pull back just enough so he can take deep breaths. "Where are you going? I'm not done with you yet, baby." Ash's voice is like nothing I've ever heard from him. It's rough and gravelly, and he sounds utterly spent. But he doesn't let me think for even a moment. He's still locked inside me, though he's growing softer, but then he brings his fingers down to touch me again, and he finds me wet and wanting, and I'm aflame all over again.

He's merciless with his movements now. This isn't the gentle caress from earlier. No, he's going to make me cum, and it's going to be right now. It takes less than a minute for his clever fingers to bring me over the edge again, and this time I scream his name as I clench around that part of him still in me. I cum so hard I'm light headed, and all I can do is slump against him.

I close my eyes and listen to the beat of his heart against my ear. It's soothing even though it's beating like crazy. Ash places a kiss against my hair and then he just holds me while we calm down and the sweat cools on our skin.

He gets up to dispose of the condom, but he returns quickly and pulls me back on to his lap so we stay wrapped around each other. It's a tender moment, sweet, and everything I've ever wanted from a partner.

"Mika, that was amazing. Thank you," Ash says, his voice barely above a whisper.

"I've never had anyone thank me after sex, but I'll take it." I try to laugh it off, but I know why he's thanking me, and I don't want us to think about that right now. We're here in this moment together, in a new relationship that has the chance of being something really wonderful. I don't want to undermine Ash's growth, but right now, I want us to just have this moment, and we can talk about everything else later.

He laughs with me and tilts my chin up so he can kiss me again. The kiss quickly heats up again, and before I know it, we're ready for round two.

Then three.

We finally make it up to the bedroom for round four. Eventually sleep takes us, and I drift off surrounded by Ash, his arms, his scent, his breaths against my neck. I want every night to be like this. I've never wanted something so bad in my life.

CHAPTER 16

ASH

Being with Mika is... I don't even know how to describe it. The best I can come up with is freeing. Mika doesn't expect me to play by her restricting rules that change without my knowledge. She's so aware of my limits and comfort that she never pushes for more than what I can give.

I was worried that my hangups with sex would be a deterrent to her. But she takes it slow with me, letting me lead when I need to have some control over what we do. Other times, she leads, and I let her do whatever she wants. I thought I would hate the feeling of giving up control since for years I didn't have any with Adele. With Mika though, it's different. When she takes the lead, it's not about her pleasure, it's about mine. I'm her sole focus, and I can't remember ever feeling this wanted, this, I don't know ... desired.

Still, I don't want to rush things with her. We have a solid base as friends, but I'm still barely just over half a year out of my relationship with Adele. Part of me, a big part, wants to spend all my time with Mika, more than usual. I wouldn't even have to push to spend most of my nights at her place, just fucking each other into oblivion. But that would be too much too soon, and I know that's not what I need.

I tell this to Danny in one of our sessions two weeks after I became Mika's boyfriend. "You're worried about making Mika your identity like you did Adele?" he asks, and he's really nailed how I'm feeling.

I slouch in my seat. "Yeah, I am. With Mika, I know I would be safe if I did, but that's not how I want to be. I completely lost myself with Adele. I was a shell, and she got to fill me with all the hate and degradation she wanted. Mika isn't like that. But I don't want to put myself in that situation again where I could lose myself. Even with someone as great as Mika." I pay him for my honesty, and it's been working so far.

Danny makes a thoughtful noise. "That's smart. We call that progress, Ash. You are setting a boundary for yourself, and that's good. Keep to that. If Mika is as great as you say, and I bet she is, she'll respect any and all of the boundaries you set. From what you told me, she has some relationship baggage herself. Just remember: you're not in the relationship to fix each other. You're in it to help each other grow individually and start something new together."

He's right, of course. I don't want Mika to think of me as a project, just like I don't want to think I can fix all her trust issues. We've both been hurt in different ways, but it's not a competition of betrayals, and it's not the other's job to try to fix the problems that came before.

"You share all the same friends, but it might be good for you to make some outside of your gaming group. You can have friends as a couple, but it's good to have a support network outside of that. And before you say anything." He holds up his hand because I open my mouth to say there's no way I'm able to do that. "I know making friends as an adult is difficult. Especially because you work from home and do your own thing. I'm not saying go out to a bar to strike up friendship. But maybe join a club or do some volunteer work that will get you around other people. Find something you like that will get you around people you can connect with. Socializing is good for you." He laughs, like he's trying to lecture a teenager on why leaving their room is a good thing.

Even before Adele, I had a lot of social anxiety. Being with her just exacerbated the issues I already had. Somehow, I'm going to have to work through that, and without Marco or Mika holding my hand to do it.

"So, you're saying I need to get a life," I deadpan, though Danny's advice seems pretty sound.

He laughs. "Yes, Ash, that's exactly what I'm saying. Get a life outside of what you already know. Find a hobby. Do something that makes you happy that you don't feel compelled to do with one of your friends or your girlfriend. This is DC. There's plenty to get yourself involved."

After therapy and sitting back at my desk in my living room, I think over what Danny said. He's not wrong. I do need hobbies. I've spent the months I've lived in DC either playing B&B or hanging out with everyone from B&B. Outside of my work and my side hustle, there's little else I do. On days I'm not with Mika or the group, I sit at home watching Netflix or working on a new book cover. I don't even know what I like for fun anymore outside of that.

The only thing I have that is truly mine, the thing that not even Adele could take from me, is my art. It has been the one thing I've always had since I was a kid. Mom was so proud of me when I got into art school, especially since I got in on scholarship. There's a decent art scene here from what I know. Maybe that could be my thing. I just don't know how to get involved and what that would look like.

I do a little research and find something called Paint and Chill on Friday nights that's not far from my apartment. I buy a ticket and add the details to the calendar on my phone. There, I did what Danny said and found something that doesn't involve anyone I already know. I only have to wait a day, so hopefully that's not enough time to talk myself out of going.

I think Mika will be proud of me, putting myself out there to do something I enjoy. I want to tell her, so I pull out my phone and text her.

[Me: I signed up to do this painting thing. My therapist says it's good to have hobbies.]

Mika never makes me wait for a response. She's one of those people who can't let a text go unanswered. Just another thing I like about her, even if it's something small and simple.

[Mika: That's freaking awesome! Want me to come with? Or is this just a you thing?]

[Me: Just a me thing. If that's okay with you.]

I don't want to panic and overthink, but that's exactly what I do. *What if Mika takes it personally? What if she thinks I don't want to do things with her? Shit, this is a bad idea.* I should just text back and tell her I want her to come. Her response comes in and stops me mid spiral.

[Mika: That's good, because one, you need your own thing. And two, I am terrible at art.]

[Me: Lol, I'm sure you're not that bad. But thank you for understanding.]

[Mika: You don't have to thank me for that. We're not attached at the hip, honey. You can do things without me. Don't feel guilty about it.]

How can this woman read my emotions over a text? Because that's exactly what I was feeling: guilt. I know it's not entirely my fault. Adele made me feel like wanting anything for myself was just selfish. Everything had to be done together or not at all. And we only did what she wanted. If I even brought up going to do something alone, she would accuse me of going out to meet other women.

[Me: You're pretty great, you know that?]

[Mika: Yeah, I am pretty awesome. You're not so bad yourself. You're definitely my favorite person.]

[Mika: Don't tell Stella.]

[Me: Your secret is safe with me. See you Saturday?]

[Mika: You bet your ass you will!]

I set my phone off to the side and focus on work the rest of the day. I want to see Mika sooner than Shabbos lunch, but I can be patient. And it's good for us to maintain our own lives and not spend every waking moment together, though the idea sounds really good.

Tomorrow, I'll go to the Paint and Chill thing and hopefully have a good time. Then I can spend Saturday with my girl. I should probably pop over to Marco and Lena's tomorrow to check in on them. They still have a lot of help around the house, but it would be good to see them and the baby.

With my weekend plans all set, I concentrate on the color palette I'm assembling for an upcoming customer event. Later, I'll get to work on a book cover for my favorite husband and wife writing duo. For the first time in years, I'm really happy with my life.

I arrive at Paint and Chill a little early and even still, it's half full of people. Easels are set up with little stations of paint at regular intervals to form rows of semicircles. I take a place toward the back where there currently aren't any people seated. That doesn't last for long, and soon there's no more space left.

On my right a middle-aged, dark-skinned man takes a seat at the easel. He's bald and sporting a Commanders t-shirt. He gives me a nod as he looks my way, and I nod back in greeting. When I turn back someone is taking the spot on my left. She's blond and looks to be a few years younger than I am. She's cute in the college girl kind of way with her sorority letters on her sweatshirt. She smiles brightly at me as she sits down. My return smile is tentative, and I quickly turn away.

The program starts, and soon we're all painting away while music plays around the room. It's upbeat and fun to paint to, not loud enough to be too distracting, but not soft enough where I have to strain to hear anything.

Around me, people chat to one another, some clearly in groups that came together, some just people talking to people because they are near. "Wow, you're really good at this," the blond to my left says, leaning over to get a better look at my canvas.

I shrug. "I just enjoy painting." I have no idea how to take a compliment from strangers. I look over at her canvas, and it's already looking gorgeous. She clearly has a lot of talent.

"Oh, me too. I wanted to major in art, but my dad refused to pay if I went into anything other than political science. Political parents are the worst. I'm Liza, by the way. My mom named me after Liza Minelli. She's a big fan." It all comes out in a rush. Liza is clearly one of those people who can befriend anyone in half a second.

"Ash," I say, and we lean over and shake hands. She holds onto me just a beat too long.

"Ash, that's a great name. And wow, you have a great handshake, too." She looks at our hands before letting go and straightening on her stool. Again, another compliment that I don't know how to take. So, I nod because what else am I supposed to do?

We lapse back into silence and focus on our own paintings for a while. Then Liza speaks again, pulling me from the colors before me. "First time here?" she asks. *Am I that obvious?*

I nod again. "Yeah, I thought it would be cool to try something new."

She smiles at me. It's a good smile, but not nearly as perfect as Mika's. "For sure! I like to get off campus and do stuff like this. It's the only way I get to do art. Otherwise I'm buried under homework. Reading especially. There's so much reading in poli sci. I'm not even unusual in my major. I swear, like, half the people are kids of senators or congresspeople. Okay, probably not that much, but there are definitely a lot. Your parents in politics?" Liza finally takes a breath and waits for my answer.

"Ah, no. I'm from New York, so most of my family is still up there. No political figures in my line," I respond, happy that Liza is at least steering the conversation.

For the next two hours, Liza keeps up a steady stream of chatter. It's more at me than with me, but I don't mind. I give her answers and respond where needed. She's not bad company, but I don't know how she gets any painting done because every time she really gets going on something, she stops and waves her brush around for emphasis. Both of us have little flecks of paint peppered across our skin and hair from where she got a little enthusiastic.

The event wraps, and I already know I'm coming back next time. I look at the work I've accomplished and feel happy. There was no expectation for this; it was just something I did. At the end of the two hours, I don't have to turn this into anyone for their approval or critique. I just get to tuck it under my arm and go home.

"You headed home now?" Liza asks, throwing the strap of her purse over her head. She looks at me expectantly.

"That was the plan. I don't want to be out all night since I have plans tomorrow." Maybe I'll text Mika to see if I can come over. It's only 9:00 p.m., still plenty of time for us to have fun or even go out if she wants.

"Boo, it's Friday night, and it's still early. Why don't we hang out? Get a drink. It'll be fun." Liza looks at me with hopeful eyes. And maybe she needs an outside friend too. Someone not part of her everyday world.

Still, I hesitate to say yes, and the old fear and guilt creep in. Adele would have lost her shit over even the idea of me hanging out with another woman just for fun. What if Mika isn't cool with that? We haven't discussed what she's comfortable with me doing, and it's not like the situation has ever come up to begin with. It's not like I'm going to do anything with Liza other than hang out and maybe make a new friend. That was the whole point of this outing. But the guilt is gnawing at me that I shouldn't hang out with another woman alone.

"Hey, Benji, want to grab a couple drinks before you head back to Macy? I know your mom is still visiting and probably already has her down for the night." Liza calls over me toward the man on my right whom I didn't speak to all night.

Benji stands, stretches, and gives her a toothy grin. "I like that idea, Liza. I love my baby girl, but this is the only time I get to myself outside of work. Mom can handle her for a while longer. First round on me?"

And just like that, my guilt is gone. Because this isn't a one-on-one thing with a strange woman—this is exactly what I wanted. A group of people on my own. "I'll come. It'll be good to stay out of my apartment for a little longer," I find myself saying, and I mentally congratulate myself for going outside my comfort zone a bit.

Liza's smile lights up her whole face. "That's the spirit. Okay, let's get out of here." The three of us leave the building and head down to an Irish pub a few blocks down. It's crowded—it's a Friday night after all—but we find a table near the back, and Benji goes up to the bar to order a round of stouts. I'm not a big beer drinker, but I decide to just go with the flow on this outing.

Benji and Liza are hilarious together. There's about a twenty-year difference, but the two act like they have known each other for years. Benji is an accountant and a single dad raising his seven-year-old daughter Macy. He's born and raised in DC and never felt the urge to leave. I can understand that.

Liza's father is a representative from Virginia, so she grew up near DC. She shares an apartment with three of her sorority sisters, none of whom are in her major. She's graduating next year, and her father is pushing for grad school at Harvard like him. "I hate the idea of Harvard. Like, I know my dad went, and my granddad went, and my sister is there now. But like, I think Columbia would be more my vibe. What do you think, Ash? You're from New York."

"I don't know anything about Columbia. I'm from the Bronx." It's easy for people unfamiliar with New York to think of it as one homogenous thing rather than several separate cities slammed next to each other. "I went to Pratt over in Brooklyn," I add.

Benji claps me on the shoulder with a laugh. "You're an art kid through and through. I saw what you were working on. You're really good. Do you do anything with your art?"

His hand is warm and heavy. It's comforting, like I imagine my dad's felt like. "Uh, yeah, actually. I work in graphic design for a marketing company. I also design book covers for indie authors. If I could make a career out of that, I would, but right now it's just a hobby."

I've dreamed about it before. Owning my own little business where I could just work on book designs and character art for authors. Maybe do some pre-made covers that authors could buy. It was something I really focused on in college when I started doing the book covers as a way to make extra money. I thought I could turn it into something bigger; let it be my career. But once again, I let Adele convince me it was a bad idea. I needed a real job, she said. One that would actually pay the bills. At least I held firm to it and continued making the covers even when Adele hated it. That was the only piece I kept to myself.

"I wish I could do that. Just make something because I want to. Let it be my whole focus. But then I would have to pay for school on my own, and I totally can't afford that. Maybe I'll make a Patreon and do art commissions for fun when I can. Do you have a Patreon?" Liza chatters away over the music of the bar, and I'm amazed how she can still go with so much noise around her.

I shake my head. "No Patreon, though I've thought about it. My clients hear about me through word of mouth. Shout outs on social and all that. I keep a website and Instagram for that," I say, drinking the last of my beer.

Liza leans across the table eagerly. "You should totally get a Patreon. You have to monetize yourself. Release some fun small pieces every so often and let people give you money for small goodies. I can totally show you how to set it up if you need help. My friend Rachel runs one for her little crochet pets, and she's making bank. Which really just pays for her crazy expensive yarn."

"I'll look into it. I would have to think about what kind of perks I would put out. But yeah, might work." And I intend to actually think about it because Liza is right: I need to monetize myself more. If I want to actually do what I love full time, why shouldn't I hustle more for it? My corporate job is okay, but it's not what I look forward to every day. It's just there because it needs to be at this point. But, dammit, I have an art degree, a bit of a name for myself already, and a modest following on my art's social page. Maybe I could do this—follow my dream or whatever.

I decide, while sitting at a table in some random bar with two people I barely know, that I'm going to do something monumental to change my life, starting with the baby step of opening a Patreon. I'm eager to tell Mika, and hell, even Danny. He'll be proud of my progress.

But I know Mika will be even more proud. Knowing my girl, she'll be the first person to sign up to be a patron. Just another thing I love about her.

Did I say love? No, I like that about her. Because if I know anything, it's too soon to fall in love with Mika. Then again, she just makes it so easy. There's no trying to love Mika. She just is, and she's the most wonderful person I've ever met. So maybe I'm falling for her. I'm okay with that.

"I should probably get going. I'm having Shabbos lunch with my girlfriend's parents tomorrow, so I shouldn't keep drinking," I say. I'm tired and want to be home so I can text Mika, but I'm also reluctant to go. "This was nice. Thank you both."

"Girlfriend? Ah damn, and here I thought we had a vibe going. Oh well, guess we'll just have to get married, Benji. There's no other alternative." Liza smiles over at Benji, and it's big and full of perfectly straight white teeth. There's nothing flirty in her tone. I think she just likes Benji's company.

Benji's returning smile reaches his eyes, and his whole face lights up with humor. "Just say the word, Liza, and I'll make an honest woman out of you." They laugh together and then we say our goodbyes.

I leave the bar feeling good about tonight. I got out of my comfort zone and did something new. I met new people who I think I could see myself becoming friends with, even if they are as completely different as night and day. I'm proud of myself for doing this, and I'm definitely going back next week.

[Me: I had fun tonight. A few people took me out. I think I made friends.]

[Mika: That's so awesome. I'm so proud of you for going out and doing your own thing.]

[Mika: I can't wait for you to tell me all about it tomorrow. If you want to. No pressure.]

[Me: I can't wait to tell you.]

[Mika: *heart emoji*]

I put my phone away and head home, thankful that it's just a few blocks away. I'm ready to crawl into my bed and sleep. Fun as tonight was, it's still really taxing to socialize with people.

CHAPTER 17

MIKA

I love Nico to death, but oh my god, he is the worst GM to ever lead a B&B game. The man waltzes into my house, eats enough for four, and when it's time to play, he pulls out a single piece of paper that he had shoved into his back pocket and gets to it. There are exactly five bullet points on the whole page and that is it. I checked.

"What are we doing, Nico?" Stella has lost her patience with him an hour ago, and we've only been playing for that long.

"I don't know. Maybe like head into the forest and see what's in there," he responds as he flips through the *Creature Compendium*.

Ash leans toward me, making sure our sides are pressed together, so my whole left side is touching him. "Is he usually like this? Because this is pretty awful." He tries to whisper, and luckily Nico is distracted enough that he doesn't hear.

"Awful? This is a good session with Nico," I whisper back. And it's true. Normally Nico just comes in and wings it. At least, this time he had something written down. But this is excruciatingly bad. Maybe it's because we've been spoiled for so long by Marco's GMing style, but even then, there's zero structure or idea of what we're doing. And that makes it no fun to play. The part of a good GM is to move the story along, to set up the world and encounters. Nico kind of expects us to do all the work while he just throws an enemy or two here and there.

A few minutes later, and mostly just our characters wandering around the woods doing absolutely nothing, Stella throws her pencil down. "Okay, I'm calling it. Nico, I love you, but I've had to prompt you three times in the last fifteen minutes to have us do nature checks or really anything else, and nothing is happening. Again, I love you, but none of us are having fun." Stella can seem harsh, but she's also not wrong. We're not having fun. It's exasperating and more like we're going through the motions of the game.

I feel bad, but it is what it is. Nico isn't the kind of guy who takes it personally though. He's at least self-aware enough to realize when he's not succeeding at something. "I know, I know. I'm not good with this stuff. Doesn't help that I compare myself to Marco and realize I'll never be as good as Marco, so why try?" He folds up his GM screen and slouches in his chair.

Now that is not typical Nico behavior. He always rolls with the punches and never takes it to heart. Nico always jokes about his GMing. "Alright, what's going on?" I say because I can't stand the thought of Nico thinking less of himself. Not to mention all the other things going on with him lately. Being on time, being more responsible, hell, even saying he can't come for a night out because he already has plans. We know it's not work because we always go to his bar.

Nico doesn't even try to brush it off or play it cool. "I have something to tell you guys." And the way he says it, there's no grin, no playfulness to his voice. This is Serious Nico. I've never seen Serious Nico.

"Oh fuck," Stella says from across the table. Her lips are set in a grim line and her eyes are wide. She's never encountered Serious Nico either.

"It's not really an 'oh fuck' thing. It's just, I'm thirty now, and I realize I haven't been too serious with my life. A few weeks ago, I met someone. Her name is Alexandra. She's a librarian at the Library of Congress. How metal is that? Anyway, she's great, and we've been great, and it's got me thinking about life. I love being a bartender. I'm great at it. I love my band. But I know we're never going to make it big; we just like to play. So I'm thinking it's time to like grow up and stuff." This is the most eloquent Nico has ever been, and I'm flooded with so many emotions. He's been seeing someone and just now telling us? That's strange, but okay, it's something different for Nico.

"Oh my god, are you breaking up with us?" Stella shrieks, and I have to admit, it does sound like a break up. I chew my bottom lip because now I'm worried about Nico leaving us, and my heart just can't take that.

Nico's eyes go wide. "What? No! Never! I love you guys. You're my best friends. And I love playing B&B, just not GMing it. What I'm saying is ... fuck, this is harder than I thought. Alexandra is pregnant, and we want to keep the baby. It's still super early. I haven't even told my family yet. We're still doing the dating thing, totally not like moving in together or anything. But I wanted you guys to know because I'm going to need your help. I have no idea what I'm doing."

"Nico!" I yell and then I'm out of my seat and throwing my arms around his shoulders while he sits. Stella is out of her own chair in a second and hugging him from the other side. I'm surprised when Ash gets up and hugs the three of us from behind Nico's chair. I hear Nico sniffle and realize my shirt is wet from where he's buried his face in my shirt. "We're here, babe. You always have us, and we're going to make sure your kid has an amazing life," I say and my heart swells. Our little B&B family is growing.

"Everyone is having kids all of a sudden. Mike, you're not pregnant, are you?" Stella looks over at me, and I can see the tears in her eyes.

I laugh. "Nope. The factory is locked up tight right now." I let my eyes wander up to Ash, and he's looking back at me, a soft smile on his face. It's way too early to think about kids, but now I can't stop myself from thinking how we would make some pretty adorable kids. Not the time though. This is about Nico, and Ash and I haven't even dropped the love bomb yet. Lots of time to think about that later.

Nico wipes his eyes on the back of his sleeve. "I love you guys so much." And there's his big goofy grin again. Nico may be in the process of doing some growing up, but there are some things that won't change about him. He's still our favorite himbo.

"How did you meet a librarian? You don't strike me as the bookish type," Ash says when we all finally break out of the group hug.

"Funny story. So you know Ariel, my drummer? Well, she's working on her PhD and has been doing loads of research at LoC. I went with Jason a few times to take her to lunch because once she's in deep, Ariel forgets to eat. That's how I met Alexandra. She yelled at me for bringing food into the library. Did you know some women are extremely attractive when they are pissed at you? Anyway, Ariel asked her to join us one day, and she said yes. The rest just kind of happened." He grins through the whole story, and of course, Nico would fall for a woman who was mad at him for breaking the rules.

"And then you baby trapped her," Stella said, though she is laughing.

Nico looks sheepish. "Okay, that part was an accident. Classic condom breaking, you know how it goes. Guess I'm joining Marco in Club Dad."

We spend the rest of the evening just hanging around talking. Nico is excited about what the future is going to bring him, and it's crazy to think he's going to be a dad. We make plans to meet Alexandra soon because she's stuck with us now, whether she knows it or not.

Once Stella and Nico leave, Ash and I cuddle on my couch for a little longer. "It's so weird to think Nico is going to be a dad. Like out of all of us, I never would have thought he would be the next one to be a parent. Hell, I never thought he would have kids." I'm running my hand up and down Ash's leg with my head on his lap, facing the TV. He strokes my hair, and it's just a simple and perfect moment. I wish we could stay like this.

"Pretty crazy. But life has a way of being like that," Ash says, keeping up the gentle strokes on my hair. "Hey Mike," he says after a beat of silence.

"Hm?"

"Do you want kids?" He tries to sound casual, but I can hear an edge of anxiety in his voice.

My hand stills on his leg as I take a moment to respond. "One day. I'm not like super eager to get to baby making, but I think I would like to be a mom one day. Have to make more Jews to replenish our numbers and all that."

I resume stroking his leg, trying to convince my heart to slow down a bit, because it's racing. This conversation is way too early in the relationship.

"Yeah, me too. I mean, kids yes, but not any time soon. And you would want to raise them with Judaism?" He's really trying to be nonchalant about this, but the strain in his voice gives him away. Ash does very little with nonchalance.

I sit up and sit so I'm turned toward him. "Well, I mean technically, they would be considered Jewish anyway because that passes matrilineally. But yeah, I would. It's important to me, even if I'm not that observant. I would want them to know their family history and to know what we lost because of what we are." I think about how my Bubbe never knew her father, never knew anyone in her family because they were all gone before she was born.

"I can understand that," Ash says, looking into my eyes, like he really gets when I mean.

But we're totally not having this conversation anymore. It's weird to think about. We've only just started dating, and I don't want to begin thinking about a long-term future yet. Things are still in the honeymoon period, and there's a chance that once we slow down a bit and aren't constantly screwing each other, we won't be so compatible. I mean, we can be sexually compatible without being emotionally compatible.

"Anyway, it's very exciting for Nico. Have you been to visit Marco lately? I was there yesterday. They both look so tired, even with alternating overnight feedings." I go back to toying with Ash's leg, a good distraction from baby talk.

Ash seems to take the hint and follows my lead on topic change. "Yeah, I went Friday before the painting thing. I hung out with baby Maria while the two of them napped. Rosa went back home last Wednesday, and Shazi had to get home to her mother. Sorry to tell you, but Maria is my best girl now."

I laugh. "Of course she is. I don't mind being replaced. She's hard to resist." We lapse into comfortable silence, just enjoying each other's company on my couch. It's getting late, so we head up to my bed, but we don't go to sleep right away. Not until we bring each other to orgasm, in my case, a few times. Then I wrap myself around Ash like I'm holding on for dear life, and we finally fall asleep.

I go to Shabbos at my family's alone this week, and I'm actually grateful for that. Not that I don't love bringing Ash or my friends, but sometimes it's nice just to be the five of us again.

David is late, as usual. We really should start telling him we're starting early just so he'll show up on time. Bubbe is on her second glass of wine before the meal even starts, and I have to hand it to her, she never misses a chance to enjoy life as much as possible.

"There's my darling daughter. Unattached today? I'm used to seeing you with your groupies," Dad says as I enter the kitchen. He's standing over the stove, stirring something that smells like caramel.

"Just me today, I have to give my groupies a day off every now and then, or they start to unionize and demand better pay." I slide onto a stool at the kitchen island and watch my dad putter about the room.

He nods. "Ah, can't have that. So, how's life, kiddo? Anything happen in the last week?"

I think about my week. Obviously, the biggest news is Nico and his new girlfriend having a baby. But I feel like that's something Nico will tell my parents when he's ready. I opt instead to tell my dad about my visit with Marco and Lena and work. My dad doesn't need to know the intricate details of my relationship with Ash, so I just tell him he's good and how he's enjoying his new painting event. Dad hums in approval at everything I say, half focused on me while the rest of his attention stays on the food he's preparing.

"Where's Mom?" I ask because normally Mom hangs around the kitchen while Dad cooks. I already know Bubbe is in the living room watching her murder mystery shows.

Dad waves in the general direction of Mom's home office. "She's finalizing some details for the party coming up in two weeks. Which I know you absolutely didn't forget about." He gives me a look over his glasses.

I totally did.

"Right, the party. Yup, definitely remembered that. I plan to go shopping with Stella for a dress this week." I tell myself I need to text Stella to let her know that's happening.

Dad doesn't buy my obvious lie, though. "Uh huh, just don't forget. And maybe bring Ash. It's always good to have a date to a party."

And now I have to remind myself to text Ash about the party. Only if he wants to go. Ash and social situations do not exactly mesh well. But he is trying to get out of his comfort zone, I just don't to push him too far out of it. One of my mom's parties would definitely be considered toeing the line of comfort.

"I'll ask him," I say noncommittally. "I think I'll go shame Mom for working on Shabbos." I leave the kitchen and head to my mom's home office. The door is shut, so I knock gently just in case she's still on the phone.

"Come in," my mom's voice calls loudly from inside. I open the door and slip in, leaving the door open behind me. "Mika, darling, there you are. Just you today?" She looks over my shoulder just to see if there's anyone else with me.

"Just me. I'm here to tell you off for working on Shabbos. Party planning can happen tomorrow," I say, leaning against the door frame. I smile at my mom. We're not super observant, we're not like shomer Shabbos, so like besides family lunch, we just have a normal day on Shabbos. But it's still good for my mom to take some time away from working all the time.

"You're right. I'm being bad right now. It's still two weeks away, but you know how it goes, caterers book up, especially this time of year. Halls have reservations and no room. Just getting my ducks in a row." Mom stands from her desks and stretches out. Clearly, she's been here a while. Her phone pings on her desk.

"Unless that's David texting to say he'll be late, as usual, don't answer it," I chastise her while she picks up the phone to check it.

"It's David, and yes, he's running late again. I swear I need to set that child's clocks fifteen minutes ahead just so he'll show up when he's supposed to. How he made it through medical school, I'll never know." We leave her office together and head back to the kitchen, where Dad is pouring what appears to be a caramel sauce over a tray of chopped almonds.

"Making my famous Roca. It's for a charity event at your grandma's temple. Chocolate, almonds, and caramel, can't go wrong," my dad says brightly, smoothing the hot caramel over the nuts. I'm totally going to have to swipe some before I head home.

Bubbe ambles out of the living room only when David finally arrives, and we all sit down to eat. The chatter between my family is nice. Saturdays always make me feel grateful that I have them. We're all close, and I'm know that makes me lucky.

"Okay, I have an idea." I announce to Ash at lunch the following Monday. He looks up from his food and waits for me to continue. "Well, it's more like a favor, but it's helping both of us. My mom is having like this party thing next week, and I have to go and be the dutiful daughter. It's on the same day as the event she-who-can-rot-in-hell wanted you for. So instead, you can be my date to this party, and I won't have to go alone and talk to a bunch of old DCites who still think I'm sixteen."

He thinks it over, taking a drink from his glass of water. "Sounds awful. I'm in."

We make plans for the following Saturday. I really hate these things, but it's part of being Esther Levenberg's daughter, so I put on a mostly modest dark blue dress that hits just below my knees with cap sleeves and a scoop neckline. I picked it out on the impromptu shopping trip I dragged Stella on last week.

My pink hair is pulled up with just a few curls hanging down to frame my face. Not a bad look overall, though more buttoned up than I normally go for. I prepare to smile my face off for a few hours.

Usually, I just hang with David through these things, but now that my big brother is all Dr. Levenberg at Johns Hopkins Hospital, people actually want to talk to him. Nobody finds what I do particular interesting. They probably think I'm the family disappointment. Joke's on them. I don't care and neither does my family.

Ash shows up to my house early, and honestly, the man can wear a suit. It's perfectly tailored to his toned body, the black cutting seductive angles on him. The shirt is stark white with French cuffs while the cufflinks are a simple square silver design. The tie is narrow and actually properly tied. I'm glad he didn't try to gel his hair back. Instead, his dark hair is mussed just so and looks perfect on him. Yeah, that's my boyfriend, and I'm near melting.

Mom wants us there before the party, so he's there by 5:00 p.m., and we take a Lyft up to Chevy Chase, getting out at a swanky building I've been coming to periodically since I was a teenager.

"That's a lot of red, white, and blue banners," Ash says as we walk up to the main doors holding hands.

I laugh. "Of course, she's gotta look patriotic for her re-election fundraiser."

Ash gives me the side eye and a confused expression. "Re-election?"

Oh, he doesn't know. That's weird, considering he's spent several Shabbos lunches with my family. But then again, we make it a rule to not talk work at all when we're together. "Yeah, Mom's a Senator. She's been in Congress since I was like fifteen."

"Oh. How did I not know that?" he says, genuinely surprised. We walk into the hall, and it's fitted with "Re-elect Levenberg" signs everywhere, mixed with tasteful decorations and round tables already set for dinner.

Mom is standing near the stage with Winnie Gumphrey, her top aide. Winnie is just a few years older than I am, but she has the demeanor and spine of a woman twice her age. She takes no shit, and I love her to pieces. She's been with my mom since she was fresh out of college and has practically been a big sister to me.

"Mika, darling. And Ash! How wonderful to see you both. Are you two hungry? I know I made you come out early, so why don't you head into the kitchen and grab something from the caterers? Everything looks amazing." I give her a hug, and she practically crushes Ash to her in a bear hug. If my family liked Ash when we were just friends, they love him even more now that we're together. I'm like ninety-nine percent sure my Bubbe has the entire wedding planned, and the dates marked for when her first great-grandchild will be born.

We head off to the kitchen to grab a snack. It's going to be a long night, and I've learned from experience to eat when I can because someone will always interrupt you while you are stuffing your face.

I eat nearly a whole tray of canapes myself with a little assistance from Ash, who insists he doesn't want to spoil dinner. Such a rookie mistake.

"So, is your mom like a Democrat or Republican? I know it makes me stand out in DC, but I don't really follow politics." Ash leans against a counter that is currently empty, though it won't be for long.

I shove a celery stick into my mouth, my last one, I swear. "Ash, honey, she's a rich Jew from Chevy Chase. Obviously, she's a Democrat."

He nods his head. "Of course. So this place is just going to be crawling with politicians?"

"Mh hm, just the friends of my mom's. And then of course, the most important people: political donors. That's really what this is about—raising money for her campaign. It's the home stretch, and she's really making that final push." Dad thinks she might run for president, or at least, that's what he keeps telling me. But I don't see her ever doing that. She likes being a senator and has said on multiple occasions that being president is the shittiest job in the world.

"How long will we have to mingle before we can dip and make out in the coat check?" Ash asks as we head back into the hall. His grin is so fucking sexy, I'm thinking of pulling him into the coat check now and spending the rest of the night in there.

But I do have to play the dutiful daughter tonight, and honestly, I don't mind doing that for my mom. "A few hours at least. As enticing as making out in the coat check is, we still have to be present and mature adults for this. Besides, I think being caught making out in the coat check for the third time will have people saying I have a bad habit."

Ash gives me the side eye as we walk. "Third time?"

I nod, pulling him along toward the stage again. "First time was Mom's first victory party with Chelsea Wagner when I was sixteen. Second time was Tripp Blackthorne at a fundraising gala when I was twenty-one. Only, we weren't just making out that time. I couldn't look at my parents for a month." Yes, I was a bit of a wild child in my younger years. "Now Tripp is a state representative in Connecticut with a wife and two young kids. He still sends me dick pics when he's drunk, which for the record, I do not ask for nor want."

"He sounds like a douche," Ash responds, and I worry for a minute that I've made him uncomfortable.

"Oh, he's a total douche. His wife is a total sweetheart though. I hate to be the asshole to her, but whenever he sends his dick pics, I forward the messages to his wife. She thanks me every time, and I usually get an Edible Arrangement two days later." I laugh, and I feel better when Ash joins in. And not with his fake laugh, but with his real, full-bodied laugh.

"You are a force to be reckoned with, Mika Levenberg." He leans over and kisses me tenderly. This man, I swear, makes me weak in the knees on the daily.

"I get it from my mom, the badass herself, Senator Esther Levenberg," I yell out dramatically as my mom walks over to us. If she's stressed about the fundraiser or the election for that matter, she doesn't show it. She's already plastered on her politician smile. I prefer her real one; it's softer and only her family gets to see it.

She does a little twirl as she comes to a stop next to us. "I am a badass, aren't I? Anyway, your brother is finally here. People are starting to arrive, so just be sure to mix and mingle. And no making out in the coat check."

"I'll keep her in line, Esther. Don't worry," Ash says with his "trust me" smile. Mom is not fooled. She gives us both a parting look that says she'll have her eye on us. I don't know about Ash, but I plan to be on my best behavior tonight. I've had enough incidents at these types of events in my youth that I'm trying to show the old politicos that I'm actually a mature adult now.

Ash and I stick to the side of the hall as we watch people start to filter in. I shake hands with other rich people who have been contributing to my mom's campaigns forever. They are all old and make the same comments about how much I've grown, and then a charming anecdote about how wild I was in my youth, which they share with Ash accompanied by a knowing wink. The aides of other senators and the senators themselves greet me with hugs and ask after my work. I see plenty of them on a semi-regular basis, so it's not like they miss much of my life.

I introduce everyone we meet to Ash, and calling him my boyfriend gives me a little thrill every time. Dinner time rolls around and those of us with zero political clout get relegated to a table off to the side of the stage. Not that I mind. The table is filled with my favorite people: my dad, David, Ash, and Winnie, who is mostly there in case she needs to jump in quickly. That woman won't actually sit and eat. Mom sits at a table full of her top donors because even while eating, she has to woo them.

Just as I suspected though, people come up to our table throughout the meal to talk to dad, David, or me. David is the most popular at our table since he's Dr. Fancy Pants. I love seeing my big brother in his element talking to other people in the medical profession. Medicine has never ever interested me, too much blood, but the way David talks about it, well, he's very passionate.

I keep checking in on Ash just to make sure he's comfortable. He doesn't say a lot, but he squeezes my hand reassuringly. Still, I let him know we can always bail if he needs to. After the speeches, things are going well. Ash is even able to meander a little away from me to have conversations. I'm proud of him. This isn't his world, but he's holding his own.

CHAPTER 18

ASH

Two hours into the fundraising party, and I'm surprised to find I'm actually having a good time. Having Mika at my side makes it easier, but I also have her dad and David, and they are good company. There are plenty of other people to talk to, and even though I know basically nothing about politics, it's like they can detect I'm not one of them, but rather than alienate me, they inquire about my work and congratulate me on wrangling a great girl like Mika.

Mika wasn't kidding when she said my face would hurt from all the polite smiling. I don't think I've ever smiled this much. But it gets easier as the night goes on. There are a ton of speeches after dinner. Esther Levenberg really knows how to work a room. She's a fantastic orator. Rather than deal with flowery, overblown promises, she's direct and hopeful. It's no wonder she keeps getting re-elected.

"I'm going to get another drink. Do you want anything?" I ask Mika as I stand from our designated table.

She's giggling at something her brother said but still turns her attention to me. My girl gives her full attention no matter what.

"Yeah, that would be great. Thanks, honey," she says with light squeeze of my arm. I love how she always tries to find little ways to touch me. It's comforting while also setting my whole body to tingling. I can't wait to have those touches later with no clothing between us.

I walk over to the bar that's set up off to the side. They went all out for a full bar, so I order two rum and cokes for us. While I wait for our drinks, I notice out of the corner of my eye someone else sidling up to the bar. I don't turn though. It's someone else ordering a drink.

"Hello, Sebastian," a sultry feminine voice says.

I would know that voice anywhere. And there's no way she should be here. Not this party. *Of all the parties in this fucking city, why this one?*

I turn toward her, and there stands Adele. She's tall, toned, and dressed in a long-sleeved black dress that hugs her figure perfectly. Her sleek chestnut hair lays in perfect waves around her shoulders, and her makeup is at the perfect spot of natural and sophisticated. By looks alone, she would be considered beautiful, but her chocolate eyes are hard, and I know what lies in her soul. There's nothing beautiful about her black heart.

Even knowing what a monster she is, I can't help the fear running through my body. I shouldn't be here. I need to find Mika and get out of here.

"What are you doing here, Adele?" I manage to force out, though the words nearly die in my throat. The last thing I want to do is stand here and talk to her of all people.

Her lips press into a faint pout. "So that's how you greet your girlfriend? DC has made you hard, Sebastian." And I hate the way her voice sounds. Because though she's making that face, and still she looks beautiful, her tone is sharp, cutting.

"You're not my girlfriend anymore, Adele. I've already told you that." I can't look at her. I don't want to look at her, so I turn my face toward the bar. It might seem like an innocent enough gesture, but I know Adele will take it as a dismissive insult.

The bartender sets my drinks on the bar top, and I grab them and turn away. "Is that for me? You know I only drink wine, Sebastian," Adele says, and I think she's going to make a grab for the glass anyway, so I pull away.

Her eyes flash with cruelty, and I know that if we were still together, she would make me pay for the slight. She would break me down, and at the end of it all, I would be the one apologizing to her. But this isn't our apartment in Brooklyn, and we're not together. Fuck, my heart is racing so fast. I can't breathe, and it's getting so hot in here I feel like I'm burning up inside.

"It's not for you. I'm here with someone else. So again, why are you here?" I keep my tone firm, but inside I am shaking so bad, it's a wonder there is still any liquid in the glasses.

She narrows her eyes at me. "You're cheating on me, Sebastian? How typical for you. What an embarrassment you are. I can't believe you." Adele scoffs at me, and I know what she's doing. She's going to do this to me right now, right here, even with other people around, even though they can't hear us or are even paying attention to us. "But if you must know, I'm here with a fellow partner at the firm. The owner is a big doner of Senator

Levenberg's. How did Bronx trash like you end up here? Sneak in with the catering staff?"

That's another thing Adele always did, made me feel less than for being from the Bronx. Hell, she put me down for my Puerto Rican heritage, like I was less than her because I wasn't WASPy like her. And for years, I let her make me feel ashamed for who I was. Something I used to be so proud of, and I'm just starting to feel proud of again.

I shouldn't rise to her bait, but I can't help it. I can't help but defend myself. I've spent so much time in therapy thinking about this moment, thinking about confronting her. But I don't feel strong enough to do this. I am not prepared. Not really.

"I'm a guest of someone who was invited," I mumble. My resolve is crumbling by the second.

The noise she makes is one of disbelief. "Whatever, Sebastian. I'm disappointed you didn't pick me up for this. I told you we were going together. God, you never listen to me. And once again, you've embarrassed me, and now I have to salvage this situation." She straightens her immaculate dress and continues to make me feel like garbage. "Now, fix your tie, and you're going to escort me around the room."

I find myself nodding but looking down at the floor. I don't want to do this. But I have to. She'll make this ten times worse if I don't go along with what she says. I realize I'm still holding the rum and cokes in my hand, and suddenly I don't know what to do. I told Mika I would get her a drink, but Adele won't let me just walk up to another woman and give her a drink. Should I set the glass back down and forget about it? Or should I excuse myself for just a second and take it over to Mika? No,

Adele won't let me out of her sight now. She'll stay plastered to my side to make sure I don't do anything further to anger her.

"Ash, everything okay?" Mika's voice is like a calming balm to my fractured emotions. I look over at my girl, resplendent in pink and blue, and she's amazing. And I don't deserve amazing. I don't deserve her. She puts a hand on my arm, and I can't stop myself from panicking. Adele will absolutely lose it seeing another woman touch me.

"This is a private conversation. Why don't you head back to whatever two-bit representative took pity on you enough to make you an aide?" The way Adele looks at Mika, like she's beneath her, like she's nothing more than an annoyance, makes me so angry. It's one thing for Adele to do that to me. I deserve it. But Mika doesn't. She is better than Adele. Mika is the sun itself.

Mika gives Adela a saccharine smile. "Ha, funny. I'm sure I just caught you on a bad day. Mika Levenberg, daughter of Senator Esther Levenberg, the one whose party you are attending." She holds her hand out to Adele, and I swear the air gets colder.

The resting bitch face Adele wears drops immediately. Her mask goes up, and suddenly she's Adele the hotshot lawyer and everyone's favorite. "Oh my god, I am so sorry. Yes, it's been quite the day. Sorry about that." She's definitely not sorry, despite the act she's putting on. "Adele Chamberlin of Gardarin, Levi, and Pine. Our firm owner is one of your mother's donors. I was just having a conversation with my boyfriend, Sebastian. I'm sure you know how men can be." Adele takes Mika's hand, giving her a dainty handshake.

I watch as Mika grips Adele's hand a little tighter before letting go. "Yes, I totally know how men can be. Especially this one, since you know, Ash and I are actually together. Unlike the two of you." Adele's face falls again, back into the nasty face she makes, the disapproving one. In all the years I had been with her, I've never heard anyone stand up against her. People tend to fall all over themselves for Adele. They think she is the perfect woman, a fierce lawyer in the courtroom and a congenial demeanor out of. Nobody else knows the truth about her.

Now I really can't breathe. The look Adele shoots Mika is so cold, it fills me with ice. I feel like I'm going to throw up or pass out. I never wanted this to happen: my past and my present meeting. I'm so happy with Mika, and Adele will ruin that just to spite me. She's still in my head even though I thought I was doing so well getting rid of her.

"Wow, so he really is a cheater. Funny, after four years, you think you know someone. I'm sorry to have to tell you this, but he's definitely taken, and he's just using you for his own gain. You deserve better." Adele recovers quickly. She's going to spin this the way she wants. Partly because she can't lose face in front of a senator's daughter, but she doesn't like to lose in general.

Mika grabs my hand and squeezes, but she doesn't take her eyes off Adele. It's like she sees a predator and knows she can't take her eyes off her. "Yeah, we all know that's bullshit. Especially since Ash has been here for months now, and yet here you are for the first time. You don't belong in my city, and Ash doesn't belong to you. I think it's time for you to leave because I am definitely not above making a scene."

With my whole heart, I truly believe Mika would make the biggest scene she could, and she would do it for my sake. She's already told me how she's trying to present herself in a better light with these people, repair her reputation from her younger years. I'll ruin that for her if I let her do this with Adele now. It'll ruin the whole party and then Esther will hate me too, and I can't disappoint that woman. I just can't.

Adele glares at Mika, running her eyes down from her pink hair to her low black heels. Assessing her. Judging her. But she doesn't move. Not yet. "I could either call for security to escort you out, or maybe I'll just call my mom over and she can tell your boss all about this. You're really making a great impression for your firm tonight." Mika darts her eyes over Adele's shoulder and raises her hand like she's calling someone over.

I see Esther wave back toward Mika and then she's coming over to us. She hugs her daughter tightly. "What a night. What's up, my darling? You two having fun? Did you get a chance to eat? Ash, dear, come here, you spilled a little something on your lapel." Esther takes out a little pocket square from her smart cut blazer and dabs a little of the rum and coke off my jacket. It's such a motherly gesture that I almost want to throw my arms around the diminutive woman and tell her all my problems. Since I've met her, she's always treated me like one of her own.

"Are you okay, dear? You look awfully pale. Mika, darling, why don't you two get out of here and back to our house? Order some pizza and beer. I love the food here, but it never fills me up. Save some for me and Dad. Ooh, order a pizza for David, too. He's staying over too. He'll eat half a pizza himself. I need to get back to mingling." She hugs Mika again and then pulls me in for a tight squeeze. When she pulls away, Esther pats my cheek affectionately. "Get some rest, dear. And don't you worry about sleeping in a guest room. We're all adults here. We know how these things work." Then she's gone, leaving me red from embarrassment. If I thought my body was burning up before, I feel like a living inferno now. My hand is sweaty and slides against Mika's palm as she retakes my hand.

I don't want to look at Adele, don't want to see her judgment, her disgust. But it's like trying to avoid looking at a train wreck. The morbid curiosity gets the better of me, and so I look up, and God, she looks ready to go for Mika's throat.

"Bye, Adele. See you never," Mika says, and her voice is dripping with venom despite the smile on her face. She pulls me away from my ex, who stands there fuming at the bar. Adele isn't used to not getting her way, and I'm going to pay for this. Somehow, she'll get back at me, and it's going to be worse than anything she's done before.

My insides are churning violently as Mika pulls me out of the hall and into the cool night air. I take huge gulps of air and try to fill my lungs as best I can, though it still feels so difficult. My heart hasn't stopped racing, and I can hear my pulse pounding in my ears. Somewhere far away Mika is calling my name, but I can't respond. I'm choking on air.

I swear the pounding in my ears is starting to sound like Adele's laugh. Not the one she uses for other people. No, instead, it's the malicious laugh, the one without any humor. It's rage, disappointment, disgust, embarrassment. That laugh is the embodiment of the only emotions I was allowed to feel when I was with her, and they were all directed at myself.

"Ash, honey, breathe. Just breathe. In through your nose and out through your mouth. Come on, breathe with me." Mika places her hands gently on the side of my neck and starts to take her own deep breaths, encouraging me to do the same.

So I do. Deep breath in and then out, counting to six as I do so. Mika keeps going with me, her hands never leaving the skin of my neck. It's just as grounding as the breathing I'm doing. My heart rate starts to slow, and the pounding laugh in my ears begins to dissipate. The flames that have been eating at me begin to simmer and fade, and I'm suddenly left freezing as the night air hits me. My face is wet because at some point I've started crying.

"Shhhh, honey, it's okay now. Let's get out of here and head back to my parent's house," Mika says, her voice soft like she's dealing with a wounded animal and needs to be gentle.

I don't want her to act like this. Because I'm not wounded. I'm fucking broken and nobody can fix me.

Not Mika.

Not Danny the therapist.

I can't even fix myself.

Over half a year of therapy and healing completely undone by spending ten minutes around Adele. Somehow, I feel worse than I did when I left her. Because now I know I'll never really escape her. She'll always find a way to get to me. Running away to DC didn't make me any safer from her, didn't keep her out of my life forever like I hoped.

What was the point of leaving then? I'm away from my family, away from everything I've ever known. Putting physical distance between me and Adele did fuck all. Even though I know, for certain, that good things have happened to me since I moved to DC, I don't think about them now. All that surrounds me and penetrates my head are all the things wrong with me.

I'm so in my own head that I don't even realize I haven't responded to Mika. I should respond. I should say something, anything, but words are so hard. What if I say the wrong thing and it sets her off? It doesn't matter that Mika is nothing like Adele. Mika is sweet, caring, compassionate, and patient. But she is still a woman I've offered my heart, and it's so fragile, so small, that I want to snatch it back from her because I can't trust anyone with that again. Even someone as wonderful as Mika.

"I can't do this, Mika," I choke out, but my voice is thin, and fuck, I'm crying again.

"You can do it, Ash. I know this has been really hard for you. We can go back to the house, and you can message Danny and get an emergency session, okay? Let me take you home and get away from her." That's exactly what I need. She's not wrong. But I can't do it with her. I need to get away from all of this. I won't let Mika see me fall apart. I won't drag her further into the dark pit that is my soul with all the baggage attached.

I shake my head and take a step out of reach. Her wonderfully warm and calming hands slide down to her side, and she looks at me with such beautifully big concerned eyes. "I can't do this, us, Mika." The words are hard to say, but now they are out, and I can't take them back. I want to take them back.

She looks confused now. "What do you mean? Listen, I know that was shitty, and Adele is a total fucking monster, but what you could use is rest and time to talk to your therapist." She reaches for me again, and again I take a step out of her reach.

A flash of hurt covers her features for only a moment, and then she puts on her brave face again. Because my girl knows I'm hurting right now and won't show anything. That's why I can't keep her. I don't deserve to have someone put my feelings over their own. I don't deserve Mika because she is better than me and always will be. All I am is a broken shell of a person trying to stuff things in the cracks to hold myself together. But all of that is only temporary. I'll never be whole again.

"I'll talk to Danny. But I can't be with you anymore. I can't give you what you need, Mika. I'm too fucked up, and tonight proves it. I'll just drag you down with me, and I don't want to do that. So, I'm done." I watch as my words cut through her, and as her eyes fill up with tears. I feel like a real monster, but I should feel this way.

"Ash—" she starts, but I don't want her to talk me out of this.

"I think I love you, Mika. But I don't deserve your love, and you don't want the shitty, broken love I can give you." I don't even think when I say the words. I don't just think I love Mika; I know I do. And fuck, it feels like I'm dying right now.

"You love me, so you're breaking up with me?" She sounds confused and hurt, and fuck, I feel the same.

"It's the best thing for both of us. I'm sorry. Fuck, I'm sorry. I've screwed this all up." Now I see the tears starting to well up in her eyes, and I feel like the biggest asshole on the face of the planet.

But Mika is strong, so much stronger than me, because even as she's on the verge of tears, she straights her spine and her face turns to one of resolve. "Right. Got it. Adele rolls into town, and suddenly you're not worthy of me or some shit. Were you just using me to get over

Adele, or do you think you have to go crawling back to her abuse just because she's here?"

I want to throw myself at her feet, explain that I would never use her like that. That I don't want to go back to Adele. All I am worthy of is being alone.

I don't get to say anything though because Mika holds up her hand and closes her eyes. "You know what: I don't want to know. We've spent months doing this dance, and I thought we were happy, and you were working on yourself because I wasn't trying to fix you, Ash. But I won't let someone play on my emotions again or make me feel like an idiot for trusting them. Call Danny and go home, Ash."

And then she's walking away from me, back into the hall, even as I hear her quiet cries filter through the dark.

My whole body feels weak and my chest hurts. I clutch at it, right over my heart, and let the tears fall. I shouldn't have come to this city. I should have just stayed with Adele forever, or at least until she got sick of me. Because then I wouldn't feel this unbearable pain. My head and my heart hurt, and now I know neither will ever be fixed.

"At least you did something right, for once." I hear Adele's voice behind me. I don't turn around; I don't want her to see my face right now. Because this is my lowest moment. Nothing in the four years I was with her was as bad as this.

I feel her hands on my shoulders and then they slide down my arms. Their touch makes my skin crawl, even though the fabric of the jacket. Her touch is poison, her words the most potent venom known to man. If only she would just disappear forever, this wouldn't hurt so bad. But her being here to witness the worst pain of my life is too much. It's just another power play to her.

"It's better this way, Sebastian. You don't deserve to be loved by anyone but me anyway, and that's only because I'm generous. Now, let's go back to your place, and you can make all this up to me. Then we'll discuss you coming home." Adele is so self-assured, like she knows I'll cave to her demands because that's what I do. That's what I've always done.

And it turns out, I'm still not strong enough to defy her, but while I don't say anything, I nod, and follow her away from the venue.

The car ride to my apartment is silent. Adele keeps a possessive hand on mine in the center seat. I don't turn my hand over to hold hers, like I would have in the past. Instead, I keep my hand still, pressed against the leather.

I open my apartment door on autopilot and continue in without saying a word to Adele. I don't want her in my space. This has been my refuge for months, a safe space away from her. Now that she's here, it doesn't feel so safe. It feels wrong.

She looks around my small apartment, judging every surface, every personal item I've put out. And she wrinkles her nose at what she sees because it's not her tasteful décor. It's messy and chaotic. My desk takes up most the living room, and it's covered with printed out copies of book mockups, my notes scribbled all over them.

"Hm, bit of a dump. And oh, Sebastian, you're still making those trash book covers. I thought you had moved past that." Her eyes are locked on the mockups, and her disdain fills up the room like a palatable thing. The air feels too heavy, and I can't find air again. I need to do something. Get her out of here or at least stand up for myself.

"I like making them," I mumble because that's all the voice I can muster, all the defiance I have right now. "I'm really tired. It's been a long night. Can we just do this in the morning?" There's no way I can handle Adele right now. I need to get a moment alone to send a text to Danny about setting up an emergency session. That's the only way I'm getting through this.

"Well, I'm not. And you have a lot of groveling to do. I came all this way. You owe it to me to make this night salvageable. Especially after how your girlfriend—" She stops and gives me a malicious smile. "Sorry, ex-girlfriend, treated me." She plops herself down on my small couch, hiking up the skirt of her dress a little and spreading her legs once she sits.

It's not an invitation. It's a demand. After everything that happened tonight, after everything she's put me through, she still expects me to get on my knees and take care of her needs. She has beaten me down enough through our relationship, and tonight I feel less than human. But even I have my limits, even in this state.

"Good night, Adele," I say and walk past her to my room. My legs tremble with every step, and I take shallows gulps of air. My heart races, and I'm sweating again, but I make it to my room and shut the door. I lock it for good measure because I know Adele will try to follow me. She won't take my dismissal of her as an answer.

I lean against the door, trying to calm all my emotions, for all the good that does me. It's only a few seconds later that I hear the door knob jiggle as Adele tries to come in. Adele is not the kind of person who will break down a door, though I'm pretty sure she could. She just always expects to get what she wants, whenever she wants it. Instead of trying the door again, she knocks. Not a pounding knock, but it's authoritative enough. "Open the door, Sebastian."

The door remains locked. I'm not stupid enough to let her into this space. I've been stupid enough for one night just letting her come here. I steel myself to respond because I have to say something. "I said good night, Adele." There's no force behind my words, but I don't need it with a locked door between us.

I hear her huff loudly. She's clearly annoyed that I'm not doing her bidding. "Can I at least get something to sleep in?" A reasonable request since she's in a party dress, so I pull an old t-shirt from my dresser and a pair of gym shorts that'll be too big on her, but it's something. There's no way I'm opening the door to hand her the clothes. She'll just push her way inside my room. I take the coward's way out instead and shove the shirt and shorts under the door. The gap is wide enough that I can easily push them through. The fabric is ripped from my hands and I hear her huff again. That's not just her angry huff. She's fucking pissed at me. Still, she stomps away and goes back to my living room. At least there's a wall and a locked door between us, and I can finally text Danny.

All I want is Mika though. Even as I type out the message to my therapist about getting an appointment tomorrow, I want to talk to her more than I want to talk to the actual paid professional who can help me through this.

I settle in my bed after stripping off my suit, not caring that I've left the nicest thing I've own in heaps on my floor. What does it matter now anyway? As I crawl into bed, I can't get the look of Mika's face out of my head. I can't believe I told her I loved her while I broke her heart. There's something so deeply wrong with me.

I go to sleep hating myself more than I ever have before.

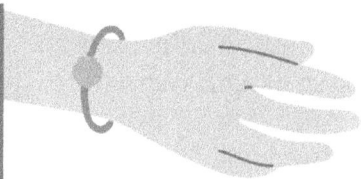

CHAPTER 19

MIKA

When I get back to my parents' house, alone, feeling like shit, I still order the pizza and beer like mom had directed me to.

David came home not long after the pizzas arrived. I have all of one slice, sitting alone at the kitchen island like a sad sack, staring at my phone, hoping that Ash will call. He doesn't. David takes one look at my face, which is certainly streaked with makeup, and wraps me up in a hug. Big brother hugs are the best after having your heart shattered. It's warm and protective.

"Need me to cut off his balls? I can do that, you know. I'm a doctor." David smiles at me as he holds me an arms-length away.

I sniffle, and even though it's thin, I still laugh. "Nah, I'm pretty sure his ex-girlfriend already has them in her purse." I tell him about our encounter with Adele and how Ash broke up with me. I don't tell him about Ash and Adele's history, other than to say it was a toxic relationship, and Ash ran away from her. "God, I'm so stupid, David. How did I let this happen again?"

My brother kisses the top of my head. "You're not stupid, Mikey. If he left her, there's probably a lot of unresolved stuff there, and he didn't know how to face it. He's the one being stupid. It's not your job to fix anyone. But if that idiot loves you like he said, he should know by now that you'll stick by him no matter what. So again, he's the stupid one."

I swipe at my cheeks again to get rid of the last of my tears and try to smile at my brother. "Thanks, David. That's exactly what I needed to hear." He kisses my head again and asks me if I want to stay up and hang, but I shake my head and go upstairs to sleep. I grab some pajamas from the overnight bag I brought. Ash left his at the venue, so I brought it back with me, and it sits next to mine, untouched and without its owner.

The last time I cried myself to sleep was over five years ago after my breakup with Quinn. I promised myself then that I would never let myself cry over another relationship again. Turns out, I'm not very good at keeping promises to myself because that's all I've been doing. Even with David's words still in my head, it doesn't help because my mind drifts back to what Ash said, how he looked. *Who the fuck tells someone they love them as they are breaking up with them?!* That same thought plays over in my mind.

What little sleep I do get is fitful, and when I wake up in the morning, I don't feel rested at all. It's not even dawn yet, and I lay in my bed in my childhood room staring up at the dark ceiling. I think of Ash's face, devasted and streaked with tears even as he tore my heart out. Months of flirty and getting closer as friends, and we lasted what, a month, as a couple. Rationally, I know it's because of Adele. Ash is a victim and being confronted by his abuser unprepared was too much for him. But right now, I'm going to be sad and angry at Ash and his choices.

Even though the sun isn't even up yet, there's no way I'm going to be able to sleep. I get up and put on the long sleeve pumpkin colored dress and black tights I packed for a lazy day around the house. A lazy day I had planned to spend with my family and Ash.

I look at his bag still sitting on the floor. It's probably not a good idea to talk to him for a few days. Still, I don't know what he's packed in there, and if there's anything he needs for today. When it's a more reasonable hour, I'll take it to him because I should. But then I have to leave right away. I don't want to talk to him. I don't want to hear any explanations or excuses. I just want to do this one thing and get out of there. He's probably left some things at my house, but I'll collect them and have someone else give it back to him.

I check my phone, but Ash hasn't texted or called. Not that I expected him to, I'm actually relieved he hasn't. Because if he did, it would be the same bullshit he was spouting at the party about how he doesn't deserve me and whatever. It doesn't matter that Adele is the shittiest person ever. He can't get over her, and I won't be put in a cycle of him feeling okay with me and then not.

Ash wakes up early even on the weekends, so around 7:00 a.m., I slip out of the house and luckily manage to get the only Lyft working this early on a Sunday to take me back into the District. Before I get in the car, I think about heading to my house first, but figure if I go home first, I'll just stay there and feel sorry for myself some more. So I have the car go straight to Ash's place in NoMA.

It's a long, quiet ride, and I'm grateful that my driver isn't a talker. At least not to me. He's too busy having a heated conversation over his earbuds in a language I don't know. He looks at the GPS occasionally but mostly just keeps talking. I thank him when he drops me off outside of Ash's building, and he waves but doesn't stop yelling back at whomever is on the other end of the line.

The walk up to Ash's apartment seems to take so much longer, and yet, not long enough. My feet feel heavy, and suddenly my bag and his feel like they weigh a million pounds. I'm in front of his door before I really have the time to process the walk up.

I take a deep breath. This won't be easy, but it's better to just get this back to him, get home quickly, and hide in my bed. I'll let him know that if he has anything else he wants to say to close out this relationship, we can do that later.

Right. Okay. Time to get this over with and go.

I knock on the door, my heart in my throat.

The door opens after a few seconds, but it's not Ash who answers.

It's Adele. Wearing one of Ash's t-shirts. Wearing only his t-shirt that barely covers her ass. She smirks at me. "Wow, back here already. That's pretty pathetic, don't you think?"

I'm going to punch her right in her fucking vagina. This bitch is pure evil. But then the realization of what her standing here means hits me. She's in nothing but his shirt, and she clearly spent the night.

I feel like I'm going to be sick.

"Yeah, go fuck yourself. Here." I toss Ash's bag directly at her stomach, hard. "Give that to Ash. He left it back at the party." She lets out an omph as the bag connects with her body, and I feel a little gratification at that.

I turn to leave, but then I hear his voice calling, and I want to shatter right here in the hallway now. "Who's at the door?" he calls over Adele's shoulder. I see him a second later, and his eyes widen with shock and sadness as he sees me standing there. "Mika? What—"

"Goodbye, assholes," I spit out, turn away from the scene at the door, and hurry down the hallway. I see Adele's cruel smile as I leave, and I hate her so much.

"Mika, wait! It's not what it looks like," Ash calls out to me, and I hear the slap of his feet behind me. I don't turn though because I don't want to hear his excuses. I don't want to hear anything from him.

He grabs my upper arm, not tight, but enough that he stops me from continuing on down the hallway. Still, I won't turn around. I don't want to see his face at all. Because I will break. I will start crying and letting whatever bullshit he wants to feed me sink in and start to believe it. And I can't do that.

"Mika, we didn't do anything. She slept on the couch. I kept my door locked. I promise. I wouldn't do that to you." His voice is cracking, and he sounds on the verge of tears. I have to will myself not to care.

It's not working out well.

"Right, sure. Totally believe you," I say, though I've never sounded so sarcastic in my life.

"Mika, please—" But I can't listen to him any longer. I tug my arm from his grip, keeping my back to him so he won't see the tears that have started to slip down my cheeks.

"Just please stick to our agreement. I don't want to see you at B&B anymore. Anything you left I'll take to Marco and Lena's for you to pick up." I don't say bye. Instead, I run away. Like actually run. Ash calls my name again, but he doesn't follow me.

I'm out of breath by the time I hit the bottom of the ground floor, and I'm full on crying now. I get another Lyft home and barely make it through my front door before I crumple on the floor and sob. I stay there until I have no more tears left, and then I trudge up to my room and crawl into bed and sleep.

I stay in bed all day Sunday. Ash tries to call several times and texts, but I don't answer any of them. I don't even look at the texts. Eventually, I will. But I can't today. It's too raw. I'm too raw.

My room is my sanctuary today, and I leave it only to get the takeout I have delivered. Then I go back to hiding. At some point, I think about calling Stella. She's helped me through this before, but I don't want to burden her with this. We'll see each other tomorrow for drinks anyway. I hope Ash has the good sense to not show up. He'll probably spend the day with *her* if she's still in town.

Monday I can barely work. I drag myself out of bed, shower, and go about the motions of my day. I eat some toast for breakfast, not because I'm particularly hungry, but I know I have to eat. I'm not going to let myself waste away over some guy.

I can't focus on work, though. Everything sounds like the grownups from Charlie Brown, like trombone noises with no words. It's like I've forgotten the English language. And judging by my work on a translation, I've forgotten Hebrew, too.

Who needs words anyway?

When it's time to meet up for drinks, I contemplate not going. I'm going to have to tell Stella and Nico about Ash, and that sounds excruciating. But I really do need my friends right now, and surrounding myself with my friends seems like the best idea for my mental state.

I arrive late. Stella and Nico already have a table, and drinks sit before them. There's an extra glass sitting before an empty seat, so I take that and immediately chug my drink.

Stella narrows her eyes at me. "What happened?"

God, I don't want to answer her. I don't want to talk about it. But these are my friends; they are like family to me. And clearly, Stella knows something happened and won't let up until I tell her something. "Ash and I broke up. His ex showed up to my mom's fundraiser party, and I guess he decided that he was better off with her than me and broke up with me at the party. I went over to his place yesterday to drop off his bag, and she answered the door wearing only his shirt." My eyes are filling up with tears, but I try to hold them off.

"I'm going to cut off his fucking balls," Stella seethes, and she downs the rest of her drink in one go, slamming the glass down on the table almost hard enough to shatter the thing.

"Hang on, that doesn't sound like Ash. Like I know I'm not as close to him as you are, Mike, but even I can tell he's crazy about you. He doesn't seem like the type of guy who screws his ex on the night he breaks up with his girlfriend. Just saying—that doesn't pass the vibe check." Nico looks like he's concentrating hard, which if I'm being honest, doesn't look right on him. He looks more like he's in pain.

"You would say that. Keep to the Bro Code and shit. It doesn't change the fact that one, he broke Mika's heart the minute his ex waltzed in, and two, that he let her sleep over. Whether they slept together or not, letting your ex sleep over literally right after you break up with your amazingly gorgeous girlfriend is fucked up," my knight in shining heels says. Seriously, Stella's wedges are covered in sparkles tonight.

Nico gives her a look, and Nico never even tries to stand up to Stella. "Excuse you, I'm a feminist. It's not Bro Code, it's Ash Code, and sure, having an ex over is shitty, but that doesn't mean he did something bad."

I love them both so much, but this isn't nearly as comforting as I hoped. "Guys, can we just not? What I need is alcohol and like fried cheese or something. This is a shitty situation, and I just need a night to not think about it, please."

My friends both give me a sympathetic look, and then by some silent agreement, Nico goes to the bar and orders another round. It would be easy to get drunk off my ass and hate myself for the hangover in the morning.

But it won't make feel better. And feeling better about this whole shitty situation is my end goal.

We stay for only two drinks before we end up at a pizzeria. It's exactly what I need, and I'm grateful that my friends just keep plying me with food. At the end of the night, I'm so full of food that at least I know I won't have to make anything when I get home. Maybe I'll even sleep better. It's not like one night out repaired the damage my heart has taken, but it definitely took the edge off the pain, if only for a little while.

I'm still a sad sack on Wednesday night. I can't bring myself to cook anything, so I order Thai. Nico is disappointed there's no dessert for him to swipe, but baking brings me joy, and I don't really feel joyful right now.

After Stella and Nico arrive, I find a few ways to delay the game because it's supposed to be my turn to GM, and while I prepared everything last Friday before the breakup, I haven't looked at my notes since then. I had originally planned to put the finishing touches and brush up my notes the night before, but it seemed like too much effort. So instead, I went to bed at 7:00 p.m.

I keep looking at my door, half hoping Ash will just suddenly step through and play B&B with us. But that's not going to happen because we had a plan. One that I never thought would actually be needed. Maybe I'm just an idiot for thinking that, but here we are.

He doesn't come, and I'm glad.

We also don't play B&B because I can't focus on the game, and it's just not as fun with only three players, especially when the person running the game can't get into it enough to try. Marco could pull off a three-person game, but I can't. Not like this anyway.

Since Sunday, Ash has called only once per day and only sent a handful of texts. He's giving me space but doesn't want me to think he doesn't care. At least, that's what I'm interpreting it as. I still haven't looked at his messages or listened to any of his voicemails. I don't want to see his words, let alone hear his voice.

Before I know it, Saturday morning rolls around. A whole week of feeling like total crap and barely leaving my room as taken its toll on me. I feel drained and look like a mess. My stomach is still rolling from all the junk

I've consumed lately. I should probably eat something green today before my body really starts to revolt.

I'm going to have to talk to my family about the breakup today. I'm sure David let my parents know a little of what happened since I didn't stick around the house long enough last week to say anything, but I know I'll be bombarded with questions regardless.

I go through the motions of getting dressed, opting for a lime green A-line dress. There's no way I'm going to dress to match my mood. If my demeanor isn't going to be bright as usual, then my outfit damn well will be.

Fixing my hair in the mirror, I make a decision. I've given myself a week of feeling sad and sorry for myself. It's not like I'm over Ash. That's not going to happen anytime soon. But I'm not going to mope around any longer. Sure, it'll hurt, but I have to get on with my life. And then, when I'm ready, I'll reach out to him to have some closure and return his stuff. That's it.

Now that I have a game plan in place, I don't feel so much dread on the way to my parents' house. I didn't invite anyone else to come along, so it's just me today. Honestly, that's what I need—just my parents, David, and Bubbe. The people who have always loved me unconditionally, even when I'm a total wreck.

"How are you, darling?" Mom asks, pulling me into a hug the minute I'm through the door. I hold her close, folding over her a little since I have a few inches on her, and just let the warmth of her embrace seep through me.

I give her a squeeze and then step back. "I've been better, but I've also been worse. So, I guess I'm coming out even." I give her a brittle smile. It's nothing like my usual grin, but I don't think I can muster up enough emotion to really smile like that.

Mom cups my cheek and gives me a small smile. Then she leads me into the kitchen where Dad wraps me up in a hug but doesn't say anything. During lunch, Bubbe slips me a flask under the table, like we all can't see her do it. But I take the offered drink anyway and enjoy the way whiskey tastes going down. David makes a *gimmie gimmie* gesture across the table, and I pass it over to him before giving it back to Bubbe, who downs the rest of it.

My family doesn't say much about Ash, and I'm grateful. I know they really liked him, more than every liked any of my previous partners, so I feel like they are hurting a little too. Instead, we just enjoy each other's company and eat the great food my dad made, which luckily does include green things. My body thanks me for that.

It's our own calm before the storm. Wallowing in my own misery this week has made me forget that the election is coming up in three weeks. Mom's, (hopefully), victory party has already been planned out, and that means I need to find another dress to wear. There will be a lot of photos that night, and some of her aides stream it on social media, so I can't hide in the corner and mope.

Mom talks excitedly about her poll numbers. It's a no contest really. Mom is a popular senator for a blue state, but still, the show has to go on. Guess I should probably let Winnie know to strike Ash from the guest list. It's going to be a lonely night at the senator's party. Nico's band got booked for the Ballot Box Blowout at some club. They almost won the battle of the bands event last year.

Stella hates any and all politicos and doesn't really want to go to an event where there will be plenty but has offered just in case I need a date. I don't want to force her, and I won't. But it's going to suck being on my own again. I guess I'll have Winnie, but she'll be frantically checking polls numbers every two seconds, and only after the results are called will she actually sit down and eat something.

My family each give me tight hugs before I head home. "Why don't you hang around for the rest of the weekend? We can play boardgames and watch *Star Wars* like we used to," Dad offers, and it's tempting. Even David agrees to stay, and it's always fun to play boardgames with my brother because we help each other cheat. All in good fun, of course.

I should stay. My family is just trying to help me through a rough time. I know David is just doing it because he feels bad, but he has a Saturday night off, and I'm not going to make him waste the rare opportunity to enjoy the weekend by making him stay in with his little sister.

"Tempting offer, Dad, but I have some work to catch up on that I didn't get to this week. I'm kind of lagging behind after everything." It's not a lie. I was not particularly productive this week. As sad as it sounds, I will actually be spending my Saturday night working on transcribing and not wrapped around a boyfriend that I no longer have.

And tomorrow is Sunday. Museum day. I make plans with myself for tomorrow to stay on my couch and watch *Star Wars* on my own and not think of where I could be if I still had Ash.

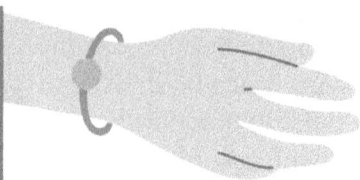

CHAPTER 20

ASH

It's been almost two weeks of absolute agony. I've been seeing Danny three times a week since Adele left my apartment. Luckily, Danny was able to get me in first thing the following Monday because Adele's leaving was an absolute shit show. For the first time since I've known her, I really thought she was going to hit me. But all she did was scream about how much of an idiot I am for leaving her. How I'm a failure because of my book covers when I could be doing real work. And my personal favorite: how I wasted the best years of her life because I was shitty partner and was holding her back from success. It took threatening to call the police to get her out. Not that I would do that. Police are no help.

I've only left the house to go see Marco and Lena. Normally, they would probably be sick of how often I'm over, but they are helping me through the chaos in my head, and they don't seem to mind that I take Maria for a bit while they take it easy.

I'm sitting at their table on Friday afternoon before Paint and Chill. I didn't go out with Liza and Benji last week, but Lena is trying to convince me to go tonight.

"Ash, you need to get out of your apartment, and I don't mean just to come here. You've been ordering take out and not showering for almost two weeks now. You're gross." Lena takes a sip of her Perrier.

"I took a shower this morning, thank you!" I say indignantly. Truth be told, before that, I don't even remember the last time I showered, or did laundry, or ate anything that wasn't terrible for me. Not that I've had much to eat. Danny and Lena have been on my ass to eat more, but I just feel sick all the time.

I play with the cap of my own bottle of sparkling water. "I don't know what to do, Lena. I fucked up so bad. I realize now that I didn't want to break up with Mika. She's the best thing to ever happen to me. I just let Adele get in my head. I wasn't ready to face her, and there wasn't an opportunity to get away from her. Four years I let her bully me around, and I'm still letting her do it."

Lena leans across the table and grabs my hand. "Hon, have you tried talking to Mika about all this? I mean, you told her you loved her as you were breaking up with her. Which, as I've already said before, was, in fact, a super dick move."

Somehow I feel even worse now—didn't think that was possible. "I've tried calling and texting, but she hasn't responded to me. She hates me, and she should." I let my head drop onto the table. I can't even bear to look at Lena. My hand is still in hers, and she gives it a gentle squeeze.

"Ash, Mika has never hated a single person in her life. Not even her ex, who was a total shithead. She doesn't hate you. But I imagine you broke her heart pretty bad, and that's not something she'll just get over. Give her time. She'll eventually talk to you again." Lena's right. I know that. Doesn't make me feel any better. Besides, it's the same thing Danny has been saying. As well as reiterating that he is not a relationship counselor, and he can't fix my "boneheaded mess," which he informed me was not a professional opinion, but still stood.

Marco walked into the room, cradling baby Maria across his chest. "I can talk to her on Wednesday. Maria and I are running a game. Aren't we, mija? Yes, we are. You'll be Daddy's little co-GM. Oh my god, baby's first TPK." He coos at his daughter. Hard to believe she's already over a month old. She responds by sneezing a cute baby squeeze on her dad.

"Babies are gross," Marco grumbles, grabbing a tissue from the living room.

I think about what Marco offered on my way over to Paint and Chill. I've been trying to give Mika space. Maybe I haven't been super great at it. I still send her a message a day in the hopes that she'll respond. But I'm not even being left on read; she's not looking at them at all.

I decide it might be my best bet to have Marco talk to her next week. Until then, I'll stop trying to contact her and give her proper space. It's not like I want to, but it's probably the best thing to do.

[Me: Offer still stand to talk to Mika at BnB?]

[Marco: Always. No guarantees, but maybe I can convince her to at least read her messages.]

[Me: Thanks, Marco.]

[Marco: np]

I put my phone back in my pocket and head in for a night of painting. Liza waves to me as I walk in the door, and I take an easel next to her. "Wow, you look like someone kicked your dog. Everything okay?" she asks while I get my stuff set up. Liza is more observant that she lets on at first. It's easy to immediately classify her as a sorority valley girl type, but that's the thing about people: they have layers and depth once you start looking closely.

I don't tell her or Benji about what happened. Our friendship is still new, and I am not going to dump my emotional damage on them. When she asked me last week, I just said I was dealing with some personal stuff. Neither of them pushed for more information. They just nodded, Benji patted my shoulder, and that was that.

"You know, still dealing with some shit. I'll be fine, though." Benji drops onto the chair across from me.

"Still looking like shit, Ash. Girl troubles?" Benji asks, getting straight to the issue. Benji doesn't pull punches, that's for sure. He isn't saying it to be mean; he's just blunt. That's what I like about him: he doesn't sugar-coat anything.

I run a hand through my hair. It's getting longer than I usually keep it. "Something like that. I did something dumb, and now I'm facing the consequences. Not a fun place to be." It's more than I planned to tell either of them, but I don't want to worry them anymore.

He nods, and I hear Liza make a humming sound on my other side. "Well, at least you can drink some of your problems away with us tonight. Right, Benji?" Liza looks over at Benji with a big smile, and the man melts instantly. He agrees and so we make plans to head over to one of the bars after class.

I let myself get lost in the painting, like I'm putting all my frustration and sadness into my brush and letting it channel to my easel. It's cathartic and the best I've felt in weeks now. My brush strokes are sure and even, and I marvel at myself that I can even keep the brush in my hand without shaking. It's been hard to get through work since that night, though I've been working a lot more. Any free time sends me back to thinking about Mika. The look on her face when I said I loved her and when I said I couldn't do it anymore. I think about how she's doing.

Is she hurting as much as I am, or has she just written me off as another mistake?

But tonight, I empty my mind using one of the breathing techniques Danny taught me and just feel the painting take shape under my hand. "No thoughts, empty brain," Danny said, and I've been practicing that for a week now. It's only just started working out for me the last two days. Progress is slow.

Once the two hours are up, I set my brush down and assess my work. There's a lot of blue. No doubt a message from my subconscious that I'm clearly in a bad place mentally. *No shit, brain.*

But there's also pink. Bubblegum pink. Mika's hair pink.

I haven't done a portrait piece in acrylic in a long time. Sitting on my canvas is Mika, her beautiful face rendered in shades of blue and black. Her pink hair stands out against the darkness, like a beacon lighting me home.

Liza leans over to look at what I've done. "That's gorgeous. Is that your girl? She's really pretty."

I stare at my own work without saying anything for a few moments. How could I ever think I would be okay not seeing those eyes every day of my life? Mika is the most amazing woman I've ever met. And even if I feel like I don't deserve her, that doesn't mean I shouldn't try. I owe that to her, and maybe I can be the type of man who makes her happy. Now if only I hadn't screwed up royally. I can only hope there's a way to fix things with her.

"Yeah," I say softly, "that's my Mika."

Wednesday night rolls around. I should be at B&B at Mika's house. For as much as I miss her, I find that I also miss playing too. For something Marco just dragged me into to get me out of my comfort zone and out of my house, it really became an enjoyable part of my life. Not just because it brought me Mika, but I got some good friends out of playing. I learned to let go of my inhibitions and reservations and just be for a few hours. Take on a new persona and live it up a bit. My imagination ran wild like I was a kid, and with all the stresses of adult life, it was something I really needed.

I sit at my desk staring at my bag of dice and *Player Tome*. Because yes, I have a whole bag of dice now. Turns out, one set isn't enough. Not just because leveling means you get to roll more dice, but because the mood struck me to buy a set. Or someone in the group would find a set that reminded them of me or my character. It's easy to see how collections can grow so quickly.

I pull the bag close to me and reach inside, feeling around until my fingers land on the unmistakable shape of a d20. I pull it out, and it's the glittery blue one Mika gave me. My favorite set.

For no reason, I lift the die and roll it across my desk, delighting in the sound of the plastic on wood. Instantly recognizable and oddly soothing.

"Natural twenty," I whisper to my empty apartment. Because of course it is. Never roll them in game, but I roll them while alone not playing. I smile anyway. It's still a lucky die, if for no other reason than my favorite person gave it to me. The one person who still has my heart even though I know I crushed hers.

Adele's voice comes to me, *You ruin everything, Ash.* But it's not true.

I know I fucked up with Mika. That's my consequence. However, it's also Adele's fault. She knew what she was doing. She knew how to break me down even if it had been months since she had the chance to. Even if I had let her do it, that's the nature of abuse. It starts out subtle until you don't even realize it's happening. And then you believe every word that person says because that is the person who is supposed to love you more than anyone else, so if they are telling you that you are worthless, it must be true.

It isn't true. It never was. I'm not worthless. I deserve love, and I deserve to be able to love someone unconditionally.

I love Mika. I just need to prove it to her. That I'm all in, and even though I'm a work in progress, I'm willing to work alongside her. It's not her job to fix me. I have to do that myself. But that doesn't mean we can't enjoy each other's company. There's no one I want more than her.

Marco is going to talk to her tonight, and if she is willing to talk to me, I plan to grovel. A lot. Like probably for the rest of our lives. And I will gladly do it.

I go back to working on my latest book cover, a monster romance featuring Mothman. It's a surprisingly soft book. The author sent me over a copy so I could get a good feel of the book's tone and translate that into the perfect graphic. I like how it's turning out so far.

I try not to stare at my phone while I work, willing Marco to text me or call me with Mika's answer. It's still early in the night. They would just now be getting down to playing after having dinner, so there's a lot of time to kill.

I flip my phone over and concentrate on the design on my computer, trying not to let the fact that my stomach is in knots distract me. Marco will let me know tonight one way or the other. I'm just really hoping it goes the way I want.

CHAPTER 21

MIKA

"**Y**ou are going to let a literal baby TPK us, aren't you?" Stella whines across the table from me. Marco has been letting Maria roll the dice for this particular encounter. I say roll loosely. She more like first tries to stick the d20 into her mouth, and then just drops it on the table. Doesn't stop her from rolling stupid high and letting our characters get pounded on. This is brutal, and even a little humiliating that an infant is kicking our asses.

I'm so proud of her. She's going to be a great GM like her daddy someday.

Marco laughs, and Maria coos in his lap, like she knows she's doing well. "The dice gods have spoken. What can I say? She has a gift."

An hour later, we end the game. Our characters have been beat to hell, but we survived despite baby Maria's best efforts to destroy us and eat all her dad's dice.

Everyone starts packing up to head home. "It's great that you brought her along. Gets her out of the house, and Lena needed the break," I say, holding onto the baby while Marco shoves his stuff into his bag. He was so excited to play, and when he asked us on the group chat if he could bring Maria, we all readily agreed. She spent the first half of the game asleep, and the second half either on Marco's lap or passed around the table. Nico paid special attention to her and kept looking down at her with such fondness on his face. That's going to be him soon enough, holding his own little baby in his arms. Which is so fucking weird and yet totally makes sense.

I hug Stella and Nico before they walk out, but Marco hangs back. "Hey Mike, gotta minute?" He sounds hesitant, and I'm pretty sure I know what he wants to talk about. I've been prepared for this. Sorta. A little. Mostly, I just haven't wanted to think about it.

"Yeah, sure. What's up?" *Please don't let this be about Ash.*

It's wishful thinking though. "It's about Ash," he says as he hefts Maria onto his shoulder to pat her back. Of course it is.

I cross my arms and keep my face neutral. I'll hear him out. I can do that.

He takes my attention as approval to go on. "He's a mess, Mika. I've never seen him this bad, not even after everything with Adele. He knows he screwed up, and he's trying to talk to you. I'm not saying you owe him anything. And I'm not saying you should get back together. That's on you two, and it's none of my business. All I'm saying is maybe consider talking to him."

It's like he knows I still haven't looked at any of Ash's messages. He probably does. There are not many people Ash confides in, but Marco and Lena have undoubtedly heard it all by now. Realistically, I know I'm being a bit petty. But he hurt me.

"Marco, he told me he loved me for the first time as he was breaking up with me. And then he went home with his ex. She answered his door half naked, wearing only his shirt. That's a pretty clear sign to me." I'm somewhere between angry and wanting to cry, so I bite my lip to keep myself from raging and crying.

Marco sighs heavily. He doesn't want to be in the middle of this, but he's doing it for Ash. Without a doubt, I know Marco offered to do this and not that Ash asked him. "It was a boneheaded move; you know he's emotionally stunted. It's not an excuse, but he is. Mika, I can promise you, on my life, Ash didn't sleep with Adele. He locked himself in his room and almost had to call the cops on her to get her out of his apartment. We don't call the cops. It just doesn't happen. So trust me when I say that nothing happened between him and Adele. He saw his therapist first thing after, and he's going a lot. Because you told him to."

I'm surprised at this. Not that Ash didn't sleep with Adele. The rational side of me already knew Ash would never. No, I'm surprised that he listened to me and contacted his therapist right away. I'm surprised he's going more often than usual. Ash is a mess, but he realizes that and did something about it. There's a surge of pride for him welling up within me. My resolve to stay away from him is breaking down because the truth is I really miss him. Not just the sex, but his companionship, his friendship, just his presence in my life.

I realize I'm still biting my lip, so I stop before I draw blood. "I... I want to talk to him, Marco. I miss him so fucking much. But I'm not going to do that if he can't get his head out of his ass."

Marco nods. "Yeah, I get that. Will you at least respond to one text? Even if it's to tell him to fuck off. Sorry." He looks down at Maria. "I mean, tell him to fudge off. Is that better? I'm trying to watch my language around her."

That breaks the tension in me, and I laugh. "Yeah, I think that's better. But you're right. I'll at least look at his messages and maybe one text. But it won't be to tell him to fudge off. I couldn't do that to Ash."

Marco smiles. "Okay, cool. Thank you, Mika. I hate to see my cousin in pain like this. I hate seeing you in pain. You two are good together, but you both just need to get your heads out of your butts."

Okay, he's not wrong, so I don't take offense. He leaves a few minutes later, and I'm left alone with only my phone full of messages from Ash for company. I pick up the offending object and open my messaging app. There are twenty texts from Ash, but nothing since last Thursday night. Maybe he's finally giving me the space I needed.

The first ones are from the Sunday evening after I dropped off his bag. They were all mostly identical. Apology after apology. Explanation after explanation. More apologies and walls of texts about how he screwed up.

I'm glad I didn't read these when he sent them because it would have made it so much worse. There would have been no way I would have believed any of this was sincere. Time away from him has given me a cooler head and more clarity.

I finally get to his last message, almost a week old now.

[Ash: I love you, Mika. I'm sorry I did this all wrong. If you ever decide to speak to me again, I want to make up for every minute I made you feel unwanted. You are an amazing person, and I want to be worthy of your love someday.]

That motherfucker!

It could have been so easy to stay mad at him after his barrage of apology texts. But then he ends with that! Like how can I just ignore that? I can't. Because if I'm honest with myself, a first in a while, I'm in love with Ash. It is hard not to be. Not just because he treated me well or that he had become my best friend.

It was in the way he treated my family, how they accepted him into their fold like he had always belonged there. How my friends took him in and let him into our group of nerdy gamers. It was out of his element and yet he kept coming back, and he seemed to really enjoy it. He let me lead him around this city to see the places I love, the places I wanted to share with him. He's still a mess. I know that. Just like I know it's not my responsibility to fix him. But that's the thing. He doesn't expect me to. He's doing that all on his own.

Ash is pretty great. He's not perfect, but he's still pretty great.

Before I can overthink it, I hit call on his number. It barely gets through the first ring before he answers.

"Mika?" He sounds out of breath and unsure.

Hearing his voice feels like a balm on my broken heart, and tears immediately spring to my eyes. "Hi Ash," I manage to choke out.

"Mika, fuck. I'm so sorry. I messed this all up, and I didn't mean to. You mean the world to me, and I'm sorry I'm such a fucking idiot with my head up my own ass, and I'm just sorry." His words are rushed, like he's trying to get it all out before I hang up on him.

I can't help the small smile. "You've been talking to Marco. He said the same thing before he left tonight."

I hear him laugh on the other end. It's not his full laugh; instead it's brittle and soft, but it's still the best sound in the world right now. "Yeah, he probably thinks it's a small price to pay for all the free child care they are getting out of it. But talking to Marco and Lena, well, and my therapist has helped me realize just how messed up what I did was."

He stops, probably waiting for me to interrupt him, but I want to hear everything he has to say, so I keep quiet. He takes it as his sign to keep going. "You know I let Adele screw with my head. I could easily blame her for everything, but I need to take responsibility too. Not for the abuse, but that the minute I was tested, I let her blow up my life again. Mika, you are an extraordinary woman. The most amazing person I've ever met. I know I don't deserve you, but that doesn't mean I don't want to try with you. I want to try so much, every day, for as long as you'll have me."

"Ash ... you hurt me. Like badly," I say because he has to know by now that it wasn't just a passing thing for me.

"I know. God, Mika, I know I hurt you. I wasn't thinking. I let my fear get the best of me. I—"

I cut him off. "Honey, stop. I know you're sorry. Listen, I'm open to meeting up and talking. I'm not going to make any promises or tell you everything is going to be okay. I just don't want to do this over the phone. I want to see you, Ash. It's been hell not seeing you." And now I'm crying, but I don't bother trying to stop myself. Let the tears flow. I need them right now.

I can hear his breath hit over the phone. "Yeah, I would like that. No expectations. I've missed you, Mika.

Everything seems wrong without you around. I feel wrong without you around."

My heart flutters in my chest. And I thought I had it bad with this guy but turns out Ash is a hopeless romantic. "I hate to make either of us wait longer, but well, Election Day on Tuesday. My mom has me booked for the rest of this week, and Tuesday I'll be stuck at HQ all day. We could do lunch on Wednesday, if that's okay with you."

It seems like a lifetime away, but I have obligations to my mom, who's been a nervous wreck all week, despite what she says. We've spent enough time apart, but one more week won't hurt us.

"Yeah, I can do lunch. Does Esther need any more help? I'm free if she needs me." Because of course he's thoughtful enough to want to help my mom with anything she needs leading up to Election Day.

"I'll give Winnie your info. I'm sure she'll have something for you. Probably like being stuck outside a voting center talking about Senator Levenberg's policies and why they should vote for her. Hope you like Howard County because Winnie will definitely give you a shitty, hard to reach location." I laugh, and it's the first real one in weeks. And it's totally true. Winnie will put him in the worst place as a fuck you for hurting me.

The next time Ash laughs, it's fuller, almost like himself again. "I will take whatever punishment Winnie dishes out. I'm team Levenberg all the way into the trenches of Howard County."

"Good night, Ash."

"Good night, Mika. I love you."

I don't say it back, but I don't think he expects me to.

I toss my phone on my bed and head down the hall to take a shower, feeling better than I have in weeks. At the very least, I want to get my friend back.

The rest of the week is spent finishing work. I barely have time for anything else. Normally I have a steady stream of work, especially for college lectures. Business really boomed during lockdown. But for some reason, the week before the elections, I'm swamped with work.

Stella invites me out on Friday and Saturday, but since I'm taking all day Monday, Tuesday, and Wednesday off to do Election Day stuff and help my mom, I really can't spare the time.

It doesn't help that I'm checking my phone a lot, just to see if Ash texted me. We didn't say that we wouldn't text, just that we were going to talk next week, but I still kind of hoped he would send me something. Even if it was just a dumb gif or meme. But he doesn't. He's respecting my space until our designated meeting time.

Damn him for respecting boundaries and all that. There's no rule that says I can't text him since I've gathered I'm kind of leading this thing we're doing, but I know that if I text him first, I'll be completely derailed from work and spend even more time looking at my phone. So I don't. Even though I really want to.

By Monday morning, I just don't want to get out of bed. I worked until midnight to finish up a week of lectures, and I'm tired. For the next two days, however, I'm for Winnie's use only, until my mom actually needs me herself. Then I get to smile, take a ton of pictures with everyone, and hopefully take victory shots with my mom afterward. Which we definitely do in the kitchen area of the venue so nobody gets any pictures of Senator Levenberg knocking back shots of Goldschlagger, which isn't good, but Mom calls it festive.

I'm already looking forward to Wednesday. Mostly to see Ash, but also, because I'll sleep in really late, and Dad makes a gigantic breakfast with only the finest hangover foods. It's a Levenberg family tradition.

Mom's campaign has taken over the house when I arrive just after 8 a.m. They'll move to HQ tomorrow where most of us will spend all day, while Mom and Winnie make the rounds. But today it's nothing but staffers surrounding the kitchen island while Dad works over his electric griddle making pancakes for the hungry masses. I swear, people fight to become my mom's aides mostly for all the food Dad makes. They are probably the most well fed staff in DC.

"Mikey!" Lila Roth, one of the interns, squeals as I walk into the kitchen. She runs over to me and squeezes the ever-loving hell out of my body. Lila is in her final year at Georgetown, almost as small as Stella, and I'm pretty sure has broken ribs just by hugging. She's sweet as pie, and I've known her since she was just a bitty seventeen year old when she volunteered for Mom's campaign the first time. She wasn't even old enough to vote yet and still had so much passion for politics. At seventeen, I was way into my poetry classes and kissing cute boys and pretty girls in areas that should have gotten us caught if we were just a little less sneaky.

"Lila!" I hug her back using what little bit of arm I'm able to move within her embrace. She's super peppy and undoubtedly has been up since 5:00 a.m. and probably downed at least one pot of coffee by now, whereas I woke up forty-five minutes ago and forgot to grab my coffee from my kitchen counter before hopping the train.

Other staffers greet me as I wiggle my way out of Lila's crush hug, and I make my way around the kitchen. Dad kisses me hello on the cheek and hands over a plate of pancakes fresh from the griddle. Take that, staffers! This is what nepotism looks like around here.

It's already super loud. Mom and Winnie emerge from her office a few minutes later, and I get in a quick hug to both of them. Then I settle back and wait until Captain Winnie gives me direction for the day. She runs a tight ship, and just because I'm the senator's daughter does not win me any favoritism.

Which is how I end up with David in his car to make the rounds to various senior centers on how they can get to their polling locations and to talk about our mom's platforms. Luckily for us, one of our first stops is Bubbe's senior center, and she does most of the work for us.

"That's right, my daughter has been the best damn senator Maryland has had in a long time. And she's going to keep working for us. You don't think that other guy, whatshisface, is going to care about us old Jews, do you? No, he doesn't give a damn about his elders. But my Esther, she listens. Even as a little girl, I never had any trouble with her. She would actually listen to me, absorb what I said, and she was so methodical in her response." Bubbe goes on for easily thirty minutes just telling stories about mom's youth. Stuff we've heard a million times, and let's be real, everyone in this room has heard a million times.

But Bubbe is passionate and believes in Mom, so nobody stops her. Seems I come from a long line of exceptional public speakers. Too bad I did not get that gene.

The rest of the day is smiling and answering questions. A few times there are some nasty comments from some of the seniors either because my mom is a Democrat, or a woman, or the classic, because she's a Jew. Antisemitism is kind of an evergreen thing.

It's after 5:00 p.m. by the time we get back to the house. I check my phone, something I kept myself from doing all day, but there's still no messages from Ash. What if he's regretting talking to me? Like what if it set him off and he realized he can't really be with me? Or wants to be with me?

I shake my head and knock the stupid thoughts from my mind. Because they are stupid. That's not Ash. He's giving me space, respecting boundaries. He understands that we will have our time to talk, and he's being patient.

So why can't I be patient?

It's not like I don't have enough to think about without focusing on what could or could not be with Ash. I just... It's been a hellish few days and an exhausting day, and I just want to hear his voice.

I slip upstairs to my old room, shut the door behind me, and call Ash before I can talk myself out of it. But it just rings and rings. Eventually it goes to voicemail. I don't leave one.

My heart sinks into my stomach. Last time I called, he barely gave it time to ring, but now he's not picking up at all. Did I misunderstand things in our last conversation? Am I the one crossing boundaries now?

I sink down on the bed and lay down on my side, my phone curled up in my hand. I'm so tired, and now I'm sad because just hearing Ash's voice would have made things just a little better. It takes effort, but I remind myself that he's not necessarily avoiding me. He does have a life and work, and body functions he has to take care of. Nobody is going to answer the phone if they're on the toilet or showering. Plus, Ash gets really absorbed in his work when he's in a flow, so he might not have noticed that I called at all.

I sigh and stare up at the ceiling. There are still a few of the sticky glow stars I put up when I was twelve and going through my astronomy phase. I made constellations across the top of my ceiling based on the winter sky since I put them up in winter. They are a comfort to me now.

At some point, I fall asleep because when I wake up, it's dark outside, and the house is not nearly so loud. I check my phone but all I have is a text from Stella with a picture of some fruity cocktail and the side of Nico's face.

[Stella: Missing you.]

[Me: I want that next time.]

[Stella: Nico's treat. He spilled this on me right after I took the picture.]

[Me: Lol, well, he had a good run. Shame he had to die.]

[Stella: Real shame.]

I get off my bed and head downstairs, smiling a little to myself. I hate missing out on Monday night drinks, but I'm glad Stella and Nico still went out. Things are changing so much with our little group, so any bit of normalcy is good.

Downstairs, there's still some staffers lounging around, but many have already gone home, ready to be back at it bright and early tomorrow for the big day. I just wish I could talk to Ash and tell him about my day.

Winnie did say she had a role for him tomorrow, so maybe I'll get a chance to see him. I can only hope.

CHAPTER 22

ASH

I have torn my apartment apart looking for my phone. Last time I saw it was Monday morning. I'm about to head out to stand outside a polling station and talk about Mika's mom on the other side of Howard County, and I still haven't found the damn thing.

Luckily, arrangements had already been made for a staffer to pick me up at 7:00 a.m., so I don't have to worry about trying to get a ride share. I worry that Mika might have tried to contact me, and that makes me a little more frantic to find my phone. It is almost 7:00 a.m., so I head to my computer and shoot off a quick email to Marco asking if he could look for my phone since I was over there yesterday. Now that I think about it, the last time I remember having it out was when I was showing Maria videos of puppies. She kept trying to grab the phone to pull it closer to her face.

Nothing I can do about it now, so I head downstairs and wait for my ride. A white Prius pulls up, and there are two people inside: an older woman in the driver's seat and a woman probably a few years younger than I am in the passenger seat. I open the door to the back seat. One side of the backseat is full of bags, but there's still just enough space for me.

"Morning, I'm Amy Saperstein. This is my mom, Caroline. You're Ash, right? Want some coffee?" the young woman in the passenger seat says, holding up a paper cup of still steaming coffee. I accept it gratefully.

Caroline doesn't speak the entire drive up to the polling location, and I'm mostly quiet in the backseat. Which is okay because Amy does enough talking for the three of us. She's in her second year at Catholic University studying English and thinks she might go to Columbia for her masters, just to get out of the District.

"How did you get involved with Senator Levenberg's campaign?" I ask, genuinely curious why a mother/daughter duo would spend the day at a polling station to convince voters on why they should vote for their candidate.

"Esther and I went to the same synagogue growing up. We used to ditch Hebrew school together when we could get away with it. Our families are very close." Caroline catches my eye in the rearview mirror, and her eyes narrow at me. Well, that settles that: she obviously knows about me and Mika. This day isn't going to be easy.

Amy, however, seems to be in the dark about things though. "Yeah, David and Mika are like way older than me, but our families still hang out some times. Are you a big politics guy? I mean, you live in DC, so that was a dumb question. How did you get on the campaign?"

I opt for the truth, or something like it. "I'm friends with Mika. She asked me to help out today. It was pretty last minute, so Winnie gave me an earful about her schedule."

Amy laughs and turns to face out the window. "From what I've heard about her, you got off easy," Caroline says, her eyes on the road. This time she doesn't meet my gaze in the mirror.

The rest of the ride is filled with Amy's chatter. I tune out but nod or make a noise every now and then when I think it's appropriate. Neither Amy nor Caroline seem to mind that I'm detached from the conversation.

I keep waiting for my phone to vibrate in my pocket, maybe a message from Mika. But then I remember I don't have my phone with me and that in all likelihood, it's shoved between a cushion at Marco's house. Not that I expect Mika would have contacted me. She didn't even read my messages for weeks, and we haven't had the real conversation yet, so I doubt she wanted to talk to me before then.

We arrive at the polling center and set up a pop-up tent, like the ones used at outdoor markets. It's only a five by five thing, but it provides us shelter in case the weather turns, and one side has a tarp wall to block the wind, not that it's particularly windy today, but it's a nice addition.

I want to say it's an exciting day, but it's really not. The morning has a slow trickle of people. Most just walk past us, but a few stop to listen and grab a one-sheet that Caroline had brought in a clear plastic tub she pulled from the trunk of the car. An occasional enthusiast stops to yell at us that we are supporting evil or something equally ridiculous just because Esther is a Democrat. I won't mention the few antisemitic things thrown out. People are so hateful for literally no reason.

There's a rush around lunch time, and I honestly had no idea how many could turn out to vote. Now I feel bad for not being more politically aware. I usually only vote during presidential years, and even then, I'm spotty.

We're here until 6:00 p.m., even though the polls close later. It's a long day, but Amy packed lunch for all of us, which I'm grateful for, since I didn't even think about bringing food. I figured there would be some place to eat around the area, but we're outside a church, and there's nothing else near the church.

"So, we're going to head back to HQ to drop off these one-sheets. You're welcome to stay for the party. Fair warning—it's crazy tense and busy until the official announcement. You'll be in for a very long night. Or we can drop you off at home," Amy says as we head back to the car.

I think about it for a moment. If I go to HQ, I'll probably see Mika, and I really want to see her. Maybe this is my time to start making things up to her, to show her that I'll be there, no matter what. But I could definitely use a shower and a change of clothes.

"I want to head to HQ, but I should probably clean up a bit. If it's not too much trouble, could you take me home?" A tinge of guilt hits me, like I'm asking too much for myself.

"No trouble. We planned to do the same, so it's not out of our way," Caroline says, pulling out of the church parking lot and heading back to the highway. We're all too tired to do much talking on the way back into the city, and I can feel myself getting drowsy in the back seat. Amy falls asleep in the front, and I can hear her faint snores.

Amy is still asleep when we pull up to my building, and I try to quietly get out so as not to wake her. "Ash," Carolina says as I'm halfway out of the backseat.

I turn back to face her. "I know it's not my place, but I'm a meddling mother. In my experience, most people are worth second chances if they really try to be better. Mika is a good girl. She deserves someone who is going to put in the effort."

That confirms she knows what happened between me and Mika. I'm not surprised. I nod and duck out of the car. I stand on the sidewalk for a moment as it pulls away and heads down the street.

When I get into my apartment, I take a quick shower and get dressed in a pair of black jeans and dark blue button down, opting to look a little more put together for the event. I can't stand the sleeves around my wrists, so I roll them up to the elbow. I can look nice and be comfortable.

I check my email to see if Marco found my phone. And as luck would have it, he found it between the cushions of the couch. I want to get to the venue as soon as possible, and it would take time to get to the Metro and get over to Marco's and then back on the Metro to get to Chevy Chase, so I tell him I'll pick it up tomorrow. It's not like I'll need my phone tonight anyway, though it's been weird not having it all day.

The train is packed because of course I waited until rush hour to head up. It's standing room only, and too many people are touching me. Internally, I'm cringing so hard, but I just have to deal with it.

What feels like hours later, I've finally made it to the venue serving as the campaign headquarters. There are a few people pacing outside, talking loudly on their phones, or taking smoke breaks. I keep my focus on the doors and head inside.

Outside had been slightly chilly but still a little warm for early November. Inside, the air is warm, and the place is crowded. A stage is set up with an empty podium, and two large screens flank it, showing initial poll results as they come in. There are tables set up for people to hover around and grab food. Drinks seem to be flowing already, judging by the amount of people holding glasses. And phones are everywhere, people checking and refreshing pages of poll numbers.

I make my way in and find a spot along a wall to look around. There's only one person I want to see right now, and it's not the elder Levenberg. It should be easy to spot Mika. In a sea of dark blues and blacks, her bubblegum hair usually sticks out. But as I scan the crowd, I don't see her anywhere.

There is one Levenberg I do see, however. David stands near the stage, talking to Winnie, who looks very much like she's trying to escape the conversation. I walk over to them and greet them both.

"Thanks for helping today, Ash. Sorry, David, I have to check on something," Winnie says, flashing a brief wave before half running away.

"Wow, it's like she couldn't get away fast enough," David deadpans, watching Winnie's retreating form. He turns his attention to me once she's out of sight, and he frowns. "What are you doing here anyway? Come to fuck with my sister's feeling some more?"

Okay, I deserve that. David and I always got along, but that was before I made the dumbest mistake ever. Naturally, he would be a protective brother, and for a moment, I wonder if he'll hit me. Take me out back and kick the shit out of me for hurting his little sister. Can't say I don't deserve that.

"Mika asked me to help out today, so I did. Listen, David, I know I fucked up. Like really fucked up. I never meant to hurt Mika. I just had this stupid idea that I was doing what was best for her, but I know that wasn't my decision to make. So if you want to hit me, that's completely valid, and I won't try to stop you." I mean it sincerely. I'll let David wallop on me even, if it'll make him feel better. Though I'd rather he didn't.

David's face remains stoic for just a few seconds before he cracks a smile and slaps me on the arm. "I'm a doctor, man. The whole *do no harm* is kind of ingrained in my brain. Besides, I already talked to Mikey about everything, so I already know everything. You screwed up, but you don't seem like a total douche, so once you're done groveling to my sister, we're okay."

I'm surprised at his reaction, but I give him a tentative smile because if David is okay with me, hopefully that means Mika is too. I want her family to like me, to accept me. But Mika's acceptance is the most important thing, and I need to show her how much I want to be with her.

"Now, if you want to know where my sister is, she volunteered to pick up Bubbe from her place. She just left, so it might be a while, especially since my grandmother definitely won't be ready to leave right away, and they will be waylaid by every single one of her friends on the way out."

Well, that's disappointing to hear. Yael is great, though, and it'll be good to see her again. Patience might not be one of my stronger attributes, but I can wait for Mika. Besides, there's plenty to eat and drink tonight. Maybe David will let me hang with him for a while. It's not like

I have the luxury of goofing off on my phone while I wait since it's currently sitting at Marco's place. Still can't believe how careless I was for leaving it there.

David and I chat for a while near the stage after getting some drinks. But then he's eventually pulled away by more important people. As the senator's son, he's in demand for people's attention. So, here I stand alone, with nothing to do but people watch. The room is so loud with people shouting poll numbers from different sources across the room. There's some music playing, not that I can really hear what song it is with all the noise. More people fill the room as the evening progresses until it's basically standing room only.

Esther spots me at some point, and she and Mort come over to give me a hug and thank me for helping out. But she's whisked away quickly with Mort in tow. She's the center of attention after all and doesn't have time to waste on her daughter's ex-boyfriend. I cringe at the term. I don't to be her ex anything. I want to be Mika's boyfriend, partner, best friend. I want to be all of it for her. She just needs to show up so I can tell her that.

And that's when I see her. A beacon of pink in a sea of dark colors. She leads her grandma by the arm through the crowd to her parents. She looks gorgeous in a pale blue short-sleeved dress that stops just shy of the floor. The neckline swoops across her collarbone, showing off just enough of her beautiful creamy skin to drive me wild. I want to make my way over to her immediately but decide it's probably better to give her time with her family first. Only after she's done talking to them will I go to her.

I drain the glass in my hand of whatever alcohol I've been drinking. I don't even remember what it was, and

I don't even taste it because I'm so focused on Mika. It's been weeks since I've seen her, almost a month, and it's like I'm taking her in for the first time. Only her profile is visible, but I can't help looking over every inch of what I can see. Not that I don't already know every curve and dip of her body, but it hits me all over again how much I missed her. Seeing her. Touching her. Just being near her.

I watch as Esther points in my direction, and Mika turns to face me fully. Our eyes meet, and I see what looks like relief, or longing, or both cross her face. Pretty sure I'm making a similar face. I'm hurrying toward her before I even realize my feet are moving, and she moves through the crowd with more grace than I have. We meet somewhere in the middle, and as much as I want to throw my arms around her and hold her close to me as tight as I can, I stop myself from reaching out to her. We stop only a foot from each other, and she tilts her gorgeous face up toward mine. There's a charged silence between us as we just look and look, drinking in each other's presence. Going from seeing her multiple times a week to not at all has left me desperate to see her.

"Ash," she breathes out, and I can't tell if she's happy to see me or not. But this is my chance, and it might be the only one I'm ever going to get.

"I'm sorry. I'm so sorry. I let my dumb trauma brain get in the way of the best thing to ever happen to me," I say, and my whole body is shaking from nerves. I have to get this out though. She has to know how I feel, even if she doesn't forgive me. "It was stupid of me to let Adele get inside my head again. I worked so hard to get over what she put me through, and I let her destroy that in a second. I shouldn't have let her talk me into going back to my apartment. But you have to know, nothing happened.

I would never do that to you. I would never do that to myself. She wanted me to go back to New York with her, and I told her no because my life is here, and she's not part of that anymore. I meant what I said, Mika. I love you. And I may not feel like I deserve you, but that's for me to work on, and not my decision to make for you. So, if you'll have me, I want to work on making it up to you. I want to show you that I am putting in the work on myself and that I can still work on being good *with* you, not *for* you."

Increased sessions with Danny have gotten me to this point. I can't work on myself for the benefit for another person. I have to do it for myself. That doesn't mean I can't be with Mika. She just can't be the reason I do better for myself.

My speech done, I wait for her to say something. Her eyes are shining, and a smile slowly takes over her face. It's so beautiful and bright, the sun can't even compare. She reaches out and takes my hands. Hers are warm and soft and look so small in my sweaty palms. I stare at our joined hands, and damn, I missed just touching her so simply.

"Ash, you're a mess. I know that's not your fault, and I can see you are really trying. So, while you might be a mess, you're my mess. I forgive you for making dumb choices. You were scared." She slips one hand out of mine and cups my cheek, her thumb resting on the edge of my lips. "I love you too. I want us to try this again because you are worth it."

My heart nearly stops in my chest. *Did she just say she loves me?*

The noise of the room falls away, and all I can hear is my heart start to race, like it remembers it's supposed to do that and is trying to make up for the skipped beats. Mika looks up at me with such adoration and love. How did I never see that before? Because this isn't the first time she's given me this look.

I can't hold back anymore. I need her. I bend down and capture her lips in a bruising, claiming kiss. Kissing Mika has always been an amazing experience, but this kiss is unlike any of our previous ones. Just like I'm claiming her with my lips, she's claiming me right back. It's deep and passionate, and I never want to stop. My arms wrap around her waist, and I pull her tight against me, wishing to eliminate all space between us. She's just as greedy, snaking her arms around my neck, dragging me down to her even more. I can easily see us doing this for the rest of our lives. I want to do this for the rest of our lives.

I'm vaguely aware of cheering around us. Maybe it's for us, or maybe it's for something else—I don't really care. All my attention is on kissing my girl, my Mika. It's days or maybe minutes before we pull away just enough to look in each other's eyes, though we stay wrapped around each other.

It's only then do I realize there are balloons falling down around us in shades of red, white, and blue. The cheering continues around us, and my eyes flash to the screens flanking the stage. Esther Levenberg has won re-election to her senate seat.

"Shit, I have to go," Mika says hurriedly. She pulls her arms away from my neck, and I reluctantly let her go. "Will you stay by the stage while I head up with my family?" she asks me and pulls my hand into hers.

I nod and let her pull me through the crowd toward where Senator Levenberg is about to take the stage for her victory speech. Mika leaves me right at the bottom of the steps to the stage, giving me a parting kiss before she joins her brother, dad, and grandma on stage with her mom. I stare at her rather than the senator, and while she does her best to keep her attention on her mom, occasionally her gaze wanders back to me, and the smile she's already wearing grows bigger.

While Esther Levenberg gives her victory speech on how she's going to continue her work in Washington, my thoughts turn toward a bright future. One with Mika in my life, sharing adventures around Washington DC.

Less than a year ago, I arrived in DC completely broken and poorly prepared to rebuild my life. There were no expectations other than to just learn to live without Adele's constant torment. Marco and Lena were the only people I knew. I had no friends here. But now, I have great friends, and I'm working on making new ones. I love that I get to create art every day. I get to be with the woman I love, who is so full of life and sunshine, for as long as she'll have me.

And it's crazy to think I have found the woman of my dreams simply by rolling some dice on a tabletop.

EPILOGUE

MIKA

Some time later

"Does twenty-three hit?" Ash asks, lifting his eyebrows at Marco, though he's wearing a huge smirk on his face.

Marco levels a look at him. "Mothertrucker, you know it does. He's a goblin with like five hit points left. Roll damage."

Ash rolls a d6 on the table, one of the sparkly blue ones from the first set I ever gave him. "That's nine total," he proudly declares to the table.

Marco writes something down behind his screen and dramatically throws down his pencil. "Congratulations, you obliterate him. He is strips of bloody flesh, torn asunder by your cat claws. Well, that was the last one, so I'm going to call it for tonight." We all stand and stretch. Our games don't last as long as they used to—turns out being over thirty makes you ache a lot quicker than in your twenties.

With a toddler running around, Marco just doesn't have the energy to GM all night long like in years past. Not that he's the only one with a toddler. I look across the table at Nico. He looks absolutely exhausted. His son, Leonardo, has molars coming in, and he's a little wailer. It's a good thing Alexandra stopped breastfeeding a while ago. Leo was already a biter.

Next to Nico, Alexandra also looks completely wrung out, but there's a smile on her face. She started playing with us not long after the baby announcement came. She's quiet with pretty brown-gold hair, wire-framed glasses, and a fashion style like a 1930s archeologist. Alexandra is a total nerd, so she fits right in with us. Her and Nico are such an odd pair, what with her scholarly demeanor and look and Nico's rock & roll persona. But they work. And they are doing great as parents.

"Alright, you degenerates, I need to jet. I'm bringing food to the wife since she left hers again, and if I don't bring it, she'll eat her way through the food court," Stella says, packing up her bag. It's been a year since they got married, but she still refers to Elise exclusively as her wife to everyone.

Everyone leaves quickly. We all love each other, but they all have obligations at home now and can't linger like we used to. As I shut the door behind Nico and Alexandra, I feel warm, strong arms wrap around my middle from behind.

I lean back into Ash's chest and absorb his presence. "Well, that was fun. But I am absolutely exhausted. Can we blow off dishes until tomorrow?" He nuzzles his face in the crook of my neck, and I love the feel of the bit of stubble on his chin against my skin.

"Hm. Are you too exhausted to have a little fun in our bed?" That's the only reason I'll let dishes sit overnight. One of his hands slides up and cups my breast. Answer enough for me.

"Never too tired to please my fiancé," he murmurs into my ear before taking my earlobe between his teeth. I moan loudly. It feels so good when he does things like this. My whole body is thrumming with need. It still amazes me that he can elicit such reactions from me after all this time, but I can't get enough of him. Not even cohabitating and finding out all his annoying habits have dampened my desire for him.

I turn in his arms and push up on my toes to kiss him. Then I'm running away, up the stairs and into our room. I hear him laugh behind me, and then he's chasing me, catching me just through the bedroom door. Before I can put up any resistance, I'm sailing through the air and land on our bed with a soft oomph.

Ash sheds his clothes quickly. It's going to be one of those nights where everything is fast and rough, and oh so fucking hot. He lunges for the bed and immediately pushes up my dress. My poor panties don't stand a chance as he rips them off me, like literally tears the thin fabric in his haste to get to my most intimate part.

He feasts on me like I'm his last meal, and he savors every bit. I scream his name as I rake my nails up his back. Ash moans against me, and that just turns me on even more, and I grip his hair to pull him closer. When I finally come on his lips, I swear I see starbursts, and all my thoughts empty from my head.

Once I come down enough to focus, I order him on his back and throw a leg over his hips to straddle him. We both are partial to this position. I stare into his beautiful chocolate eyes as I ride him, slamming down on him as he raises his hips into mine. Our kisses are bruising, and his fingers are going to leave marks on my ass from how hard he's clutching onto me. I love everything about this. I love everything about Ash. Every jagged piece, every shy smile, every lust-filled gleam in his eye. He's my everything.

As we lay curled around each other, letting our breathing slow, I admire the engagement ring on my left hand. It's not a diamond. No, Ash got something even better. Instead the stone is a glittering fire opal set on a rose gold band. It shines with vibrant colors in the light, and it's so me.

"I love you," I whisper against his chest, resting my cheek there, and listen to his heartbeat. He squeezes my arm and kisses the top of my head.

"I love you too," he says back, and hearing those words never ceases to send a thrill through me. We fall asleep wrapped around each other. As I drift off, I think about Ash, our life, and the Bargains & Battles campaign that brought us together. It might sound corny, but it really feels like I rolled a natural twenty on life.

BOOK CLUB QUESTIONS

1. Were you interested in the snippets of the Battles & Bargains game? Did they add to the overall story?

2. Ash deals with extreme anxiety, especially in social situations. Can you relate to the anxiety Ash feels?

3. How did you feel about Mika being with another person on page before being with Ash?

4. A big theme involves characters moving on to the next stage of their lives. Do you think Ash and Mika mature well into that next stage?

5. Do you feel like the conflict between Mika and Ash was believable? Was their reconciliation earned?

AUTHOR BIO

Kait Disney-Leugers is an author of romance books with a little magic thrown in. Originally from Ohio, she has a degree in history from Ohio University. She now lives in Maryland with her husband and two kids and uses her history degree to be insufferable while watching historical movies and shows.

When not writing in the dead of night once everyone else is asleep, she enjoys playing D&D, trying in vain to get through her giant pile of books, and baking bread to 90s hip hop.

More books from
Kait Disney-Leugers

Antique Magic
Blood Magic
Heart Magic

Discover more at
4HorsemenPublications.com

10% off using HORSEMEN10

Milton Keynes UK
Ingram Content Group UK Ltd.
UKHW031950281024
450365UK00008B/416

9 798823 205146